METAtropolis
Book 1: METAtropolis: The Dawn of Uncivilization
Book 2: METAtropolis: Cascadia
Book 3: METAtropolis: Green Space

DATE DUE

METATROPOLIS

METATROPOLIS

Edited by John Scalzi

Original Stories by

JAY LAKE
TOBIAS BUCKELL
ELIZABETH BEAR
JOHN SCALZI
KARL SCHROEDER

SUBTERRANEAN PRESS 2009

First Edition

ISBN
978-1-59606-238-2

Subterranean Press
PO Box 190106
Burton, MI 48519

www.subterraneanpress.com

TABLE OF CONTENTS

INTRODUCTION

JOHN SCALZI

'm not sure if the book you hold in your hands is a first, but if it's not, then it's something very close to it, because it's a book that was originally an audiobook, rather than the more typical other way around. Early in 2008, audiobook seller and producer Audible.com contacted me and asked me if I would be interested in putting together an audiobook anthology. I thought it was a really interesting idea; I've had novels performed as audiobooks, but writing directly for the form was new to me and seemed like an interesting challenge, especially if I had some willing collaborators.

But what I didn't want to do was the usual anthology idea, in which writers are given a theme and then set off to work in isolation. It's been done, and sometimes the authors and the ideas are a bad fit together. What I thought would be more interesting would be to collect a set of smart, engaged authors and have them build a world together, and having established the world, then go off and write their stories. We would get the advantages of a communally-created setting—everyone in the same world—and all the advantages of the individual writers, creating stories in their own style. The notable previous example of this is Harlan Ellison's classic anthology, *Medea: Harlan's World*, Plus, we know the writers would be well-matched with the world, because, after all, they helped create it.

The key would be the writers themselves, because they would provide the ideas that would build the world. And in this we were very fortunate to have the group we had: Elizabeth Bear, Tobias Buckell, Jay Lake and Karl Schroeder (as well as myself, since I was penning a story as well as acting as editor of the project). If you're a current reader of science fiction, these names need no introduction, but I'm going to brag on them anyway: Our little group has three previous John W. Campbell Award winners (and four nominees), a multiple Aurora Award winner (that being Canada's highest SF award), two Hugo winners, two authors who have showed up on the *New York Times* Bestseller list and one who has had his novel listed as a *New York Times* Notable Book.

And, to top it all off, they'll all smart as hell and fun to brainstorm with. As the project editor, I have to say these writers were my "A"-list—my first choices for the project—and I was delighted to get them. I figured that would make me look like a much smarter editor than I really was.

I was right about that. Karl Schroeder got the ball rolling by proposing the general idea of "future cities"—but not just the standard-issue Jetsons future cities, or another take on the city states of medieval times, gussied up with technology, but the idea that the cities would be something like an "interstitial nation"—that the people of a future Detroit or Portland might have more in common with the people in Hong Kong or Johannesburg than they might with the people right down the road—and what it would mean for the way we lived if city dwellers acted on that.

This was the starting point for the conversation, but as you'll read in these stories, it definitely wasn't the end of the conversation. The title of this anthology is "Metatropolis," which means, more or less, "the city beyond." The cities you'll be reading about here are meant to be just that—a step beyond what you know, or what you may have expected.

Being the editor, I'm biased here, but I think these authors have a really amazing job of opening up what the possibilities of cities are, and what they will be. The stories, separate but interconnected, create a world I think you're going to really enjoy visiting. All I ask is that you pay attention—this could be your future. I hope you're ready for it.

IN THE FORESTS OF THE NIGHT
JAY LAKE

One of the most clichéd pieces of writing advice out there is "write what you know"—but the reason this advice is cliché is that it happens to be true. And one of the interesting things about the METATROPOLIS project was how each author incorporated what he or she knew into their own stories. In the case of Jay Lake, this included locale. Jay is a proud citizen of "Cascadia"—that metropolitan corridor that stretches from Portland up to Vancouver, British Columbia—and it's here that he sets his story.

Now, writing what you know is all well and good, but this is also speculative fiction, so Jay's Cascadia is different from the Pacific Northwest you know (or think you know). Jay's touch with world building is impressive enough that it made sense for us to put his story first and let it be the one that gives you a sense of the world we created together.

And so, in the beginning: There was Jay Lake.

INTROIT

I t would be nice to say that Tygre arrived in Cascadiopolis on the wings of a storm, riding the boiling front of electric darkness and lashing rain like a tall, handsome man out of some John Ford western. Or that he came through shadow and fire by a secret tunnel through the honeycombed basalt bones of these green-covered mountains, a hero out of templed legend following the journey of the gods. It would be nice, but inaccurate. Tygre arrived the way almost everyone comes to Cascadiopolis: either by accident, by judicial design or by following the damp silences between the trees higher and higher until there was nowhere left to go.

In Tygre's case, all three.

His name was Tygre Tygre. Spelled the way Blake originally did, T, Y, G, R, E. Or, if you prefer to file it by last name as so many sentencing authorities and similar busybodies do: Tygre comma Tygre. Not that he had a file, which made him unusual for someone who wasn't otherwise born and raised completely off the grid. But then Tygre was unusual from before we ever saw him to long after we laid him down in the forest loam beneath a simple stone marked only with a stylized flame.

Death improves everyone's reputation. For some, it also multiplies their power.

Bashar grunts. A familiar, weary look nestles in his narrowed eyes, visible to the pickets even in the deep, green-black shadows of a Cascades evening. The men and women who stand at Cascadiopolis' first line of defense know better than to give him cause for challenge. Not when he is in this mood.

Even the new fish like Kamila understand this with the same brute instinct that keeps young cats alive in the face of a battle-scarred neighborhood tom. Still, she is not so smart as she should be. Spiked into camo netting forty feet up a Douglas fir, she tries to sneak a hand-rolled smoke.

Cigarettes are so twentieth century, the pocket-sized equivalent of an SUV these days, but there's been a fad for them in the cities up and down the I-5 corridor. Every generation ignores the lessons of the one before. It's not tobacco—long haul transport is too difficult and expensive for something that doesn't pay good Euros by the gram—but a mix of locally-grown herbs and good old fashioned ganja. Rolling papers can be sourced regionally from the old Crown Z mill up on the Washington side of the Columbia.

Everyone knows this. The old hands, meaning anyone who has been on the picket line for more than a week, also know that Bashar hates cigarettes with the same passion that he hates concrete, white people and internal combustion.

Kamila does not know this, so she clicks her sparker and takes a drag inside a cupped hand. Bashar has the hearing of a bat, they whisper to one another when the commander is on the far side of a basalt-ribbed ridge line. He stops, pressure-rifle suddenly cocked, and without turning his head says, "Miller."

She accidentally swallows the butt, then chokes hard on the mix of hot tip, raw smoke and an inch of lumpy paper going down her throat. "Sir," she squeaks.

"Drop it."

The new recruit almost says, "Drop what?"—a relic of oppositionally defiant teen-hood so recently left behind, but the absolute silence from her fellow pickets warns her. Cautiously she casts her sparker down. It hits the mossy ground with a muffled thud to be swallowed by the shadows at the base of her tree.

"The fag, Miller." Now Bashar sounds bored. That is when he is at his most dangerous. "Drop the fag."

"I don't have it," she whispers, then belches smoke and paper shards amid a searing pain in her larynx.

Still not looking over his shoulder, Bashar snaps off a three-needle burst from his weapon which takes Kamila in the meat of her thigh. She squeaks with the agony of the non-lethal hit as the tangy reek of blood blooms among the trees.

Whatever he was going to do to her next was lost amid a startled challenge from Ward, a hundred yards downslope hunkered down behind a lichen-riddled boulder.

Her voice crackles over the dissociated network of turked comm buds, shouting, "H-halt!" A fraction of a second later the words echo through the cooling air.

Bashar moves like a mountain lion on a wounded sheep; fast, hard and silent as he makes the long descent in a dozen bounds. Ward knows better than to apologize—she is no new fish—but she has the stranger in her sights.

He is Tygre, of course, though none of us have heard of him yet, and he has walked right past the outer line of Bashar's pickets as if they were a row of dead streetlights on some Portland boulevard. The picket commander meets the invader face to face in a pool of moonlight, rare this deep beneath the spreading arms of the montane forest.

For a moment, even this toughest of the renegade city's partisans is lost in the mystery of the man who would be their king.

We quote from the introduction to a master's thesis written during the last year that the Sorbonne was still a degree-granting institution:

> The early decades of the twenty-first century brought the collapse of the American project. A noble experiment in democracy and economics had transitioned through imperialism, then dove straight into the same hollow irrelevancy which had seized the eighteenth century Spanish crown—a zombie empire shambling onward through the sheer weight of its extents, but devoid of initiative or credibility. Where Spain had been dogged by England in those post-Armada years, America after Reagan was hunted by a pack of baying hounds: transnational terrorists, post-NATO powers and resource-funded microstates with long-armed grudges. All this while rotting from the inside as the true failures of internal combustion-centered urbanism were finally exposed like worms in the heart of a prize bitch.

> Hope was not dead, but it lived in strange, isolated colonies on the warm corpse of the United States.

Astronomers listened to good news from outer space in their enclaves in Arizona, Wyoming and west Texas. Green entrepreneurs only a generation removed from South Asia and Eastern Europe clustered amid the Monterey pines of Big Sur, in the cornfields of Iowa, within sealed, half-buried arcologies along Pamlico Sound. The stochastic city blossoming hidden amid the near-ruins of Detroit, silent and extraofficial as it was, prospered as no city had since the 1947 founding of Levittown unknowingly sentenced urban cores to slow death.

Cascadiopolis was an equally stealthy western answer to Detroit's secretive rebirth. Built on Federal land, its inception funded by a handful of private philanthropists, its initial design ruthlessly controlled by a Colorado environment activist who fancied himself a latter-day Pablo Lugari blessed with a much larger canvas, the city-that-was-not-a-city hidden high in the Cascades grew not despite itself but through the sort of deliberate intent not seen in North America since Pierre L'Enfant laid out the streets of the District of Columbia. Where Washington's diagonal avenues had been arranged to provide maximum opportunity for enfilading cannon fire to repel British invaders, Cascadiopolis defends itself in far more subtle, and effective, ways.

Tygre Tygre aimed to approach that city much as the British had approached James Madison's Washington. Like his historical predecessors, he would set flame to the seat of power. Like them, he would ultimately fail, while the dream that was the heart of the city would endure.

Tygre is a tall man, like all natural leaders. We are not so far from the fruit trees of Central Africa, and the same height which confers the advantages of long-armed reach and the first glimpses of danger also helps dominate committee meetings and win bar fights. Our genes know this, far deeper even than our socialization, which only reinforces the message.

The newcomer is ambiguously colored in the pooling moonlight of the Cascades night. Bashar cannot decide for a moment exactly which species of hatred he will deploy on this intruder so arrogant as to walk straight through his brutally-trained pickets. The newcomer doesn't seem to be a white man, but neither is he safely, anonymously dark-skinned. Something weird, like Anadaman Islander, or someone from the genetic melting pots of late, unlamented West Coast liberalism.

Distrust is universal, Bashar reminds himself as he slips the muzzle of his weapon up into the soft skin at the bottom of the taller man's chin. "Welcome to the end of the line," he whispers.

Tygre is unperturbed, calm as a man being handed a check by a bank president. When he speaks, his voice has a timbre that could call armies to the march, bring men and woman alike to their knees, or fill an offering plate. "I rather prefer to believe this is a beginning."

Bashar nearly shoots the man right there and then, but something stays his hand. He would be within the rules of engagement—nobody legally enters Cascadiopolis by night, not ever. "You never heard of the Granite Gate?"

That is the outpost much further down in the watershed, where the abandoned railroad spur runs out of trestle, where people with visas or deportation orders or any of a hundred essential materials cited on the ever-circulating lists can appear and apply for entry.

Even here in the heart of fog-bound anarchy, there are processes, rules, requirements to be followed. Freedom must be protected by a wall of suspicion. Only rats slip through under dark of night. They are trapped, beaten, skinned, then hung out to rot on iron poles at the farthest boundaries of the city's territory like shrike-impaled prey.

These measures are largely effective, making the work of Bashar's pickets much easier.

But not tonight.

"It was not convenient for me," says Tygre.

"Convenient," says Bashar as if he has never encountered the word before. Despite himself, he is fascinated. No one has been so utterly unafraid of him since he hit puberty. Thirty years and a near-collapse of civilization later, Bashar's very name is a byword for brutally effective security from Eureka to Prince Rupert.

"No." Tygre smiles. In that moment the true force of him is revealed like diamonds being spilled from a velvet bag. Calling it charm would be like calling a North Pacific typhoon a breeze. A tall, handsome man with a voice like bottled thunder can take on armies. A tall, handsome man with a voice of bottled thunder and that smile can take over nations.

Even Bashar is set back. "We have rules," he says weakly, a last gasp of bluff in the face of defeat. A million years of evolution have conflated with the raw tsunami of one man's power to overcome even his profound distrust. His pressure rifle drops away from Tygre's chin. "What's your name?" Bashar barely swallows the "sir" hanging at the end of that sentence.

"Tygre."

The word rolls through all the pickets on the turked comm circuit, echoes in the ears of those within shouting distance even though the man is whispering, launches into the air like the compressed chirp of an uplink releasing orbital kinetics on some unsuspecting ground site.

Some last vestige of procedure rescues Bashar from terminal embarrassment. "You have a visa, Tygre?"

"Do I *need* one?" His voice holds the infinite patience of a kindly god.

"Asylum," mutters someone *sotto voce* in the dark.

Bashar doesn't even seem to notice for a long, hanging moment. Then he echoes the word as if the thought were his own. "Asylum. You can claim it."

"I claim asylum." The gentle humor in Tygre's voice would make a stone smile.

Part of a memorandum from the Security Subcommittee to the Citizen's Executive, originally drafted shortly after Tygre arrived in Cascadiopolis:

A cursory analysis of the action reports from the first penetration will show that virtually every picket on the south slopes claimed to have seen Tygre personally on his entrance to our territory. This is clearly impossible, as the deployment patterns were not significantly disrupted that night, as evidenced by comm time-position tags.

As might be expected, the descriptions provided in those action reports vary widely. At least three pickets, specifically alpha-seven, alpha-ten and gamma-three, claim that Tygre's skin showed stripes in the moonlight. Given that first contact was made by alpha-five, and Bashar's intervention occurred within alpha-five's free fire zone, it is impossible for any gamma picket to have witnessed the encounter, and strongly doubtful that alpha-ten saw more than silhouettes.

Yet the action reports possess the intense conviction of passionate eyewitness testimony. Clearly the pickets all believe they saw Tygre.

Citizen Cole has advanced a theory of mass hallucination brought on by biological, chemical or pharmacological agents. However, she offers no possible dispersal mechanism. Citizen Lain has suggested multiple persons in stealth suits or other low-visibility gear, combined with "the power of suggestion."

It is the opinion of this office that while judgment should be withheld in the details of this matter, there was no significant breach of security other than what was documented by Bashar in his own report. While we are hesitant to simply dismiss the testimony of so many pickets as fantasy, there is no more reliable explanation available. In the meantime, Tygre will continue to be monitored closely, just as he has been since entering the city.

Cascadiopolis welcomes Tygre with dank, mossy arms indistinguishable from any bouldered stand of trees by night. He enters the city silent as mist off the river. Bashar walks before him, point man on a patrol the security chief had never thought to walk.

Prisoners not summarily executed are bound over to the Evaluation Subcommittee. That body is made up of specialists much like Bashar himself, though their focus is on information extraction rather than perimeter security. It is a self-conscious paradox of distributed self-governing communities that such experts emerge in the face of demand. Hydrologists, medics and economic theorists, for example.

Tygre walks behind the back of a man who has not yet understood where the bounds of loyalty lie. The city is among the trees, of the trees, in a way that even the great-souled visitor has not yet understood.

This is the city that is not a city, close kin to the urban pioneers of Detroit but springing from a different resource base. Where the stochastic farms were atop abandoned shopping malls and office blocks, their living spaces distributed and ephemeral within the centuries of civic infrastructure towering above the raddled Michigan earth, Cascadiopolis is built from the basalt bones of the Oregon Cascades.

Seventeen million years ago in response to a crust-busting cometary impact the region drowned in a mantle plume of molten rock that eventually grew to be a mile deep. Basalt fractures as it cools, forming hexagon pillars of seemingly unnatural regularity. The later return of the stratovolcanoes

17

lifted the recognizable peaks of the modern Cascades—Hood, Adams, St. Helens—pulling the mid-section of the Columbia River basalt flow upward with the rising line of mountains. The hidden pillars of the earth cracked as they emerged. The emerging shoulders of the young mountains birthed hidden lava tubes.

In time, all was covered with the rumpled green blanket of lichen, moss, ferns, rhododendrons, and eventually the towering Douglas firs, Western hemlock and lodgepole pines. The old growth forest tops three hundred feet in height, trees of a size unimaginable to city-raised eyes from deep in the east.

Bury your city that is not a city in long lava tubes the size of subway tunnels, build it among the natural pillars framing the cliff faces and ravines, stake it to the flanks of forest giants twenty feet in diameter, spread your trails under vast networks of rhododendrons, draw your water from glacier melt streams and seep springs.

Do all that, build no fires, and you will be invisible to satellite and aerial surveillance. Even thermal imaging gets lost in the deep shadows of those spreading canopies.

Populate your city with biotech engineers, refugee coders, third-generation hippie grass farmers, anyone with skill and will. Place them amid your shadowed outdoor halls with luciferase coldlights engineered from the firefly genome and you have an intelligent, pale constellation beneath the cold roof of night.

Tygre enters this mystical night of chilly shadows and watchful eyes. Bashar stalks before him, a squat and vengeful god already rethinking the virtues of human sacrifice. Tygre knows but does not care—his supreme indifference to the jealousies and violences of the world is among the chiefest of his charms.

The people of Cascadiopolis emerge from their camo netting. Children crawl from beneath thermal blankets tucked inside dripping bushes. A manufacturing team puts down their water-powered lathes and spring-loaded microchip pullers to stare. Fungus farmers abseil down out of the high branches, leaving their reeking troughs unattended. Currency reverse-arbitragers abandon their palm-sized terminals to leave half a million New Yuan stranded in a Flemish forex repository. Shovels in hand, the Labor Subcommittee emerges from the trench of a brownwater pipe project to stare.

Tygre has come to Cascadiopolis, and the city has risen to meet him.

He follows Bashar into the lava tube known as Symmetry. Along with the tubes named Objectivity and Innovation, Symmetry serves as secure storage for anything requiring metal concentrations or chemical shielding, as well as the chambers for the governance necessary to any functioning anarchy. Symmetry is where the Security Subcommittee maintains its weapons caches and its interrogation rooms—those elements of their work not subject to the decentralization ethos by which Cascadiopolis governs itself.

Government is very much on Tygre's mind, of course, because he has a purpose in all things he does—most of all in stealing a march behind the wall of the most reclusive city in America. Being his own Trojan horse, in effect.

He steps carefully along the resin-soaked fir logs leading down into the mossy darkness of Symmetry. There he will face the first passage of this, his final and greatest performance. The great man whistles as he passes within, a song out of religious history which gives pause to the watching multitudes behind him, their eyes shining with the pallid echoes of destiny walking.

GRADUAL

Happiness Cardoza stalks the Granite Gate. She has spent most of a week in a tiny high-altitude survival shelter buried in leaves and mud almost a half a mile east of the site. Greenie patrols have passed with a dozen feet of her at least twice since then, but she continues invisible.

Though she can be dangerous in the way of hard, competent women and men of her generation, her only weapon on this hunt is a fluid-lens scope. It is a South African import, turked from the far side of the world to bring her a small miracle of static electricity and focused monopole magnetics. Not being a fool, she has much more lethal hardware cached nearby. Just in case.

She doesn't pretend to understand the physics of the scope, but she certainly understands the operation. Cardoza can count the pimples on the chin of the young greenie currently front-lining Cascadiopolis' doorway. She can even dial in a fish-eye view of each individual ruddy excrescence.

Quit scratching yourself, Otis, she thinks toward the kid. *You'll have a happier life later on.*

No bullet for the guard this mission. His lucky day. Instead she is watching process, to see how often the greenies vary their routines. Cardoza is looking for patterns amid the variations. She knows those patterns are there—no human being is capable of truly random behavior.

Not even the legendary Bashar.

There are only so many viable patrol routes, for example. They have to follow different paths to avoid leaving a trackway in the forest. At the same time, the terrain itself dictates where those patrols must travel, to be effective.

Likewise the guards at the Granite Gate. This one, whom she has nicknamed Otis, has been on several different shifts. He and his peers switch shifts around for a few days, then rotate back to whatever other labor the collectivist hell of Cascadiopolis has assigned to them.

Their only regular behavior is the manner in which would-be immigrants and traders are processed. A necessity, of course, for such dealings as the greenies have with the wider world. That consistency is the defenders' weakest point, but it isn't Cardoza's ideal approach. Bashar is the polar opposite of a fool, and expects just such a line of attack. Cardoza is certain that if she approached with papers or trade goods she'd be found out.

Perimeter probes had proven disastrous. If her employers

were lucky, they might identify the body from the skinned corpses hanging in the forest glades. More often, the operatives just vanished. Dead, or swallowed up by the greenies.

Cardoza's plan is to watch at least a week. She has been creating a baseline of the behaviors at the Granite Gate, identifying all the interdiction activities in play along with whatever she can observe of their patterns and metapatterns of deployment. She also carefully watches who is admitted and who is turned away, in case some detail in that process suggests an approach despite her intuition. She is empowered to make a reconnaissance into Cascadiopolis, opportunity permitting, but no one expects her to do so.

Least of all Cardoza herself. She doesn't do suicide missions. Not even against greenfreaks.

Eventually she'll withdraw and make her way back down into the foothills to where her bike is hidden. No two wheelers on these rough slopes. Down below, a long night's ride to Portland's West Hills will bring her back to her employers.

Mostly she scans, makes notes, and thinks.

Oregon's Willamette Valley had been spared much of the worst of what has overtaken the ruins of America. An area once blessed with an overabundance of rainfall retreated into mere shortages, as opposed to the wholesale drought which depopulated the Southwest from central Texas to southern California. Likewise the summer heat was merely unbearable, while the winter hurricanes which first began in the century's first decade lashed the Northwest without drowning it Gulf of Mexico style.

Still, Portland these days was more like historic Cairo with its cycle of flood-and-drought depositing permanent layers of mud in the downtown streets and rendering the old industrial district of the near southeast virtually worthless.

Most of the money had long since retreated to Dubai, Johannesburg and other centers of twenty-first century wealth.

What remained in Portland had climbed the West Hills, bought out the zoning rules and created a series of glittering arcologies for itself. These Escherian constructions were anchored against the already-bizarre fixture of the OHSU hospital complex atop Marquam Hill, folding reliable access to antibiotics, nuclear medicine and worthwhile trauma care into the blanket of such wealth and privilege as remained to dominate the Oregon landscape.

William Silas Crown sat in the sky-spanning penthouse of the Council Crest arcology and stared east toward where Mt. Hood would be if the air were clear enough to see it any more. Crown could recall easily enough his youth when the mountain was a snowbound chevron floating in the silver skies. He still knew where to find it, even if no one under thirty could point to the peak with any confidence.

"Streeter," he said to the empty air. "Has there been any update on Project Verdancy?"

"No sir," replied his executive assistant, stepping in from the office next door. She was a willowy woman of mixed Asian extraction, with that strange hyperefficiency that sufficient money could buy. Or at least put on the payroll.

"Meaning reports without status changes, or meaning no reports at all?"

Streeter didn't even glance at her wrist. "Asset Chi has been bouncing a chirp off the Galileo-II Eurosats on schedule. Keepalive only, no updates. She is in place and observing as planned.

"Asset Tau penetrated the target last night. No status check since, which is within operational parameters."

Crown tapped his teeth with his index finger. "And our sources inside?"

"Current status unknown, sir. There has been no evidence of recent compromise."

"Of course there hasn't." Bashar was too good for that sort of thing. Crown would never know, until he realized he didn't know anything at all.

Still, such a mare's nest of rogue talent and soft-path tech simply couldn't be ignored. He was long past believing in the sanctity of much of anything, but some things just shouldn't be kept hidden.

Not that Cascadiopolis itself mattered a whit. The green-freaks could go camping in the woods until the entire range burned out for all he cared. He didn't have timber rights, possessed no interest in access control.

Crown was far more interested in the innovation arising from that misguided band of anarchists. Once the geek-American community had wrenched itself away from the forty-year side-show that had been the software industry and gone back to good old-fashioned hardware—not to mention good new-fashioned biotech—the game had changed. Barely in time, either.

The case study was around gas-in-a-jar. Several California startups had engineered petroleum-producing microbes in the late 2000s. The oil shocks arising from the American failures in the Middle East produced the necessary economic boost to kick-start development, but lacking a terminator gene, the bugs had gone home in the pockets of too many lab assistants tired of six dollar per gallon gas.

Within another decade anyone with a high school science education and the talent to brew beer was in the oil production business. And *nobody* had made any damned money off the greatest revolution in energy production since Colonel Edwin Drake started digging holes in Pennsylvania farmland back before the Civil War.

If these idiots weren't smart enough to capitalize on their own intellectual property, he would damned well do it for them. The world needed those quiet innovations. At least if anyone planned to keep the lights on much longer. Beachfront condos on the Beaufort Sea were fine for sun worshippers with enough money, like Crown himself.

There were a few billion people starving in place. The green-freaks weren't going to keep it all to themselves. Their intellectual property was too damned valuable to be pissed away on hippie dreams. Better someone who could do some good got hold of it.

Crown realized Streeter had been speaking.

"I'm sorry, Evelyn," Crown admitted. "I lost track for a moment."

"Carbon, sir."

"Carbon?"

"They've been sourcing carbon nanotubes in laboratory quantities."

"Not industrial quantities?" he asked.

"No, sir. Not unless they're running a very small industry."

He turned that over in his head. Why would the greenfreaks need nominal quantities of carbon nanotubes?

Because they'd found a way of making their own up there in the woods. Charcoal ovens or similar crap, tended by some hyperfocused hippie with a set of nanomanipulators.

"Reference testing, Streeter. They've figured out something important, I suspect."

"May I congratulate you on the fortuitous timing of Project Verdancy."

Crown laughed bitterly. "In the past five years we've traced eleven significant innovations in manufacturing, data management, distributed systems and closed-loop resource management back to Cascadiopolis. And that's only what we can account for. All of them released open source, so widespread before they were detected that any IP action would be profoundly meaningless, even with an airtight license in place after the fact. Frankly, I would have been more surprised if we didn't cross paths with some new initiative of theirs."

Streeter met his look with a small, tight smile. "Very good, sir." Something odd hung in her tone.

"Very good indeed." He sighed and tapped his teeth again, wondering what was bothering her. Time to change the subject. "How are you doing on those power futures contracts?"

Cardoza sees her opening when Otis is relieved from his post just before moonset. One of Bashar's lieutenants, whom she thinks of as Chophead, comes out of the shadows followed by a kid even younger and more pimply than Otis. Chophead yells at them for a couple of minutes, then slides back into the deep woods, leaving Otis to walk the new kid around.

The Granite Gate stands empty, an unguarded trilithon which could lead to an earlier age of history. She is not so stupid as to rush it in a quiet moment. There are triplines, monitors, quiet watchers sleeping lightly. No, the opportunity she sees is for social engineering.

This new kid doesn't know his shoes from his shirt, that much is obvious. Something's up inside the city, if they're pulling back all the experienced hands. Cardoza thinks he'll be on shoot-to-kill orders for anyone who crosses the perimeter— here, that being the path leading from the stub of the old logging railway trestle and down through the ravine to the Granite Gate atop the other side.

Even now Otis walks New Kid around stumbling in the dark, pointing out the perimeter markers, the colored stones that provide ranging points for covering fire, the visible paths and the hidden ones—things he needs to understand and will not remember. Cardoza knows perfectly well there's no point in bracing Otis, but she's pretty sure she can keep New Kid from toasting her the minute she comes down the public trail.

It takes time and effort to train someone to kill. New Kid doesn't have the look. He's a placeholder, filling in here until someone can push him through some live fire exercises and have him kill an aging yuppie or something, just for the practice.

Cardoza settles in and chews quietly on a cranberry bar. Local produce from the bogs up by the mouth of the Columbia. As if she was a greenie. They aren't completely crazy, after all. Just a bad case of misplaced priorities. She keeps an eye on the Granite Gate while Otis and New Kid wander, listening to the cadence of their voices as they whisper like bulls blundering through a wheatfield.

Subtle, these young men were always so subtle. She smiles in the shadows and allows her ears to continue to reconnoiter.

Eventually their voices recede, echoing through the ravine, after which farewells are murmured. Cardoza never catches the rhythm of challenge-and-response. New Kid really is a bookmark then, and nothing more. What the hell is going on up there? In her days here she hasn't yet seen anything remotely this lax. This was city-grade mickeymouse, like she'd expect to see on the Edgewater contract-security perimeter at Boeing-Mitsubishi or Microsoft.

She's been given latitude in her mission parameters for a reason. She's just found that reason if she wants to take it. Even so, a walkup was dangerous. Had to get within earshot to run a talking play. New Kid might get excited, might get lucky, squeeze off a headshot or something.

But Cardoza isn't paid to be safe, she's paid to be smart. This could be a real smart way of getting into Cascadiopolis, escorted every step of the way

She raises herself back up and zooms in on New Kid with the scope. The starlight is almost pulsing this far from any power grid, but still faint as ever. Even so, the scope is smart enough to deal with that, at least as long as there's some skyshine. New Kid looks nervous to the point of throwing up. He fingers his rifle the way a fourteen year old imagines a woman might want to be touched. Cardoza swallows a silent laugh.

His pimples really are worse than poor Otis. *Kid*, she thinks. *After tonight, you'll never pull guard duty again.*

I promise.

Taken from an anonymous retrospective on early-to-mid 21st century business practices, published under a Creative Commons license:

Though corporations as such are by historical nature tied to the sovereign authorities which issued their charters, by the time of the late nineteenth century the multinational or transnational model held sway. While wealthy individuals could and did function in the role of corporations under specific circumstances, the combination of distributed risk and accumulated capital was too seductive to resist over time. Even those parts of the world where socio-economic structures varied significantly from the Western European model were not able to combat the allure of corporatism. Imperial China, Communist China and the Sunni Islamic societies all surrendered. Even al-Qaeda, that great anti-Western bugaboo of the decades bracketing the turn of the century, owed far more organizationally to transnational corporations than to any historical Islamic tradition.

Then the Westphalian model of sovereignty which had prevailed for over three and a half centuries abruptly collapsed. Though sovereign states by no means ceased to exist, their absolute control over many aspects of the global economic, diplomatic and military systems was fractured beyond repair. Corporations were already tenuously tied to their charters and nominal countries of origin through the continual liberalization which had begun when the United States Supreme Court first opened to the door to corporate personhood in the Dartmouth decision of 1819. Now they became *de jure* sovereign to match their long time *de facto* sovereignty; not by positive legal assent, but by sheer default on the part of the chartering bodies.

Given the chaos of the times around rising sea levels, worldwide crop failures and energy wars in the Middle East and Africa, few people outside economics faculties even took notice of these changes.

It was the ultimate triumph of libertarian free marketism and Straussian neoconservatism. The disasters foretold by twentieth century economic liberals came to pass, but again, were no more than a candle in the catastrophic winds blowing across the people and lands of the Earth.

What no one predicted was that the corporate actors would soon become foundational to the maintenance of continued peace and public order. The first, immutable law of capital is that it will be preserved.

ALLELULIA

Tygre might not have arrived on the wings of the storm, but he certainly brought chaos with him. The dungeons of Symmetry are not deep, or extensive, but they are as fearful as the workrooms of the Inquisition. That lava tube was the source of all discipline in the undisciplined community of Cascadiopolis.

Not that the freemen of the city need fear it. Only outsiders go below, more often than not without returning to anyone's sight.

Except for the birthright Cascadians—children brought to term under the spreading branches of the Douglas firs—everyone here began as an outsider. Everyone here had been interviewed, at the Granite Gate, by one or another committee, around the common tables and in whispered intimacy beneath the ever-dripping rhododendrons.

A few of us have even descended down the moss-damp steps into Symmetry. We especially know what Tygre faced there. Not racks, or arcs of voltage and pain, but the deadly combination of pseudocognitive databases and conscious sedation.

We gather together, as we so rarely do, to see if this new man will emerge. We sense a world borning in the mucky loam beneath our feet.

Still, we do not know what passes within.

Tygre ignores the dermal patches. For all they seem to be affecting him, they might as well be dewfall. His smile echoes in its affable silence, an expression strange on his mighty and passionate face. The leather straps holding him to the chair seem almost insubstantial, somehow.

Bashar has already begun to understand this man's secret. His knowledge is nonverbal, or perhaps preverbal, buried deep in the hindbrain where the triggers of reflex flow. The same instincts that make Bashar a deadly marksman have already surrendered to Tygre. It will be some time before the security chief can unwind his reactions sufficiently to contemplate betrayal.

For now he simply mirrors Tygre's smile and watches two women from the Security Subcommittee attempt to work the man over. In a way, the sight is funny.

Anna Chao is stumpy and angry, with dynamic ink tattoos crawling up and down her arms in a fair representation of the Divine Wind overwhelming the Mongol fleet. Sometimes Bashar thinks he can see aircraft carriers sinking in the storms, their stars-and-stripes flags burning to ash. Anna's primary work detail is supervising the stonemasons who quarry basalt from the ravines and crevices of the mountain beneath their feet, careful to take their slabs and pillars in such a way as to leave a natural-seeming void behind. This has given her the muscles of a stunted giant, but strangely, no patience at all.

Her interrogation partner in this game of bad cop-bad cop is a little person of African-American descent. Gloria Berry just manages to top three feet in height, and she is built like a bowling pin. Gloria is also the single meanest person Bashar has ever known in a long life filled with evil-minded sadists and good old-fashioned neck breakers. She is also rumored to have more lovers than any other woman or man in Cascadiopolis.

The two of them stacked together would barely be tall enough to stand duty at the Granite Gate, but they'd broken many a testosterone-laced hulk in their time.

Tygre just smiles.

"I don't freaking care how you got in here," Gloria says with an incongruent echo of menace in her piping voice. "I don't freaking care who you know, who you've done, or who you've bought off to get here." Her fingers fly through a haptic interface of microwatt lasers and passive motion sensors, teasing data out of piezoelectric Malaysian quantum matrices embedded in stone blocks. The tease is not going well. "What I do freaking care about, my sweet, sweet man..."—Bashar's spine shuddered at that—"...is how you've come not to exist anywhere in western North America."

Anna checks Tygre's patches with a worried frown. For all that she swings a hammer on the day shift, her delicacy is a butterfly's. "He's taking it up, Glo. It's just not, well, doing anything."

Tygre's smile widens. He clearly has all night to spend here in the delightful company of these women. Bashar's hindbrain stirs, prompting him to speak out of turn. "I don't believe you'll get anywhere with this one, ladies."

The look Gloria shoots him would have maimed a lesser man. "We don't tell you your business, soldier-boy, don't you be telling us ours."

Anna reaches into a toolbox which was once bright red but is now covered with layers of stickers in an archaeology of protest and outsider music trends. She brings out an ancient pair of pliers, the handles wrapped in grimy medical gauze. The tool seems to smell like an old wound, even to Bashar lounging fifteen feet away. Tygre looks with polite interest, then speaks in that divine voice. "You need help fixing something, ma'am?"

"Only you," says Anna.

"Am I in need of some adjustment? If you wish to know something, you have only to ask."

Here Bashar has to laugh, though he keeps the noise behind his lips. The gruesome twosome have been working Tygre over for an hour, datamining, reading his eye reflexes and the set of his jaw, but they haven't actually tried direct questioning.

Which admittedly rarely works on people making an involuntary visit to Symmetry, but still represents a deeply amusing problem.

Gloria glares at Bashar again, then with both hands elbow-deep in her data, turns the hard-eyed look on Tygre. "Name?"

"Tygre."

"That all of it?"

"Tygre Tygre, actually." There is a benevolent warmth in his tone. "Spelled the old way."

"Right," says Anna in a withering tone. In a city which is home to people with names like Starbanner, Undine and Taupe Pantyhose, Bashar finds this hardly fair.

Gloria eyes her display suspiciously. "Where you born?"

"Nowhere."

Anna clacks the pliers, miming the breaking of a knuckle, but Gloria waves her to silence.

"How'd you get here?"

"Walked."

"From where?"

"Further downhill."

Admirably truthful answers, Bashar realizes, and profoundly useless. Still, there is something on Gloria's face.

"Anna, come here," she says quietly.

Tygre maintains his mask of amity while the other interrogator slips around to the far side of this segment of the lava tube. They don't bother to speak aloud, or tell Bashar anything at all, but both heads are quickly focused on the glowing, buzzing universe of information projected above the pile of broken stones.

"You ever own an automobile, Tygre?" Gloria asks after a few minutes.

"Never."

"Scooter? Registered bike?"

"Never."

"No bank accounts," says Anna.

"That's hardly incriminating," Bashar offers in spite of himself. "Half the people here have never even touched folding money, let alone held an account."

"He is *not* half the people here," Gloria mutters.

Anna steps over to Tygre with her pair of pliers. "Tell me, man. What happens if I use these?"

Tygre's smile widens. "You probably would prefer not to find out."

"Wrong answer, man." Her eyes cut to her own enormously muscled bicep.

He follows the line of her gaze with a lift of his hand. For a moment they touch, finger to arm, and Bashar realizes how enormous Tygre truly is. Anna is not tall, but her mason's arms are thicker than Bashar's thighs. Tygre's fingers look overlarge even laid upon her tattoo.

The tattoo storm calms beneath his touch, a sunbeam breaking through the clouds—something Bashar has never before seen.

"Right answer, woman." He stands, shrugging off the restraining straps as if they'd never been buckled. "I believe this interview is over."

"It's done when I say it's done," Gloria answers hotly.

Anna is fascinated by her own tattoo and does not reply.

"Have you found any data trail on me whatsoever?"

"No..." she admits. Her voice is grudging.

"Then under which security rule are you holding me?"

With Bashar in the interrogation room, Gloria could hardly declare a security emergency. And Bashar himself would be the arbiter of any imminent threats. In this moment her role is confined to the vetting. With or without prejudice, but the moment for Medievalism has already passed.

Tygre turns to Bashar. "I would meet your people." He then gravely nods at first Gloria, then Anna. "Will you ladies accompany me?"

"I'll skinny dip in hell first," Gloria snarls.

Anna smiles and takes the big man's hand. Just by size alone, she could have been his child, giant daughter to a giant father.

They head back out the deeply shadowed hallways of Symmetry, past salvaged cubicle partitions and homemade concrete dividers. Bashar trails behind them. From the deepest part of the lava tube, Gloria's steady, monotonous cursing washes over them like waves upon a distant shore.

An excerpt from the Bacigalupi Lectures:

The concept of "soft path technologies" is at least as old as Aldo Leopold. Twentieth century culture had barely noticed the idea, discarding it unused like so many other potential salvations. Much like water, capital seeks the easiest channel. Infrastructure re-investment requires enormous commitment to long-term planning, or the resources of a stable government.

Wall Street would never spend the money in any given financial quarter, and it never looked into the future past the next quarter.

Cascadiopolis took its inspirations from the same wellsprings as the urban pioneers in Detroit, along with their daughter-colonies in Buffalo, Windsor and else-where: the hippies of the 1960s and 1970s, the Green movement of the 1990s and 2000s, the apocalyptic undergrounds of the decades of the twenty-first cen-tury. While the individual thinkers and tinkerers who provided the underlying soft paths were scattered throughout history, only in the opening decades of the new millennium was there sufficient social will to imple-ment these on a scale larger than family farming or microcommunities of shared intent.

For the first time since the invention of coinage, social capital was able to trump financial capital. Social capital itself is perhaps the greatest of those soft path technologies.

The root causes of such change are as fantastically varied as the root causes of any cultural movement, but the proximate causes are stunningly clear. The failure of governmental institutions outside of the defense sector was a deliberate strategy of late twentieth century Republican leadership. By the early twenty-first century conservatives had succeeded beyond their wildest imaginings, only to meet with disaster. Instead of a libertarian paradise of unrestrained capital lifting a rising tide of employers, workers and households, an economic apocalypse emerged which made the Great Depression look like a post-Christmas sales slump.

At the same time, two hundred years of aggressive industrialism combined with a deliberately self-censored policy of abusive neglect of climate change trends came home to roost in an overwhelming way. The loss of New Orleans was not a fluke; it was a harbinger. Mobile, then Charleston, then Miami followed within years. The upper speed of hurricane winds increased by forty percent during that period, forcing a revision to the Beaufort scale. Sea levels rose as currents shifted to bring polar meltwater south.

The financial disasters on Wall Street and Main Street were echoed for anyone who lived too close to water.

Suddenly solar-powered hot water heaters and windowbox greenhouses didn't seem so silly, even to dyed-in-the-wool conservatives convinced that the six-meter waves pounding the Gulf Coast were somehow a political conspiracy concocted by the left.

Even then, as always, most people were incrementalists. The balance of power shifted in that the activist minority grew from a noisy fringe to a major movement within American society. In this, they were welcomed by their Green brethren in Europe and the Third World.

And so Cascadiopolis was built, one soft path at a time.

We don't know what to make of him, we who stand like owls ranked in the darkness. Mother moon has set early, so the shadows under the trees are nearly as dark as the shadows beneath the stones. Still, we wait out the time of blood and screams and query hacks, watching the tunnel's entrance as if our own deaths lurk within.

When Tygre emerges, he stands tall with fists cocked upon his hip and sweeps his gaze across us. More than half of the city's shifts are present by then, over two thousand souls crowded shoulder to shoulder on branches and along paths. We breathe as one beast, mutter as one many-headed animal, shift our collective weight and stare.

The man himself is almost luminous. His skin shines out of the shadows, and his eyes flash as if target-painted by distant lasers. He looks back and forth, taking us in, then tilts his head, takes a great breath and speaks but one word.

"Hope," Tygre says in a voice which ripples through us all.

At that we dissolve into twice thousand tired, grumpy people looking for sleep, sex, food, explanations. Whatever has bound us together dissolves like cardboard in the rain and we dribble away from the majesty of his presence like cats pretending they'd never seen a dog in the street outside that screen door.

He just stands and smiles until we are almost all gone save a few stragglers. Flanked by Bashar and Anna Chao, the large man looks over the city as if it were his own.

Eventually he speaks again. "They're coming for you, you know."

"They been coming for us all our lives," Anna answers him. Her tone is offhand, but her words are the story of protest in a new American century.

He glances sideways at her, a strangely ordinary movement. "This is different. Not authority. Capital."

"What does capital care for us?" Bashar asks.

"Don't be naive," Anna snaps at him. It is clear she already sees the lines radiating outward from Tygre's statement. Authority has its own constraints—statutes of limitation, boundaries of time and districting and election cycles. Capital knows no limits, is the beast that shouted "profit" at the heart of the world.

Bashar is not naive. He knows his own world. It is filled with firing solutions and perimeters and ways to stop, break and kill his fellow human beings. Capital is a distant evil he has always resented from the wrong side of a badge, but finance was never a mystery fit to catch his interest.

"And you've come to save us?" she asks, her voice turning oddly sweet as she addresses Tygre.

"I have come to save no one." His words are oddly prophetic, given what was to unfold. "But one can prepare better against an enemy one can see at the gate."

"Capital doesn't sneak through the dark and cut tripwires," says Bashar.

"Oh really?" Tygre lets the words hang in the dark.

After a long, tense moment, they move toward one of the canteens. It is late, even by the standards of the largely nocturnal world of Cascadiopolis. Food here, like most other things, is communal—made and served in groups, by groups, for groups.

There is a test in the minutes which follow, the kind of test that gets people not killed but gently expelled. Tygre walks into the camo-netted kitchen with the hot ceramic cooking tubs and steam tables. There he takes up a fine German knife and dices down a peck of fiddleheads waiting to go into the stew, moving as smoothly and casually as if he'd been working the kitchen here for years.

Only Bashar realizes how frighteningly quick and precise Tygre's bladework is. Anna seems entranced by the big man's economy of motion, the grace which he applies even to the most menial tasks.

When he begins to dip into the spices, even the other cooks step back slightly. A delta tang soon wafts from the stuttering pots as the fiddleheads stir amid salmon fillets, jerked magpie and tiny, stunted carrots grown haphazard in the high meadows amid their cousins the Queen Anne's lace.

He finally looks around. "Tomatoes?" Tygre asks hopefully.

No, there are no tomatoes, but there are peppers. Someone fetches a basket of withered green onions that bring more flavor than substance. Word passes, more vegetables and herbs arrive, strings of last year's braided garlic, dried Hood River apples coated in nutmeg and turmeric.

It would be a dog's breakfast of a stew in lesser hands, but Tygre divides his pots, explores different flavors, shifts from Cajun spice to Bollywood to lazy Mediterranean with the most unlikely combinations of substitutions. He is dancing with the flavors now more than before. We come and gather round, the army of owls reconvened by the scent-lure.

The evening which began with an expectation of blood ends in a sunrise feast. Our bellies are sated and our souls are piqued by this man who has made for us a sacrament of our own wine and bread.

The only flaws are Gloria's distant grumbling, and later, distant shouting of some new crisis as dawn's pink light peeks across the slopes of the mountain looming close to the east.

If you build your city well enough, it will be portable. Not in the sense of snowbirds towing their homes behind straining fifth wheel rigs that burn the last of the freely accessible oil before being parked to rust. Rather in the sense that a few-score backpackers with good data storage and the right training can make their way to Vancouver Island, or the forests around Crater Lake, or even more distant locations, and create anew what has been built before.

It is never the same. This is no greenfreak McTropolis to be stamped cookie cutter from loam and rock and sculpted wind towers. Rather, each locale has a different watershed, biological resources, landforms and contours. But the principles propagate—self-government, specialization at need, information density and power parsimony. The engineering holds true at high level, even as configuration requirements change and available feedstocks shift with rainfall flight and spikes in net available sunlight.

Like their similars in urban Detroit, the citizens of Cascadiopolis have made of themselves a virus, a transmission vectoring in the heads and hands of everyone who has passed through their loamy avenues. Their city—your city—walks on scores of feet in every direction to bloom wherever fallow soil is rich enough and the land runs wide enough. A virus, an invasive species, a wave of change designed to outlast the marbled halls of capital which already burn in Seattle, Chicago and the paved-over Northeast.

TRACT

Cardoza walks straight toward New Kid with her rifle on her shoulder. The rest of her freshly-retrieved weapons she keeps hidden. She wills him to see her as he expects: a tired soldier coming home. He wouldn't know a frontal assault if she dropped a flash-bang down his shirt, but New Kid ought to recognize an approaching friend.

Even if she isn't.

The fundamental disorderliness of the greenfreaks works to her advantage here. They'd never acknowledged the value of uniforms, barely possessing basic security discipline. Cardoza figures she could talk her way past an even more experienced guard, with luck and no reinforcing authority close to hand.

So long as this young fool doesn't shoot her in the dark, she'll be headed up the hill soon enough. Still, the cranberry taste from her dinner bar is turning sour in her mouth.

Nerves kill more operatives than the enemy. A maxim she's always lived by, regardless of its statistical truth.

"H-hey," New Kid says, not quite shouting. He's got an old Mac-10—*What happened to the bolt-action rifle she had spotted earlier?*—too easy to make a mistake, shoot to kill in a moment of reflexive panic. The weapon has a short barrel and inherently lousy aim, but a dozen rounds on fast squirt could make anyone get lucky.

"Can it," Cardoza says in a tired voice. "I been out on extended perimeter all god-damned night. And who the hell are *you*, anyway?"

Angry sergeant gets them every time. Even fish like New Kid, who's never seen a sergeant before. Kind of like a pissed off older brother, Cardoza guesses.

"S-sorry," he stammers. The Mac-10 wavers, droops. Something clicks loudly.

She realizes the fool has pulled the trigger. Wisely, Otis has not left him with any rounds in the magazine.

"Do that again and I'll feed you that god-damned weapon." Cardoza mounts the last few steps to New Kid's watch station. "You going to walk me in or what?"

This is the critical piece of social engineering. Getting him to let her in isn't all that difficult. She's already won that battle just by standing here and scaring him into lowering his weapon. But getting him to walk her up the hill into Cascadiopolis— that's the important part here and now. Because without the escort, she'll be tripping over every alarm and booby trap that Bashar's foetid mind has dreamt up.

In without an escort is meaningless. In *with* an escort, well, she'll figure out what to do next. Whatever's going on up there, she needs to know. Her employers need to know.

"I'm not, not supposed to abandon my p-post..." His voice trails off, torn between a question and slow-building panic.

"Shithead," she says with a heavy sigh. *Don't overdo it.* "You're not abandoning your post if I tell you to walk me in, are you?"

Somewhere he finds unexpected courage. "My n-name is Wallace."

Great. Now if she had to kill him, he'd be halfway real to her. Handles like New Kid are so much easier when you need to gut someone like a perch. Real people are harder to handle.

"Of course it is, Wallace." She smiles, confident that even if he didn't see her teeth in the dark, her voice would bend with her lips. "So show me you know the way up the hill."

"Ma'am, you already know it."

She leans in close. Even at this range he was barely a darker lump in the starshine, without her scope to help. It might be time to kill him now. "Don't make me write you up to Bashar, kid."

A moment of indecision writhes between them like a wounded puppy. She catches the sweat-and-piss scent of his fear, musky even over the heavy fir-sap odor of the mountain air. He makes a small noise in the back of his throat, then shoulders the Mac-10. The tip of the barrel narrowly misses her hand.

"This way, ma'am."

"Good," she says to no one in particular.

He steps through the Granite Gate. She follows, marveling that it could ever be this easy. Together they hike upward amid the rhododendron flowers almost luminous in the deep, deep dark.

A key advantage of micron-scale technology is the sheer scale at which projects can be undertaken. While this statement may appear at first blush to be counterintuitive, consider the problem of distributing optical surveillance systems. Wiring-in even miniature cameras the size of gum packs requires a dedicated team and a van full of equipment and parts. But a coffee can full of microcameras can be scattered like wheat on the wind, to settle around the target area in a spray of heavy dust.

They require no maintenance, and are sufficiently cheap to simply ignore once their quantum batteries run out. No single lens sees much, not with that aperture and depth of field, but the array of lenses is astonishingly precise. Remote processors modeled on the brains of fruit flies handle the disparate constellation of related images, but that investment needs to be made—and protected—once, while the camera dust can be scattered a hundred times.

More to the point, those hundred scatterings cost less than the parts and labor to install a few dozen miniature cameras.

There is a direct trendline from the Big Science projects of mid-century America—Grand Coulee Dam, the Apollo missions, the Interstate highway system—and the spread of micron-scale technology in the twenty-first century. That trend was charted by budgetary analysts, return on investment calculations, and the self-preservation of big capital.

The error that big capital made in this arc of change is Gödelian in its self-blindness. No single activist, no network or membership organization, could compete with the capital costs of projects in the old days. By the dawn of the twenty-first century, the same distribution of materials cost and dissolution of labor expense which serviced big capital's ROI requirements had enabled technology transfer into the hands of any greenfreak with a little cash and some technical acumen.

Mob tech.

Nobody but the government could have built Grand Coulee Dam. Any fool can lay down a line of whale-fluke microturbines in a streambed.

The same micron-scale technology that was meant to bind the economy and the populace to the invisible will of big capital was soon turned against the power of money. "Green" went from signifying financial assets to another meaning entirely. That change rode into Western culture on the back of fractionated surveillance and widely distributed power systems.

Wallace—New Kid—leads her upwards along a path that is straightforward but by no means straight. Somehow Cardoza has expected more sidestepping and long pauses. New Kid knows his backtrail, or seems to at any rate. They made the first half mile of the climb unchallenged by anyone or anything other than passive systems which remained passive.

She is unsure of what surveillance has reported, but trailing New Kid with her chin tucked down, Cardoza feels safe enough. Cascadiopolis will in no wise be miked and monitored like downtown Seattle—the greenfreaks don't stand for that kind of oversight. If she gets in among them, she'll be safe enough until it's time to run.

At that point, her choices will be different. She has her uplink tucked into her undershirt. Her contract includes an evacuation bond. So long as no one kills her dead, Cardoza figures on getting out of the green city.

When New Kid is finally challenged, she is almost surprised. A change in the air tells her they are close. Hundreds of people in close proximity bring their own warmth to the chill of a Cascade spring night. Likewise the faint odors of smoke, of metal, of food, of oils.

Sniffers would have found this city, she realizes. Smarter minds than hers have worked on this problem for some time now. Sniffers couldn't just walk in like she has done.

Until now.

"Wally, who you got?" The voice drifts down from a Douglas fir. A faint violet spot circles the loam in front of New Kid, targeting something which would have no difficulty shooting in the dark.

"She's, uh…" New Kid's voice trails off as he realizes the flaw in his current plans, such as they are.

"I'm one of Bashar's specials," Cardoza says with a rich confidence she does not in fact feel. It's total bullshit, but that slang is regrettably common. "No names will be mentioned."

"You're not turked out," the voice drawls. "No comm bud, *buddy.*"

"Not where I been," Cardoza responds. "Now get out of my way, or explain yourself to Bashar later."

A grunt from up in the tree. With a click almost too faint to hear, the violet spot vanishes. "Explain things to him your own self, then."

Cardoza follows New Kid on up the hill, watchful for drifting violet spots. If the sentry is tracking her, they have her sighted in mid-back, where she can't see.

Her spine itches terribly.

From *The Daily Oregonian Newsblog*:

Eruptions at Three Fingered Jack?

Observers in Santiam Junction have reported explosions along the flanks of the extinct volcano. "There was a rumbling for a little while first," said Yellowjohn Hackmann of the Cascade Range Patrol, a citizen's militia which controls Highway 20 through the Cascades. "We thought pulse jets at first, maybe running out of McChord AFB up north. Now it looks like a city burning up there."

The University of Oregon reports that Three Fingered Jack is considered extinct. The geology department was executed by Creation Science activists during the Newport Crisis, but professor emeritus David Bischoff commented that government or private activity was a far more likely explanation than a geological rebirth. "Besides that," he asked, "Where the hell is the ash plume?"

Fires raging along the treeline have made any efforts at direct observation impossible. Local residents have opened a reverse auction for satellite imagery, with no success yet reported.

She arrives at the city amid the sounds and smells of a feast. Improbably, most of the population of Cascadiopolis seems to be out among the shadows. The clack of chopsticks echoes along with the clink of soup spoons. They eat, these greenfreaks, even as the sky lightens above the shoulder of the mountain and the mist rises off the night-damp leaves.

Cardoza knows perfectly well that this is a time for quiet retreat and the covering of fires. Patient, stable airships circle high above watching for the flash of metal or color when dawn's first long rays stab down among the towering trunks, the line of sunlight briefly following the contours of the land here on the west slope of the Cascades. Just as they search for the screened heat signatures and energy discharges, so they look for this.

Everyone goes to ground when the light changes because that is the moment when shadows turn traitor.

Still, they are here, clustered ever tighter around something she cannot yet see.

"Reckon Bashar's in the middle of that crowd," New Kid says sullenly.

Wallace, she thinks. Wallace.

He stares at her with an air of expectation.

"Get back down the hill, kid," she tells him in a weak moment of mercy. "You've done your duty by me."

Though Cardoza has no intention of confronting Bashar, she pushes into the milling crowd as if she seeks the center. She can feel Wallace's eyes on her back like that microwatt targeting laser down along the path. Screw him, she let him live. If he's smart, he'll just walk away.

Though she only means to lose herself in the crowd, the scent draws her onward. It is a spell, this smell, bait for the monkeys inside all our heads. The call of the tribe, the campfire, the oldest camaraderie from long before basic training and hazing and politics and congregations.

Strangely, they are almost silent, far more silent than such a large group of human beings has any business being.

Thinking very carefully about what she is doing, Cardoza joins a line spiraling through the crowd. Exposure is risk. Crowds are cover. Lines are not crowds. Her worries circle like a mantra until she finally reaches the hotline as the shadows shift from gray to orange and the sun flares along the ridgeline.

A truly enormous man is serving. He looks vaguely familiar to her as their eyes meet, which makes no sense. He is ethnically diverse and overwhelmingly handsome.

"You are the last," he says in a voice which floods her soul with sorrow.

Cardoza takes the proffered bowl—turned from some mountain softwood, she sees—and shrugs off the spell. Charisma? Pheromones? That doesn't matter. *This* man is not the key to *her* lock, whoever the hell he might be.

The temptation pisses her off.

She steps away, realizes Bashar is giving her a hard look. Cardoza hopes like hell he does not remember her as well as she remembers him. Fifteen years earlier, she was a uniformed security hack just beginning to learn what he'd already known a decade on by then, one of a pack beating on a cornered greenfreak terrorist.

He'd broken a dozen arms and legs and killed two of her peers escaping. In time, this man had led her to ask questions. Cardoza had been a girl in a reflective visor back then. Now she is a dangerous woman among dangerous people.

With the slight nod of one professional to another, she steps away with her steaming bowl of paradise. The eyes which bore into her from behind are not Bashar's, though, but the big cook's. Somehow she knows that without ever turning around.

Then the singing begins.

Crown reviewed reports. Sometimes he believed that was all he ever did—review reports. Someone had to make the damned decisions, after all. The world was running down, and no amount of rewinding seemed to help.

Someone had dumped a load of hot death on a blank spot in the map in the mountains south of Portland. While not directly impacting Crown—his timber interests were confined to the much safer Coastal Range, and even the apocalypse still seemed to require toilet paper—the fact that someone could airdrop that much hell into his neighborhood was pause for thought. Warfare had been irretrievably asymmetrical for decades now. Truck bombs in urban areas were one thing, but it took a lot of juice to loft that kind of firepower. One of the few things governments were still good at was covering airspace.

Uncle Sam might not be able to fix a highway any more, but he had orbital assets which could tell whether you'd dyed your hair this week. Which meant that whoever had flown this load had done so with payoffs in Colorado Springs.

Not inconceivable, even for William Silas Crown, but damned if he could see the value proposition of such an effort.

He had a much nastier feeling about the business, too. A hundred thousand acres of heavy timber didn't get nuked just for the entertainment value.

"Streeter!"

It wasn't her shift, he realized a moment later. A clerk would be covering, but he didn't want a clerk. He wanted Streeter. She was old school. Maybe the oldest. Good people stayed bought.

More reports—old recon and traffic records for Highway 20. Rumor mill stuff off the nets, all three generations. Correlations of arrest records, at least where those were still used.

Had the greenfreaks been building another city a hundred miles south? Cloning Cascadiopolis, maybe. He'd known for a long time that was possible, even reasonable. Trying to capture their tech was like trying to capture minnows. Every now and then you got something, but most slipped away like moonbeams.

But burning out an entire city by air express?

Short of pure, unreasoning hatred, he didn't see the point. And hatred didn't pay a lot of bribes in Colorado Springs.

SEQUENCE

Tygre lets his voice flow outward. Like the morning mist rising off the damp loam to fill the spaces between the massive trees, so his singing fills the space between the tired voices of the people of Cascadiopolis.

It is an old song, almost the oldest most people know. The doxology, unmoored from the trappings of Church and Eucharist in this post-denominational community, still holds great power among the people. "Praise God from whom all blessings flow." The tune is simple and old as the modern English that they share. And no one who lives on the shoulders of the Cascades can avoid the infusion of spirituality which seeps with the glacier melt out of the cracked basalt rock faces.

His singing weaves through theirs, carrying a strange contrapuntal rhythm to undergird their threading melody.

It is not the habit of Cascadiopolis to sing a sunrise hymn. It is our habit to rest uneasy during the time of transition, then for most working shifts to lie quiet during the hours of daylight. Some jobs require the sun's presence—Anna Chao and the other masons would not cut stone in the dark for fear of simple attrition of fingers. The Security Subcommittee likewise never sleeps easily.

But today the people are out, as they have been since his arrival. Today they sing with a strange sense of liberation about them, as if the burden of being free and green has fallen away and they are merely innocents in the forest.

Gloria storms through the group, enraged. She lashes back and forth with an old lacrosse stick made heavy at the tip with tire weights, shouting: "Shut the hell up, you stupid bastards. They can probably hear us down in Estacada. Idiots! Everybody in this place is going to get a god-damned extra work detail if you don't move it right now."

The song dies a rippling death. People scurry away, vanishing amid the heavy green leaves, the bright ferns, the deeper shadows, all to their various lairs and dens with a renewed sense of purpose—stung, shamed, regretful.

In moments there is only Tygre with his escorts of Bashar and Anna, facing Gloria's quivering indignation. A few others loiter close by, either bravely eavesdropping or foolishly slow to remove themselves.

No one from the Citizen's Executive is present except for the two of them.

"What do you want here?" Gloria demands, brandishing her lacrosse stick.

"What everyone wants," says Tygre. By daylight he is rendered strangely prosaic. "Food. Shelter. Freedom."

"You will destroy us."

Bashar stirs now. He has tired of defending this man who is not his, but no one has asked the right question yet, issued the correct challenge. "We're not down inside Symmetry now," he tells Gloria quietly. Anna Chao looks uneasy.

The edge in Gloria's voice turns on him like a swallowed razor blade. "What do you mean by that, Bashar?"

"I mean you are not interrogating this man." Bashar lacks the grace to look uncomfortable, but he forces a frown for the sake of diplomacy. He has never liked Gloria. Still, visible glee at her discomfort would suit no one's purposes. "He was released from your custody."

"He walked *out*."

"And you let him," Bashar reminds her. "Out here is my domain. Who stays or goes is up to me." He glances around at the watchers, the listeners, frowns at the woman who seems familiar but isn't. A question forms on his lips, but Tygre interrupts again.

"I destroy no one," he tells Gloria. The big man steps from behind the hot line and drops gracefully into a lotus position, bringing his eyes almost level with hers. It is somehow incredibly dignified and horribly patronizing all at once.

Bashar knows this woman has killed for lesser offenses.

"You are walking death," she breathes. "The Lord of Bones." She begins to shake, something coming loose inside her.

He reaches an impossibly long hand out and touches her forehead. "You do not know me. No man knows me. But I am here for all of you. Even you who would spear my side and leave me behind cold stone forever."

Bashar wonders what the hell is happening. Anna Chao looks no more enlightened than he feels.

Gloria slaps Tygre's hand away. "I'll stop you, you big buck bastard." She turns her back and walks. There is a sobbing sound, but it cannot possibly be her.

Looking for the woman he does not know, Bashar finds everyone but Anna Chao has made themselves scarce.

"I'm going to patrol the perimeter," he announces.

She nods, too overwhelmed to speak.

Tired as he is, Bashar can still walk like a hero into the rising sun, and so he does.

Part of a retrospective report from the Security Subcommittee to the Citizen's Executive, compiled from notes made during Tygre's stay in Cascadiopolis:

Subject joined in several work details during his first days in the city. He demonstrated considerable physical skill in aiding the Labor Subcommittee, but also displayed craft skills. He was able to braze the leaky Lyne arms on the Recreation Subcommittee's number two and three stills. This act alone won him general acclaim.

The unusual social effects seen on his entry to the city were not noted again in those early weeks. Gloria Berry continued to agitate against the subject, until she was advised by the senior directorate of this subcommittee to cease her activities and resume her ordinary work assignments.

In this same period news came of the bombing of Jack City. No verifiable rumors or hard data accompanied the reports, though the social chatter was overwhelming. Subject's arrival was timed very close to the date of the attack, such that certain members of this subcommittee were concerned about his role as a spotter or spy. Ms. Berry herself cleared that issue, showing that the last data netted from Jack City via smartdust was far later than the subject's possible departure time, given his known presence in Cascadiopolis. Subject's general invisibility in the datasphere has never been properly assessed, but Ms. Berry's analysis presumes that had he been present in Jack City, his data trail would have been available to us, just as it is in our own systems here.

After several weeks in Cascadiopolis, Tygre joins the unarmed combat circle. They meet each day under the aegis of Bashar or one of his lieutenants in the hours after dusk. The goal is to provide a training regimen and support for anyone tasked with security, but also for anyone interested in fitness or defense.

Large as he is, the newcomer draws immediate challenges from several middle-rankers—those who have risen high enough in the standings to feel the need to make a show against him, but not so high as to be secure in their position.

Tygre just laughs. "I do not attack," he says. "I come to watch you defend."

With a nod from Bashar, Reynolds rushes Tygre. He steps into the attack with a smoothness unlikely in such a large man. Hands slide slowly, far too slowly to anyone's view, then Reynolds is over his hip and windmilling into the loam.

No one has thrown her in at least two months.

The man turns, arms wide, and smiles at his watchers. "I will not challenge, but I will not be taken down."

That, of course, is the worst challenge of all.

One by one they step into the circle. The affair quickly assumes the aspects of capoeira more than the mill-and-kill of defense-grade unarmed combat. There is a dance, a measure of beats and moments which passes between Tygre and each opponent in turn. By the time he has thrown his third, the others are softly clapping tempo.

They dance, deadly and beautiful in the moonlit darkness at the edge of an old burn clearing.

Tygre effortlessly works his way through the juniors, then the other middle-rankers who should have stood with Reynolds. After twenty minutes, he has not even broken a sweat. Moments later, it is over except for Bashar himself.

And Anna Chao, who steps into the circle.

She has been alternately stewing with an inexplicable crush on this man and sparring with Gloria Berry, whose anger has grown boundless. During her days she has cut more rock lately than any mason in Cascadiopolis' brief history. Slab after slab of basalt has come down in recent days as if sliced away by some godlike knife. Frustration in the fracture lines. Unrequited passion amid the dust and splinters.

Now she is covered with gray from another shift on the slopes. Tiny beads of blood glisten black in the pale silver light of the late evening. She is almost a revenant, a ghost from beyond.

The gentle clapping picks up the tempo. These people know they are about to see a battle. Anna is one of the few who can stand against Bashar, and he has been known to defeat a moving truck with his bare hands. Her mason's muscles and torturer's ruthlessness combine to make her unstoppable.

Her infatuation with Tygre is a seam painted on her armor with bright lines.

He clasps his hands and bows to her.

She does the same, and begins to circle. Tygre does not respond in kind. Instead he merely stands, arms loose at his side, smiling slightly as she passes behind him. The profound vulnerability of his exposed back combined with his proud, uptilted chin inflames everyone's passions.

Anna feints from behind. Tygre knows it, he *must* know it, but he stands still as the Douglas firs as if to take the blow. A headstrike from her could be carelessly fatal.

Now she passes to his left. Frustration makes her quiver. His smile widens slightly, just enough for all to see.

It says: *Come to me, woman. Be mine.*

She spins toward him in a classic tae kwon do strike, foot flying toward the unprotected side of his knee, fists arcing for a follow up. He steps in so close to her they might have kissed in passing The knee blow misses completely. Tygre stops her fists with the broad grip of his own hands.

Anna grunts as one of her wrists snaps. Someone among the onlookers keens in sympathetic pain. She just stares at him.

"Impossible," she says.

"Nothing is impossible," Tygre replies. He takes her wounded arm in his hands and sets the bone with a nerve-rending scrape. Her breath passes her lips like fire in an oxygen line, but she holds steady. "You should have that seen to," he tells her, releasing her bad arm to the care of the good.

With a bow that turns to include them all, Tygre walks away.

Bashar has had enough. "You are not finished," he tells the big man.

Red mist is rising in his vision. Bashar knows what this means. He once killed an entire town when the red was upon him. Cascadiopolis is a place where the red stays far away, exiled from the country of the green. Tygre is a man who soothes some part of his soul that Bashar did not even know was damaged.

But still, to so casually break one of his city's strongest people—that is a cruelty to which cats could only aspire.

Tygre looks over his shoulder. "Yes, I am."

All Bashar sees is red mist and an exposed, retreating back. He begins to run, toward Tygre, then past him, into the darkness beyond where night swallows all sins and regret is invisible.

He will have to kill this man, and soon, if something does not change. Bashar hates himself most of all for the realization.

How It Works: *The Newcomer's Guide to Cascadiopolis:*

Cascadiopolis is a self-organizing anarchist collective which aspires to the self-actualization of all citizens in accordance with green principles. Welcome to your community.

When decisions must be made outside of the context of the collective consensus, the Citizen's Executive sits in proxy for the will of the whole. Subcommittees of the Citizen's Executive in turn manage specialized tasks which might require unusual knowledge, special experience, or organizational efforts beyond community norms.

Any citizen of Cascadiopolis is free to volunteer for the Citizen's Executive, but the coordinators are appointed by the will of the whole. An election may be called at any time, for any reason, by any citizen, so long as a minimum of ten percent of their fellow citizens agree.

This practice is a compromise between our anarchist principles and the unfortunate realities of existing in a world of governments, corporations and capital-intensive infrastructure. Every citizen's core aspirations should include a dedication to the day when the Citizen's Executive will wither away and we are all self-actualized without interference from each other or the city as a whole.

Tygre arises from his bed of heather and ferns and muslin. He has been sleeping in the higher slopes, where the elk browse. This is well within Cascadiopolis' perimeter, but far away from most dosses inhabited by his fellow citizens.

Privacy is a limited commodity in the green city. Tygre has his reasons, two of which are yawning themselves awake now in the little hollow he has just left behind.

A little mystery is good for the soul. It does not follow that a lot of mystery is better.

He knows better than to silhouette himself against the skyline, but there is a rock knee he climbs halfway up every day to crouch in a niche and look west into the failing light of dusk, toward the Willamette Valley, the Coastal Mountains, and somewhere beyond, the limitless depths of the Pacific Ocean.

This place has a smell and sense of home beyond anything Tygre has ever experienced. It saddens him that his project here will almost certainly fail. In the short term, at least. But the game is long, lifetimes long if one takes the most enlightened view.

He has come from a very hard school, hidden deep within the folds of the culture since long before this latest round of collapse-and-apocalypse was played out. Heresies within heresies, ancient wisdoms hiding in plain sight.

The school, nameless as the wind, had gone to a great deal of trouble during the last century to make itself and its precepts a cliché. No one would know to look, think to question, or believe what they found.

Tygre stretches in place against the rock. His skin seems to blend in to the lichens, so even his two lovers of the night before don't glimpse him as they scowl and stare about.

Go on, boys, he thinks. *The day is just starting.*

Fuddled, they do just that, the two young men gathering their clothes and heading down into the deeper trees, unself-consciously holding hands. Even now, especially now, that is difficult in the cities.

He watches them with a tinge of sadness. So many never find what life intended for them. Or who.

In time, his thoughts turn to the woman who came late to the singing the night he arrived in this place. Bashar was obviously concerned about her, but she has vanished into the shadows. This is Cascadiopolis. No one carries an ID. Subcutaneous chips are pulsed to ash. It is a reputation economy, assisted by labor traded for value without the intermediation of State authority or capital markets.

That's what they tell themselves, anyway.

The result is that a woman who doesn't make trouble, gets along well, and moves quietly among the dripping night-dark trees can vanish in their midst. Tygre is fascinated by this. Those crafts are not unknown, but they are rare. Even in a place as populated with exceptions as Cascadiopolis.

He has thought since the beginning that either Gloria Berry or the man Bashar would be the one who turned him. Now Tygre is beginning to wonder about this woman-who-isn't-there.

It would be nice to talk openly with her a while. They could stand in the center of some chuckling stream, in an open space where passive listeners or ordinary eavesdroppers would be unlikely, and mutter to defeat distant lip-readers. He can imagine the conversation, the ground they might cover, the common interests their divergent agendas ultimately represent.

Collapse will kill everyone, eventually. His school sees that as clearly as the die-hard defenders of capital do; as clearly as the generals in Colorado Springs; as clearly as the muftis in Baghdad and Mecca. The days of denial are long gone, swept away with the collapse of American politics and Wall Street. The days of agreement will never come.

But still, they have common interests: survival, prosperity in some form, clean air and water. Children, even. A future that will arrive no matter what.

Tygre knows full well he will never speak with the woman. She may be the knife in his back, she may be no one at all. It does not matter. He is a culture-bomb in search of a fuse. She is hiding from Bashar and the Security Subcommittee.

Everyone is who they must be.

In time, he climbs down from the rock, gathers up his clothing, and wonders yet again if this will be the day.

OFFERTORY

Happiness Cardoza has come to hate this city with a passion. She is a hunted animal. Not in actuality, of course, for the greenfreaks could have run her down in the first twenty-four hours if they'd been willing to call a general assembly, then have security beat the bounds while most citizens were locked down.

That isn't the way Cascadiopolis minds its business. Not inside the perimeter. Instead of the ruthless efficiency of corporate security, or the brutal force multipliers of the military, Cascadiopolis wars with weapons of rumor and shadow. The same people who would gut her like a line-caught salmon if they found her outside don't even look twice at her on the inside.

The dispassionate part of her mind, the internal observer, is fascinated by the dichotomy. The city is too big—know-your-neighbor security doesn't work among several thousand people with a churn in transient population. That's a tribal practice, useful by the dozens or the scores. There is a reason military companies were sized the way they were. You know everybody.

This place isn't a company. It isn't even a battalion. It's a brigade. Only there is no brigadier.

If it were not her life at stake, she might laugh at the way these people are betrayed by their own anarchist ideals.

Instead she keeps her chin tucked down, works in the saw pits concealed deep in ravines where deadfall and the harvests from ultra-low-impact logging were processed into usable wood. She doesn't ever sleep in the same place twice. People talk here, all the time, in soft, pattering voices, but they never ask questions.

A capable woman willing to work a two-man saw for an entire overnight shift is an asset not to be doubted.

She has met hauliers, bargemen, teachers, engineers, farmers, lifelong activists, bereaved parents, orphaned children, people lost within their own drug-addled souls, and even one ancient, renegade venture capitalist who likes to talk about the old days on Sand Hill Road down in Silicon Valley. Cardoza says little, but when it is her turn to tell some story she talks about a fictitious childhood on Vancouver Island, recalling lost Victoria before the winter hurricanes and the sea level rises finally overwhelmed that city.

"I'm just here," she says. It's a common refrain, one heard time and again.

Sometimes watchers from the Security Subcommittee pass by. Cardoza has made herself shorter, wrapped herself in tie-dyed muslin with lumps beneath that mask her muscles. They will not do face checks, these people—against what they stand for—so the pit boss just nods and security moves on.

All it takes is one chance meeting on a path, or one question too many, and she is done.

Her weapons and body armor are stashed amid a cache of such personal gear. They would mark her out in a moment, but she does not need them now. She has only kept the chirper, to bounce the simplest codes off satellite overflight and report back to her employers.

Cardoza is in, but there is no obvious next step.

This is not a city which can be set on fire. There are too many people to kill them all in their beds. They are too spread out to be gassed or strafed.

It would take fire from the sky, as has happened further south along the Cascades recently if rumor is to be believed, to stop these people.

Worst of all, in her hiding, she has not seen the singing man since. Tygre, his name is, and it's on everybody's lips. He spends too much time around the Citizen's Executive, around that stone bastard Bashar—people she can't afford to be near. Close, but not close enough. Far, but not far enough.

So she clicks out her simple codes, ignores the whispers about government spies in hiding, and watches the path ahead of herself with the paranoia of a hunted animal. Something will break soon, Cardoza is confident. So long as it is not her, she will survive.

Crown stalked his office, worried. Two weeks had passed since the bombing at Three Fingered Jack. He'd sent people into the resulting burn zone. There had definitely been something there. A fraction of the size of Cascadiopolis, perhaps a hundred people total, but it had been there.

Like aspens spreading along a mountainside, the greenfreaks sent out runners.

What drove him nearly to distraction was a complete vacuum of information about *who* had ordered the strike. Colorado Springs was uncharacteristically silent—the Air Force leaked like a sieve at command levels, when the right questions were asked by the right people at the right cocktail parties. Not this time. Likewise corporate chatter was mute on the subject. Not even Edgewater was talking, and that hit was very much their style.

Strange.

It was a wildfire, nothing else. Nothing to see here, citizen, move on, move on.

Reports from his Cascadiopolis assets were just as thin. Asset Tau had fallen silent, though Asset Chi had indicated in code that Asset Tau was still active in the city. Their codes were too thin to communicate everything Crown so desperately needed to know now, though.

"Streeter!" he shouted.

Another silence, which was even stranger.

Crown stared out the window, looking across the sullen brown waters of perennially flooded Willamette toward Portland's east side. Despite the recent rain half a dozen smoke plumes rose. More warehouse bombings, some street front rising against the dammed capital represented by stored merchandise.

"What the economy does not kill on its own, we kill for it," he whispered. "Streeter!!!"

A clerk stepped diffidently through the door. Berry, his name was. A fairly recent promotion to his personal staff. Crown couldn't remember the young man's first name.

"Ms. Streeter has gone out for coffee, sir."

"Coffee?" Crown was incredulous. "Seven years here, she's never gone out for coffee. Besides, we have catering."

Berry shrugged.

Crown realized the young man was dressed oddly too. Though his coat was cut the same as all staff uniforms in the arcology, the weave was too dark and glossy.

Even before he'd framed the thought as to why someone would be wearing Kevlar in his presence, Crown sprinted for his desk. He dropped and rolled as Berry opened fire with something that hissed like a fire extinguisher. The blast-grade window behind him rattled hard under a rain of darts.

A riot gun was clipped to the bottom of each pedestal of his desk. Crown snatched the right-hand one free, flipped the slide, rolled once, and fired through the modesty panel. It was sheathed in the same mahogany of which the desk was built, but thin fibreboard on the inside for precisely this purpose. The scattershot from the riot gun left a cloud of splinters.

Beyond the ragged hole, Berry slipped in his own blood.

Crown put a second burst into the young man's head as he fell. He counted to three, listening for footsteps, then low-crawled around the left side of his desk.

Nothing. No one.

And killing Berry meant no questions could be asked.

He rose, dusting himself off. He'd been played, and he knew it. Streeter was compromised, possibly beyond repair. A little too old school, maybe, to stay bought. And Asset Tau was in the same position. No one on his staff could be trusted now. Not even for money.

Only Asset Chi, a *contractor*, seemed to have remained loyal—out of reach of the infection here.

Riot gun at the ready, Crown tapped out 911 to reach arcology security. That at least was answered.

"What is your emergency."

"Suite 900," Crown said. "Challenge Buster."

"Seven niner Eugene," security replied promptly.

"I need a hard team up here now. Trust no one except me."

Strobe lights began to flash as blast doors slammed all around his level.

Waiting for rescue or death, whichever came first, Crown tapped out a coded message to Asset Chi. Whether the asset would ever receive it was an open question, but he had to try.

Maybe something could be salvaged. If not here, with his backups in Istanbul or Hong Kong.

The chirper embedded in the seam of Cardoza's micro-fibre camisole buzzes as she works a log. A week on observation and two on penetration, the only message she's received from her employers was a single-bit ack to her informing them of the contingency penetration. Now she's on one end of a two-man saw and the stupid buggers want to *talk*.

She ignores it. The chirper's memory will keep the message in place until she can sensibly retrieve it. No way to parse the click code against her skin when she's working this hard. And stopping to scratch where it itched isn't her way.

They work a while, she and her saw-mate—a whippet of a boy named Mueslix still struggling to be a man. Human saw-mill is hard work, but at least the wood stacks up like bodies so you can mark your progress. Mueslix has a very mis-guided case of the hots for Cardoza, and smiles too much, but he's okay.

His callowness makes her wonder what ever happened to New Kid for abandoning his post and bringing her in. Cardoza has stayed away from anything to do with security, for fear of discovery. Not to mention fear of Bashar.

Cardoza has missed something Zazie the gang boss called out. She can feel Mueslix slacking off through the change in the tension of the blade, so she slows her own effort.

Moments later they are all silent. This is a day shift, for safety reasons, so everyone can see Zazie just fine.

"We're on a stand down," she says, her voice carrying despite its softness. Zazie has a command voice Cardoza has admired, much more difficult for a woman to accomplish than a man. Deeper voices mean bigger muscles, after all.

It's all monkey politics in the end.

"What's up?" Mueslix asks.

"Security Subcommittee says we might be seeing incoming soon."

Crap, Cardoza thinks. Someone sussed her inbound signal. The chirper has no battery, only a static accumulator powered by the movements of her body, and it's small enough to pass anything but a very thorough pat-down. A tight enough sweep with the right gear would detect the fragment of silicon and carbon fiber. Or a strip search.

I am just one of two thousand here, Cardoza tells herself.

They drift off into the woods by ones and twos, leaving the site behind but taking their tools. She finds a moment's privacy and scratches where it itches despite her principles. She must ditch the chirper very soon, and wants to understand the message that could yet be worth her life.

An excerpt from the Bacigalupi Lectures:

We talk about secret societies all the time. The Masons, the Illuminati, *Opus Dei*. Paranoid fantasies, right? How secret could they be, with their temples and their lodges?

Nonetheless, behind the glare lie simpler, harder truths. From the earliest priestly cults in mud brick cities lost ten thousand years ago to the politic parties of today, memes propagate through channels of secrecy and trust. The cell system so beloved of revolutionaries has always existed. We call it family. Friendship. Lovers. The 1950s housewife gossiping over the back alley fence with the milkman. The beat cop having lunch with the City Hall reporter.

We no longer have beat cops or milkmen, any more than we have priests of Baal Melqaart. More's the pity, some people might say. But they're wrong.

Those relationships still exist. And with the world dying around us, they are stronger than ever. Secret societies of two and three are everywhere. The true unit of economy is the exchange between individuals. Forget capital markets and balance of trade. I give you something, you give me something else. Tomatoes from your windows box. Ammunition. Sex. Information.

It doesn't matter.

We are all secret-keepers. We share with our intimates, share less with our tribe, and tell nothing to the Man when he knocks down the door to ask questions. Some people know where to score good blow, other people know the true reason for the street layout of Washington, D.C.

The substance of the secret is irrelevant. The form of the secret is everything. Carry what you know into the world, gather what people have to tell you, and you are one of the Illuminated.

We began in light, so shall we end in light.

Cardoza hunts. The message was clear, one of her employer's own conditionals. She has a termination order.

This has become a suicide job. She's almost certain of that. There are large bonds which will be paid in the event of her death, money to flow to a sister she hasn't seen since early childhood. She doesn't care so much now. Walking away would probably be just as fatal at this point, and accomplish less.

Newcomer, the message had said when she unpacked it. Terminate newcomer.

She knows who they mean. Tygre is everyone, everywhere. People say he'd already joined the Citizen's Executive, the tenure and seniority requirements waived. Others say he'd charmed Symmetry's torturers, and they do his bidding now.

Her body armor is still in the cache. She slips into the carbon mesh panels, tightens the straps with all the weight of ritual. She sorts through her weapons—some things cannot be carried openly here, even now in the end game. A gas gun with shellfish toxin-laced needles will do, she thinks.

Turning, Cardoza find Mueslix staring at her. *How had he gotten so close?*

"You're on the Security Subcommittee," he says, his voice shaking. "You was spying on the log gang."

"Right," she tells him. The lie is convenient, he already believes it. This way she might not have to kill him.

She is getting soft.

"It wasn't nothing but a little dope." Now he is whining.

Dope? she thinks. That's not even against the rules around here, unless you're handling weapons or delicate equipment. "Look, kid," she says, letting exasperation creep into her voice. She really *should* kill him—his dead body will cause far less trouble for her than whatever he might say to Zazie or anyone else on one of the subcommittees. "Go back to your squat, lay low, and don't come out for a day or so, no matter what."

"You going after Zazie?" Now the fool sounds almost eager.

"I'm going after you if you don't skid out of here and keep your damned mouth shut!"

At that, he backs away through the brush which conceals the hollow where the cache is located. "I-I'm sorry," he says from outside.

"Me, too, kid," Cardoza responds.

Her earlier burst of fatalism notwithstanding, she already considers her possible lines of retreat once she has terminated Tygre.

COMMUNION

Gloria Berry takes up the hunting knife she uses for emergencies. The blade is longer than her forearm. She has carefully blacked it out, keeping only the edge sharp and bright.

Everybody is on high alert suddenly, and she knows damn well why. Tygre has finally betrayed them.

She will serve him his own fare, blood warm. And if that fool Anna Chao stands in her way, Gloria will serve her as well.

We are disturbed, we of the city. One of the wire mesh dishes strung high in the Douglas firs has picked up a signal, confirming the ghosts which had muttered at the edge of confirmation in the weeks since Tygre has come to us.

Something is on the move. A bombing, a murder, or simple old-fashioned betrayal. It does not matter. Cascadiopolis' years of paranoia are bearing fruit.

In another lava tube called Objectivity, the Citizen's Executive meets in a rare closed, emergency session. The man Tygre is not present. It is well into the day, and most of us should have been sleeping long ago.

"Anyone who has entered the city in the last months," shouts the Chair of the Labor Subcommittee.

Manufacturing and Craft shakes her head. "We already know where the problem is. That bastard will have us all dancing to his tune in another few weeks."

"Do you seriously believe Tygre is taking orders from outside?" Bashar asks quietly.

"He doesn't have to," mutters Manufacturing and Crafts. "He's plenty dangerous all on his own."

"Popularity is not danger," Bashar replies.

"Ever heard of demagoguery?" demands the Chair of Political Education and Theory.

Bashar cracks a small, deadly smile. "Leaders emerge from among the people."

"We are a collective," the Executive Chairman says. "We don't have leaders."

In that moment, Bashar knows they have lost. He rises. "Excuse me, but I need to go supervise the security arrangements."

"Against an *air strike*?" demands Labor.

"Against Tygre, if you must know." Bashar shakes his head. "And for him. Either one."

A children's call-and-response chant, used by early childhood facilitators in Cascadiopolis.

> Why are we green?
> Because nature is green.
> Why do we hide in the hills?
> Because nature lives in the hills.
> Who do we trust?
> Ourselves. And nature.
> Who do we fear?
> Everyone outside.
> What will we do?
> Grow and grow, like nature.
> Until when?
> Until the world is green.

Tygre heads back to the kitchen where he cooked the first night. It is time to cook again. Wine at the wedding, catfish and cornbread for the crowd, blood beneath the plow boards—food is the oldest sacrament.

He has been here long enough to know more about the ingredients. Wood ears grown in the deadfalls on these slopes can be as rich as a steak. Wild onions and sweet herbs from the water meadows provide a flavor which speaks of these high places. Saps boiled to bitter syrups add a tinge.

So he makes a stew, humming the Doxology. Different words are in his mind now than the old hymnals would have it, about the quiet green cathedrals of these high slopes and the basalt bones buried in the loam beneath his feet. Tygre is not sure whether he will share them.

The stew comes along slowly and he hums. Cooking by daylight is not so common—smoke can escape sometimes, and most people shift their meals in the early evening and later night hours, to be well abed by dawn.

But he knows a strike is coming. Probably not the orbital kinetics which reduced Jack City to ash, though that is possible. Even the oldest schools, the most ancient secret-keepers, have some very modern codes. And their own quiet, bloody disputes.

Except he is not weapon, but target. The hurried busy-ness around him confirms that. It might have gone differently, lasted longer, been sweeter, but this is of no mind to Tygre now.

One way or another, these forests will burn bright, even if no match is ever set. Like those pines which only germinate amid flame, this city will not truly spread its seed until the threat is overwhelming.

The dandelion flower must die before its children can fly.

With that thought, he smiles and cuts dried trillium into his stew.

"Was it you?" Bashar asks. Close behind, silent. The man is an arrow fired in the dark.

"It was always me," Tygre says pleasantly without turning. He can smell the musk of Bashar's desire for him, that the other man will never admit. Bashar barely acknowledges women, finds men no fit object whatsoever for lust, but the scent will not be denied. "But I did not breach communications security, if that is your question."

"Could you have?" Bashar sounds fascinated.

Tygre slices thin strips of garter snake jerky, then scrapes them into his pot. This will be a stew of the high places. After that, he faces Bashar. "Couldn't any of us?"

Tygre's clicker has been heel-smashed to black sand in the stream bed these past three weeks. That city man's contract had its uses in getting him close, passage through certain difficult barriers, but had never been his true purpose.

"You're in trouble," Bashar says.

"With you?" Tygre cocks an eyebrow.

"With everyone, I think. The Citizen's Executive is stirred up. There are other rumors, people with difficulties."

"Everybody loves me." He grins at Bashar's stone face. "Well, almost everybody."

"Everybody is coming for you. Jack City scared us all."

"Jack City is dead," Tygre says. He ladles out of a bowl of stew. "It would be better if it sat up for a shift or two. We don't have that much time." Handing the bowl to Bashar, he continues, "Here. Take, eat, and be comforted. Jack City is dead, but Cascadiopolis is going to live forever."

Bashar plucks a spoon from the tabletop and eats. Everything he does around this man is wrong, he knows it. The flavor stops his thoughts. It tastes of the city, of Mt. Hood, of all the vanishing green in the world. High slopes and deep loam and the bugling of elk across the valleys. Glacier melt and the buzzing silences of the burn scars in summer.

He is consumed by a moment of transcendence, and in that moment, sees the future.

There is a woman with a gun. Another woman carries a knife with dire intent. A committee votes orders for their man Bashar to carry out. A satellite rotates on its axis, acquiring a target in the Cascades.

Children run through the bear grass shrieking at the flowers. City-building manuals are stored in quantum matrices embedded in small river cobbles that fit in the palm of a hand. Silences amid the high forests remember times before even the first nations had passed here on calloused feet.

The world is running down, but it will always be reborn. Coastlines retreat, and there are new beaches. Floodwaters recede and there is a dove on a drenched olive branch. Empires fall but people still break the ground for grain, and their grandchildren need to keep records, and so it begins again.

Capital, rebellion, chaos, climate change. It all comes together so it can all be pulled apart once again.

We wonder if it matters how he died. The city-kill will come soon enough—this day, next season, ten years down the road. There is no real difference.

Tygre's stew, his song, his folding of the place of the green city into a simple taste and a few words—these are the winds that will scatter the seeds. Different mountains, different meadows, estuaries that have never seen a volcano piercing the sky. It does not matter. The city will be born and reborn again until stamping it out will be like stamping out worms after a rainstorm.

And *this* time, capital and rebellion and ancient scholarship have combined to ensure the future restarts without having to repeat every lesson of the past. We crossed a threshold, shed our Big Science and Big Industry in favor of little things which could be carried in a pocket and last a generation.

Ideas, ideals, and no small measure of love in a cruel and dying world.

Bashar sits with Anna Chao as she carves the marker. Such delicate work is not truly suited to her style of shaping stone. She is better at ashlars and slabs. Still, someone must do this thing, and by daylight, for it is too delicate to be worked in the shadows.

Though Anna carves a flame, the city has not burned yet. People are leaving anyway. Not in a rush seeking refuge, but in twos and tens and scores. The secret societies of couples and the tribalism of work gangs.

They all carry stones, and each stone is filled with data. Most carry tools as well, enough simple wedges and hammers and crucibles to jump start the first year of effort in some other wild place.

The grave contains three bodies. Tygre lies in the embrace of two women who did not know one another. The blood is on Bashar's hands in the end. That is who he is, that is what he does, killing the only man he will ever love, and striking down the enraged assassins in the moments which follow.

His days are shortened, too. The darts which ripped into his arm have left him with a paralysis which will be fatal in his line of work. Bashar does not mind so much. He just wants to see things set to rights before he walks off on his own. "I may be some time," will be his epitaph, borrowed from half-remembered history but still true enough.

A stranger approaches through the woods, a man clearly not accustomed to running down roads. Bashar meets the newcomer's gaze, an old but serviceable pistol ready in his still-good left hand.

"You won't need that," says William Silas Crown. "I just wanted to come see for myself." He nods at the grave.

Bashar knows there is no point in asking how. Tygre's flame was all too visible far from the night-dark forests of Cascadiopolis. He does have one question, though. "Did you send him?" Bashar asks Crown.

"I thought I did," Crown answers slowly. "But we were used alike, you and I."

Bashar, Anna and Crown stay by the grave til evening, watching the satellites transit the sky. One flares, possibly turning into the sun, possibly launching kinetics at some ground target.

It would be nice to say that Tygre arrived in Cascadiopolis on the wings of a storm. He did not, for he came as a man. But he left with every one who walked away before the end, his power multiplied by his name on all their lips.

His stone yet remains, if you know where to look, blackened by ash, covered by creepers, silent and cold as the mountain itself.

STOCHASTI-CITY

TOBIAS S. BUCKELL

During the world building discussions the METATROPOLIS authors had, prior to going off and writing our own stories, I remember Tobias Buckell being very passionate about the idea of building some of our future cities not on some new piece of land, but in the very heart of existing cities. In Toby's specific case, he was fixated on Detroit. This made sense to me, since Toby lives not too far from the motor city and travels there frequently, and has had ample opportunities to see the city up close.

But beyond that, I think Toby was also interested in making sure, for the purposes of his story, that the cities of the future also looked like and had connection with the cities of the present. In other words, that the people of our METATROPOLIS didn't just look like suburbanites wearing tunics, or something similarly ridiculous. And also, to be blunt, that the people of our METATROPOLIS didn't look all white and privileged—something that could easily be assumed given the genre, but which would have been entirely false for how America is shaping up in the 21st century, ethnically and economically (although hopefully we'll fix that latter part).

And so Toby's Detroit is a city that feels like the urban areas of today, populated with the people who live there now and will be there when the future arrives, however it comes. It's also a place where just a little bit of co-operation—in its many different forms—makes the city move. Take it away, Toby.

The day before the city rioted was a day, for me, like any other. The day before Maggie pulled me deep into the shit.

I was up late that night, bouncing at ZaZa's, just barely covering my bus pass for the month. Same shit, different day.

I had this funny feeling that I'd be moving on soon, which I did every couple years, as a shrimp of a man stared up at me and asked, "What are you looking at?" And I thought, there had to be somewhere more interesting to be than Detroit.

I'd gotten into a rut here.

The shrimp pushed at me. Spoiling for a fight.

I've found that the trick to bouncing, just as much as standing around and looking perpetually annoyed, was negotiation. Not negotiation as in the I'm-going-to-give-you-something-for-something-you-agree-to-do-for-me kind, but the sort of negotiation where you agree not to stave in some drunk bastard's skull in exchange for his leaving the club.

And although that doesn't sound like negotiation, with a drunk, it really is. Because it takes a lot of circuitous explanation, leading, and alternate phrasing to make them realize they're in for a load of shit.

"Stop. Breaking. The pool cues." I used a calm, patient tone. It was, after all, a calm and reasonable request. Even if it wasn't a request, really.

"What are you going to do about it?"

Even with all the negotiation, however, you also end up negotiating how much shit they might be in.

It was a Monday night. Usually a slow night. No jumping DJ using their antique original iPods lacquered in sparkling silver to run the floor. No girl's night. No happy hour. No nothing.

Just the regulars, quietly slinking their way towards an easier form of despair, hunched over the hump of the stained wood surface at the bar. Huddled against each other, backs turned to the expanse of the empty, unlit dance floor.

Just the core regulars, and this belligerent asshole who was up in my face.

"What are you going to do about it?" he repeated.

He must have thought he wasn't three inches shorter than me. Or that he wasn't fifty pounds lighter. This little one had something to prove.

Screw it. I grabbed the yappy guy's hand before he even realized it and twisted him around in front of me. He struggled a bit, so I half-nelsoned him quick, then marched him right past the bar. Several customers turned to watch, beers raised in a mocking half salute, as I gently shoved the shrimp out the doors.

He tried to turn around and come back in, so I sucker-punched him.

As he sagged to the dirty concrete I grabbed his collar and threw him against the brick facade of the club, the ZaZa's neon sign blinking and fitzing in front of us. Both of us looked eerie orange, then green.

"Come back in, I break something," I said, and left him there with one more good shove.

He got it. Negotiations finished.

Back inside the gloom the new bartender, Maggie, looked up from setting a beer mug down in front of an old man with a long, white beard. "Want me to call the Eddies?" She was probably too young to be pulling bar duty. But she was good at listening to wasted customers. She was also pretty enough to pull in the extra tips she needed, and surprisingly tough. The electrified deterrent clothes she wore were remarkably effective too. I'd seen patrons writhing on the floor after a butt pinch. Now they kept clear of her like cows from an electric fence.

"Nah." I leaned against the bar on my elbows. "If he's got an issue with me now, imagine what he'll be like when he wakes up with a bill after spending a night in the drunk tank. Last thing he needs is a lien on his house or something stupid. Call a cab. And where the hell is Lawrence?"

"Still running late." Maggie tapped the phone in her ear. I noticed she had a bit of a bruise under her right eye, covered with makeup. I wondered what from. Asshole boyfriend? Did she like her men wild and dangerous? It was certainly none of my business...

She cocked her head. "Want me to call him again?"

"Forget it." I'd have to sleep in the storage room until morning. The last bus would be leaving downtown Detroit any second. "I'll hit the cot tonight." Besides, it'd save me some money.

Whoever the pipsqueak drunk was, he was lucky. He was a downtowner and could get home in a cab without spending a good portion of his day's wages. He could afford to get drunk.

"That's three times this week. Go take a nap when Lawrence gets here, I'll drop you off."

"Maggie..."

"Reg, I insist."

No one called me Reg. Except her. I'm Reginald. Reginald Stratton. But she could get away with Reg.

It was the cheerfulness, I guessed.

Maggie let her car drive us there with a cheerful abandon, setting the vehicle's profile to aggressive and letting it weave in and out of traffic as it whined its way on. From the somewhat revised downtown, then on past the decaying warehouses and skyscrapers of the heydays, and from there into the sudden change of the nice suburbs. The ones within a short, very short, driving distance.

I didn't live there, though: I lived in the decay of the Wilds.

The further out you got, the longer it took to drive, the more gas it cost out where battery cars like Maggie's and bikes couldn't easily get to, the rougher it got. And that's where I lived.

It began with the abandoned tract houses. Many just slumped over, windows shattered, roofs failed or riddled with pigeons and shit. I grew up somewhere like this, a dead end an hour and a half away from any major urban center.

A safe place, a protected space, to raise your little ones.

Or so we thought back then.

All the while burning our way via car to and from work.

Back then.

Now those artificial greens and wooden houses were abandoned, for the most part, given away for the land to reclaim as its own.

At the very edge of the Wilds I had Maggie pull over into the driveway. I pulled out a hundred, but she shook her head. "Let's take a look."

She followed me in. I wasn't sure what this was about, but then, Maggie was the only one who got to call me Reg.

"Welcome to Casa Stratton." I waved my hand at the three acres of vegetable gardens and the large greenhouse I'd built out of windows reclaimed from houses further into the Wilds.

"It's a fucking mansion," Maggie declared.

"House belonged to some formerly rich family, once upon a time. All the stone and brickwork stopped it from getting burned up for steam engines or winter heating."

"And you own it?"

I shook my head. "Course not." No one owned them. That would have meant paying taxes. These were abandoned, but couldn't be purchased because no one would claim them, as that would result in having to owe back taxes, with interest, for decades. All these buildings floated in limbo, just like the outer skyscrapers: the Slumps. Perfectly good real estate, abandoned and not truly owned by anyone, and thus unable to be renovated.

I knew a lot of people who'd give their right nut to live in the close-by skyscrapers. Instead they were guarded by private security, or even on contract by Edgewater. Those owners kept them from being reclaimed, but you couldn't trace who those owners were. They were waiting for the good times to come back.

Who wouldn't kill to live closer to the urban hub? Let the megacorp farms deliver food into where you all were easily gathered? No more gardening for myself, no more hour-long commutes and most of my month's take going into transportation costs.

"Looks nice, though," Maggie said. "You got an extra room, I'll move in. But don't get excited, this is simple business."

"Leaving him?"

Maggie looked confused, then touched the bruise under her eye and laughed. "You think it's a guy? No, it was a lot of guys. Eddies."

"What'd you do to piss the Eddies off?"

"Hiding out up in a penthouse in the Slumps. They found me."

"Ah. So you want to couch surf me?"

"In exchange for half the cost of your bus pass, my car's cheap to run." She charged up the car at work, some sort of agreement with the owners. "Plus, buses are getting less and less regular. Could all quit soon enough."

Halving my transportation costs. Sounded harmless enough.

I agreed and showed her a spare room. There were seven. No real trouble, other than having a pretty roommate who was entirely uninterested in me.

Welcome to poverty homesteading, I thought. But it beat getting flushed out of the city by Edgewater. I'd made the same mistake Maggie had when I first arrived downtown, seeing an empty skyscraper as an opportunity.

Fortunately I'd had enough on me to pay the Edgewater holding fee and get loose.

Every once in a while, I wondered what happened to the homeless the Eddies rounded up who couldn't pay.

Later in the night, once Maggie was fast asleep, I padded out into the backyard and off into the Wilds. Survival training-wise: flitting my way through forest and suburban ruins.

My bolthole was about two miles from my house, next to an old oak tree. Buried near a massive root, I had my whole stake in a lockbox.

Sure, currency could devalue, but that hit everyone equally. With cash in hand and hidden, no hacker, frauder, lawyer, Edgewater flunky, or government, could get at my savings.

Good luck finding this out in the Wilds.

Maggie, on the way in the next morning, talked about the various cities she'd bartended her way through. Living out of the back of her car, charging up and moving on. She'd seen the East Coast, she told me. Now she was moving on through the Midwest, although she wasn't sure how the car would do in open spaces. She was thinking about saving up for an ox. Or maybe a donkey. To pull it when power ran out, or when she couldn't get gas to fill the generator in the back of the car.

"Driving by day, sleeping under the stars, seeing something new every day. I don't want to ever give it up," she said.

I lay slumped against the passenger window in my usual morning stupor, watching the dirty sidewalks slip past. Lotta trash was building up. Every other week pickups.

But there was something new. Something I should have noticed on the bus rides in, but was too busy balancing in the aisle to see out the window and notice. The bouncy roads kept you busy hanging on if you didn't get a seat.

People milled around the sidewalks.

I would have said they were homeless, but they didn't look like garden variety homeless. They were all clean-shaven, well-clothed. A variety of hairstyles: punk to stiff to end-overs. A lot of them wore gray suits, others a loose poncho.

They all sat along the street, watching traffic and life pass by. Some waved as we passed them. One of them sat next to a large plastic cube that was folding itself up, deflating from where it was hooked to the side of the street. Some sort of mobile tent.

Most of them bunched up near the disused skyscrapers of the outer ring. As we hit downtown they thinned out. But we passed one last pair, sitting on folding chairs, fruit drinks in hand with little umbrellas perched off to the side.

"Listen," Maggie said. "You still hurting for cash?"

"Yeah." Two men in blue pinstripes leaned against a corner, talking into earpieces. I'd done a tour. These guys were doing recon. I'd have bet the day's tips on it.

What the hell was going on out in the Slumps? I needed to pay more attention to the news, because whatever it was, the Eddies would be on to it soon. If there was going to be any trouble anywhere downtown I wanted to know about it before it reached me.

"I wasn't just trying to sleep out there last night for no reason. There's a guy, paid me a week's worth to try and shelter in the Slumps for a night," Maggie said. "I'd run out, couldn't afford the hotel I was in anymore."

"Creepy?"

"Turk work. Anonymous. Some piece of software's my second boss. I found the job on a list. Looking for people in Detroit to do stuff around the city. Random shit. Day One, I delivered a package lying out on a counter in a hotel to a bike courier ten blocks away. Then a couple days later I had to walk up to the top of some old carpark and toss some paperballs over the side. Weird stuff. Random. Paid well. Last night it was good pay to see how long I could stay in a Slump building. Some other guy, a lawyer, turking out himself probably, came and bailed me out from the Eddies. As promised, if I got caught."

"Job listing still up?" I asked.

"Nah. But whoever's running this is offering me a bonus to refer people verbally." Maggie handed me a piece of paper with an email address of random numbers on it. One time encryption, no doubt.

"A week's worth?" Pay like this, and with the money Maggie was saving me, I might be able to think about a place in the city. I could ditch the house in the Wilds after Maggie inevitably moved on.

"Week," she confirmed.

"That's worth a bruised eye," I said.

"Damn straight."

Plus, it sounded harmless enough.

I don't know why it's called turking. Taking a complicated task and putting it up online, divvying up the parts of a task between multiple people and paying for the results, that had been going on a long time.

Say you needed someone to find a certain face in a crowd, if you were an Edgewater investigator. You could upload the photo of the perp you were hunting, and then upload pictures of crowds you suspected the person was in.

Then you put the task up online and paid whoever turned in a result. Saved you time, someone else did the idiot work, and you got to focus on higher level stuff.

But it went further than that. Suppose you had a package in Los Angeles that needed to get to New York. When I was a kid you'd go to a centralized post office, pay for stamps, and it would be taken on a special van at a certain time of day along a series of routes to an airplane, across the country with a bunch of other packages to a distribution center, and then onto more vans, to finally end up at in New York. And most of all that was run by that one company,

Today you turked the package out. Left it at a street corner with a price embedded on the package's tag. Someone going in the right direction would snag it and get the credit or partial credit for taking it as close to the goal as they could get it.

But other things were also turked out. Insidious things. And you'd never know. All you were being asked to do was walk a package a couple miles from one place to another. What was in the package? None of your business. And if you opened it, the tag could snag a picture of you or pass on the information you used to agree to grab the package with to the owner.

No sense doing that.

So there was also no sense in wondering what I was complicit in when I pinged the email on the piece of paper Maggie'd given me, and got back a set of simple instructions.

I was to stand on the corner not too far from an Edgewater depot, and when they left their compound, text a certain number.

Simple enough.

And with good pay. I'd make what I made in three or four night's bouncing to do this.

Someone really wanted to know what Edgewater's comings and goings were.

Not really harmless anymore. But still potentially lucrative.

I left work early for my street turk assignment, walking my way over to the location. I stood in the hot night, wind kicking faded pieces of litter past me. Dirt kicked up, grit stinging my eyes, and the nighttime rush of the city flowed by. I had staked out a spot on the street near an alley where part of a brick wall collapsed in. No one could walk up behind me, and I had the shadows to lurk in.

Trails of brake lights burned on the back of my retinas as cars whined past. Some even thundered past. Uncollected trash out on a sidewalk smelled rich, making the thermos of coffee I had clipped to my belt seem unappetizing.

The Edgewater compound broke into a flurry of activity as a large armored van full of men in riot gear rolled on out, a siren burping out a staccato series of wails and screeches.

I texted.

Over the next eight hours I texted three more times as the streets fell into their late night rhythm of random cars, distant sirens, and the occasional cat fight that broke out near any given garbage can.

Simple enough.

When dawn broke over the skyline I had an hour left. I was that much closer to leaving the Wilds. And it was then I heard the click of a safety catch being released in the alley behind me.

Impossible, but there it was.

I had the lid cup of the thermos filled with coffee. I slowly raised both hands, the thermos cup lid hanging off my pinkie.

The Eddies must have spotted me.

"On the ground," spat the voice behind me. I followed the order.

Once I kissed the sidewalk he ziptied my hands behind me. I heard an engine gun up loudly as a vehicle whipped around the street corner. I was wrenched up to standing and tossed into the back of the armored personnel carrier that I had watched roar out of their compound all night.

In the dim light inside they shoved me up against a metal bench. Five men in full urban combat garb stared at me. With gray fatigues and night vision goggles, they were also fully kitted out to climb buildings, blow out doors, and rush in with a shoot-first-ask-questions-later sort of look to them.

"Good morning," said the nearest Eddie. "What have we here?"

"He was staking us out," said the one who'd snuck up on me.

After Sudan I'd been offered a job as an Eddie in Cleveland.

By then, I'd put in enough time kicking down doors and trying to figure out if the grey-green blob inside my night vision goggles was going to shoot me or run screaming.

"You staking us out, you little concrete bunny?" The nearest Eddie, a pale-looking thin dude with a sour smell, leaned in. "You related to those fuckers that've been setting off little bombs and running for it, just to get us to run around all night? You getting off on wasting our time?"

Nothing I said would be helpful, but if I remained quiet, that was a problem too. They had me here in the armored carrier because they could rough me up some before getting back to the compound. They were having a long night, and now they had a target.

Straight truth was the easiest course. No running around. "I'm not sure what you're talking about," I said. "But maybe. I got paid a good bit. Street turking. Just to stand there and text a number if you guys ran out in a hurry. I'm the bouncer at ZaZa's, usually, but I'm out in the Wilds. They offered me good money to stand here. Bus fares are tight: you know the drill."

The nearby Eddie still looked keyed up to cause me some pain, but the Eddie standing in silhouette at the entrance to the carrier nodded. "Makes sense. Turk out the stake out, just like the guy last night. We'll bust you, they'll have a turked out lawyer ready and waiting. They have other turks watching this scene, if last night was any indication."

"Fuckers," the sour-smelling Eddie said.

"Take this joker to a cell and wait for bail, charge the max for loitering," the Eddie outside said. He sounded in-charge and on-top. "Might as well see some good green for our trouble."

"Shit." Sour-smelling Eddie spat something nasty and brown at my feet. "Sure about that?"

"Dee and me will take patrol, see if we can flush out the other turks." This Eddie looked young, and tired. He rubbed his face. Maybe he'd commanded a squad overseas, enough savvy to get noticed and promoted to running things when he got back.

Now he probably sensed something was in the air, something that didn't bode well for the Eddies.

Outside Eddie shut the doors and slapped them, and the carrier lurched into gear. Sour-smelling Eddie smiled at me.

I didn't like him.

Some people enjoyed their jobs way too much.

This punk was probably some kid from the Midwest, one of those who seemed to think that everyone non-white was to blame for everything that was wrong with the country since any of the various crises had hit. He took some relish in policing the city, putting certain people in their place.

Probably had a no-immigration bumper sticker on his electric pickup cart. Even though it was mostly Canada and the Europeans trying to keep us contained in our own borders these days.

He volunteered to steer me to my cell, and followed me in.

I turned to face him. "Can I help…"

He hit me hard in the stomach, but I'd already tensed and let my torso move with the blow.

Still hurt. All this bus riding and gardening didn't exactly keep me in peak shape. I needed to remember to work a bit harder on that.

I was a bouncer, after all.

Back a few steps, and I was ready for the next, but someone smacked the windows with the palm of their hand. "Hey! Gary. Knock that shit out."

The Community Management Officer of the station stood outside. CMO S. Whatten, the patch on his chest indicated. Unlike all the other head-shaved urban commandos I'd run into tonight, Whatten had a business cut going. Middle-management kind of look. A suit.

But you could see in his posture he was command through and through. Probably served in the same fields as me. Been given a pat on the back, a gas bonus, and taken private work on his return.

S. Whatten shook his head. "Gary, you lose your cut."

"What?" Gary looked genuinely shocked. "I helped pull this one in."

"He's got a lawyer outside. If you kept going they wouldn't be paying us permanent bail, idiot, they'd be getting a force-and-violence payout from us." Whatten shoved Gary back. "Keep it up, Gary, keep it up and I'll happily toss your ass out of the dorm and let you walk to work every day. See how long you last on your own two feet." A known Edgewater walking out and around. He'd get knifed in the back before long unless he was very quick on his toes. Gary didn't strike me as quick on his toes.

Gary swallowed, and with a glance back at me, left the room.

But this wasn't over. CMO S. Whatten stood in the middle of the door, looking me over. "You don't have any property to post a lien against. Got a lawyer outside. Got no money our computer can find. But no record."

They couldn't find my money because I took it out and buried it deep in the Wilds, in the backyards woods. "You going to knock me around and tell me to keep more pocket change on me so that next time you won't feel like you wasted your effort?"

"No," Whatten sighed. "Not going to waste the effort. Not going to drill through a thick grunt's skull like yours."

I chuckled. "Yeah, plus, I don't take orders anymore."

"Fair enough." But Whatten still hadn't moved. "You don't know what the hell you were doing out there..."

"You know how it works," I said. This was leading to something else, though.

"I've seen enough turked out armies in my time," Whatten said. "I look young, but I paid out hard. I've seen the ghosts merging in on you, kids with fireworks, others with guns, others with cameras waiting for you to make the inevitable mistake."

Whatten said ghosts. And he looked haunted, his wide eyes flicked back to memories of battles past in other lands.

The warlords would hand out cellphones like candy to the kids. Promise them gas or food to carry out errands. And individually, not much was going on.

But as a whole, a vast and complicated and decentralized attack, they could bring armies down to their knees before anyone knew what had happened.

I could see Whatten opening fire on some starving teenager with a toy gun, while the cameras relayed the horrible results live to some hungry, waiting news service. Then after the cameras shut off, the kids with the real guns, who looked just like the others, moved in to attack.

"You know something big is moving," Whatten said. "People staking us out, street turkers all over the place, setting up things. Waiting. Out there. You know what the revised articles of engagement are, Reginald?"

"Yeah, I know them." It's why I wouldn't ever become a damned Eddie. Or any domestic boot-stomping yahoo.

All you did for a turked army was to put a brick down by the side of a road. And maybe all it took was a few hundred other bricks placed to create a roadblock. Individually, you could claim you were just making a buck.

But that still made you an enemy combatant. Which meant you were no longer a citizen.

You didn't belong to another country, either.

There were no rules about what they could do to you then. You simply didn't exist as far as the rule of law was concerned.

"At some point," Whatten told me. "Us Eddies'll get attacked here. And we don't stay Eddies when it turns into a war. When the Nationals get mobilized, we're a subdivision of the army. Then people like Gary, and the real commandos, they'll come in shooting, kicking in your teeth, and really showing you some pain."

I shrugged. "You know of another way I can cover my transportation? Some place to stay here in town?"

Whatten crossed his arms over his chest. "So for that you're dumb enough to work for some turker you don't even know? The people you're turking for don't even have reputation points. You have no idea what the big scheme is? I've seen you around, down at ZaZa's. You're no tool."

"Heirarchy of needs, CMO. Give the indigenous infrastructure, they don't have to depend on desperate moves." That was a barb that dug deep. Whatten had commanded. No doubt he'd heard that phrase often enough. He'd have taught it, too.

Get dropped into some third world situation where they had nothing. No matter the reason, you soon found out that whoever hated your ass could drum up eager waves of hungry soldiers throwing themselves against you.

There was always some rhetoric. But when you dug deep, it always came down to the simple fact that the ready-to-die simply had nothing to lose. They'd sign up and trust the math. If enough of them attacked, maybe they'd live. Maybe they'd get something out of it. Save their family, get something to eat, live, whatever.

Now give them something to lose, then those waves thinned out.

Infrastructure. Running water. Food. Medical assistance. Homes. Roads and travel. The most devastating tools of war.

But in a world where even the first world nations struggled to provide transportation, water, and safety, well, domestic shitstorms started to look like foreign ones. What you never thought you'd see anywhere but abroad, that came home with you.

Whether the starving and displaced were in Africa, or sitting around a dike that had burst somewhere on a coast here, the pressures were the same. Particularly once the domestic dike had been broken over and over again, where citizens realized that it wasn't just a one-off, weather had changed, and the government didn't have much to help them with.

That's when your thin line of civilization faded.

Welcome home, Whatten, and by the way you never left the front line, I thought to myself.

He got it. He stepped aside to let me walk past and down the corridor. At the other end a gray-suited man with a briefcase waited for me.

My mysterious lawyer, and fellow turker.

I was pushing up a good defense for Whatten. The truth was…I was getting nervous.

I didn't know what the hell I was getting myself into. And maybe it was time to get myself out.

The lawyer asked me to keep my mouth shut until well clear of the compound: sign this, initial here, don't worry about that. Quick, assured, and efficient. I was buzzed through the thick bomb-proof doors in no time.

He had a bike outside, an old and well-traveled carbon fiber Schwinn with a GPS in the handle and a heavy saddle on the back. He wheeled it alongside me. "Your fine has been covered. Your night's work is done," he said. "Thank you."

I'd checked my account on my phone, but didn't see the rest of my night's pay. I mentioned it.

The lawyer looked over at me and sighed. "It's in the fine print. The cost of springing you is far more than your payoff, so you get nothing as a result of getting arrested by this Edgewater franchise. You're getting a good deal, trust me."

I never took too well to getting pissed on and being told to like it. "I'm not a fine print kind of man."

Had they paid me after a successful mission, where the Eddies wouldn't have had anything to take from me, I would have been up for the night.

Now all I had to show for the night's efforts was the down payment on this little affair and some very sore ribs.

"But the contract remains what it is, Mr. Stratton. Can't wriggle out of these things, you know."

I licked my lips. "I'm pretty good at not getting noticed. How'd they spot me to round me up?"

The lawyer mounted his bike. "I don't know Mr. Stratton. Like you, I was just called in to take care of this. I'm just a turker, making some side money." He picked up speed, pulling away from me. "You know how it works. I don't know who you are, or what you were doing. None of my business. I was just here to pay your fine and get you on your way."

He left me there on the quiet rundown streets. I flipped through my phone's address book and emailed the turker's address I'd gotten the job through, but it bounced back.

Annoyed, I started a quick jog after the lawyer, sucking air shallowly thanks to the bruised ribs. The money was a magnet, dangling just out of reach.

Turker or not, someone was going to pay me the other damn half of what I was owed.

Three miles later second thoughts occurred as I clutched my ribs, struggling to keep up with the lawyer's leisurely pace.

In the early morning dawn peeking over sullied and coal-stained brick I realized more and more people were filling the streets I was huffing my way through.

Again, an odd and silent community of well-off homeless stood near their collapsible mobile structures. I smelled eggs and sausage sizzling: both my mouth watered and my stomach twisted at the smell of food, not a good sign after all the jogging.

The great old Ambassador Bridge loomed over the buildings, the gaping bombed ruins of the roadway overhead thrumming in the wind. Thank you Canadian Air Force for that one...

I turned a corner, and into a scene that, for a moment, didn't make any sense. The parking lots and gardens of this area were overrun with massive tents, large RV-type vehicles with masts, lean-looking roadboats, and tens of thousands of people.

Some sort of instant Midwest Burning Man festival, it seemed.

The lawyer disappeared into the center of the mass of people, and three very burly bikers stepped forward. Dark shades already on in the morning sun, their leather jackets festooned with tiny tags and symbols.

"Where's your ID?" the first asked, long beard whipping about as a dust devil passed by, fluttering tent flaps and flags on poles all around. Roadboat rigging twanged a chorus.

"I must have left it somewhere," I said, calmly walking toward them, trying to eyeball where the lawyer'd disappeared.

"Nice try. You can't." The nearest biker bodychecked me away. "Fucking footprinter."

My ribs flared pain hard enough to make me suck air in through my teeth.

"Listen." I held my hands up. That made it hurt more. "I'm not trying to cause any trouble. But I need to talk to someone..."

"You got trouble understanding?" The biker's tone was familiar. The sort of negotiating tone used to indicate he'd agree not to stave in my skull if I agreed to leave the camp.

I backed away.

"Get out, footprinter...Get out now."

I turned around, wincing. Back to the bar, then. Only this time I called for a cab.

But things didn't exactly get any better there. Lawrence sat on a chair inside the door, but a big closed sign he'd hand-lettered had been hung on the door.

"What the hell's going on?" I asked.

"Maggie went home. No bartender, no bar."

I blinked. She had no reason to be home...it made no sense. What could she be up to? My stomach twisted. I still had a bus pass. I ran like hell in time to make the morning bus out to the Wilds.

Maggie's car wasn't at the house when I got there.

And the lockbox, two miles out in the depth of the Wilds, wasn't there either.

I sat next to the empty dirt hole, my back against the root, and flung an acorn out into the bush. Cute little Maggie, the bartender too wispy to be in a brutal downtown.

She was a nomad, stringing her way through the brutal and lawless Wilds of the continent. Maggie was probably tougher than me.

Certainly smarter.

My savings had just been wiped out, and she probably had enough to make the next leg of her journeys.

It rained most of the way back. A dirty, whipping Detroit grimy sort of rain. I watched the remains of it congeal on the outside of the bus's windows as I was jerked back and forth between the quiet mass of commuters making their way in.

I recognized one of the guys several seats ahead of me. One of the squatters in the Wilds who'd given me advice on my garden. He had dog tags hanging off a necklace, something a lot of the reclamation groups off in the Wilds had. Little kudos for each other, signs that told each other where they stood in their own subworlds.

They would be happy to welcome me into their little tribe, I had no doubt. I could teach self defense in one of their crèches. Sleep on recycled packing foam beds. Help out in their gardens.

But I'd done the farmer boy routine. I'd joined the army to leave that. Not my talent, I'd found. I'd found my talent the day seven nomads descended on the farm I was working at.

I blinked at the dirty rain. Hadn't thought about that in too many years. The crack of a gun, the screams of the wounded.

All too easy. Shooting people, that was. Easier than deer, mostly. But it left you odd, somehow. A little less human each time, but with the knowledge that you could do it if it came to it.

I thought about standing in front of the bar. Thought about all the work put into the brick house. Thought about each bill taken home, buried near the tree.

Maggie pulled one over on me, and I didn't hate her for it. Not a bit. I hated myself for falling into a routine, a sense of complacency and tired resignation. A miasma of life that had made it so easy for her to do this to me.

Things didn't come to people who waited. Who picked over the trash and hoped to find treasure. It came to those who grasped.

But then I wondered if that was the same attitude that had led the world to burning up its resources and leaving the dregs for us.

Lot of maybes and buzzing going around and around in the back of my head. I quashed it all. I'd made a decision. I wanted my damn money.

After that, I'd figure out what I was going to do next.

I walked to the Edgewater compound and pounded on the gates until a dubious S. Whatten ambled out to regard me through the chickenwired bars.

"What the hell do you want, Stratton?"

"The lawyer, who was he?"

Whatten's pitying look dripped scorn. "Come on, Stratton. We don't know the laywer's name. And don't play like you've never encountered one and don't know the routine."

I did know the routine. Since the Lawyer Protection Act lawyers used public encryption keys, not names, to protect their identities. Too many of them found hanging from lamp posts by their necks. "His key, give me his key." It could have been someone turked to represent the lawyer in real time, with an earpiece directing him what to say and when, or an apprentice lawyer turked out, or maybe the real lawyer.

Hard to tell these days. Risky profession.

"Expired. Stratton, what're you doing?"

"They owe me money. I want paid. I've seen him out by the bridge, hiding among some homeless camp. Who paid for my fine, maybe you know that?" They had to have something.

Whatten moved closer to the chicken wire. He didn't touch it. Electrified. "You really want the lawyer that bad?"

I folded my arms and nodded.

"Okay," Whatten said. "We want him too. We want to know what the hell is going on. You get in there, you find him out, or anything out, we'll straight up pay you for the info."

They were that fucking desperate for any tidbit. Hiding here in their sandbagged fort. I felt a shiver move up my back.

"I just want them to pay me up. Anything I find out, I'll pass on."

Whatten bobbed his head a bit, considering whether to trust me. That little cloud of desperation hung over him.

He buckled. "I'll give you a car rental chit, straight cash bonus." He named a price.

Good price.

These kids were scared.

I took it. "What do you know?"

"Your fine, it was paid by Spaceship Detroit, a non-profit."

Sounded odd. "Who they hell are they?"

Whatten didn't know.

"What do they do?"

Whatten, again, didn't know.

But it was something. I turned my back on him.

Spaceship Detroit. They'd pay up. Or give me another job. I'd get roughed up for big money.

But mainly, I could sense it out there. Something moving through the city. Something big. And I wanted to rip a piece of it off for myself.

S. Whatten knew it was out there too. He wanted to figure out what it was.

Bad enough to pay me to do it.

Things were perking up a bit.

The electric car the Eddies rented for me was fully charged, plugged into a public meter. It was a raked back egg-shaped affair of carbon fiber and plastic windshield on three wheels. I swiped the chit Whatten gave me by the window and the car unlocked itself and the doors swung up into the air.

I settled in, running my fingers over the wheel, adjusting the seat just so.

Luxurious.

My father used to take us out for special family trips in his car, when the farm had mulched up enough biodiesel in the yardpits.

Just like then, when the doors shut, it was just you inside. Like when you walked into your own house. The outside world seemed just that, outside. A barrier between you and everyone else.

It was like one of those animes where the hero puts on invincible, giant, techno-armor.

There was an appeal to this. I always found the electrics more fun than the combustion ones as well. Instant torque all the way down through to the wheels in an electric, no hesitation.

I cruised around Detroit, slipping past the downtown section. It was a fortress, new and shiny buildings with their backs to the Slumps. The hardy core of a new Detroit, where people could live in walking distance to jobs and necessities. Where the city touched the river, and boats with massive parasails for mobility delivered their cargo along the docks.

I drove out into the Slumps, paralleling the river, aiming for the Bridge, with a stop near a park where a team of kids were playing baseball.

One of the little-leaguers of some reclamation crèche was happy to sell me a bat for cash before the coach and chaperones chased me off.

The expedition continued to the edge of the bridge, where I found an alley looking out at the main street across. Most of the homeless appeared to have left the sidewalks for the strange city, just evident in the distance under the ruins of the bridge. Things were pretty quiet, just the occasional person wandering down the road on whatever errand they were on.

I fished around inside my pockets and found a pair of painkillers, which I dry swallowed.

Then it was the long wait.

Hunting was never for the patient.

Or the hungry. Eventually, after several hours of seeing homeless wander by who weren't the lawyer, I ventured out to look for somewhere to eat.

The alleyway my car was in sounded busy.

I paused after turning the corner.

The car had been cut to shit with axes, door panels slashed clean off, windows yanked free, and all of this left quickly as I'd arrived.

Everyone had fled.

I got in the car, the door creaking sadly as it swung up, and sat in. I shut the door, looking nervously around, and tapped the accelerator to get the hell out.

As the car lurched forward the three dozen well-dressed people of all ethnicities came out from their hiding places and started running down the alleyway behind me. They wore suits, or cargo pants with the ponchos. Ten of them carried sharp-looking axes, while the others had large bags. A couple of them had a sled dragging behind them.

This didn't look good.

The car was in bad shape. It coughed to a gentle stop as some part fell off from underneath onto the road.

A silent and expectant mob surrounded me as I got out of the car, the bat gripped in both hands.

I would need to grab an ax as quickly as possible after the first couple swings, I reckoned.

But the crowd moved back from me.

"We don't want any trouble," one of the axe-wielders said. "We just want your car."

"Storing carbon producing energy in a battery still doesn't change the impact of the original source of the energy!" someone shouted from the back of the crowd. "Damn footprinter."

It was the second time I'd been called that.

"Shut up Mary," the axe-wielder said. "Sir, just step away from the car."

"If you can't see how to take care of your footprint, we'll do it for you," the woman shouted.

"Mary. Shut. Up." The axe-wielder turned back. "You are not helping matters."

I still stood there, bat in hand, keeping everyone at bay. "What do you want out of me?" I asked.

"Just your car," the man said, exasperated.

"What the hell is going on?" I really wanted to know. I felt like I'd fallen down a hole into some alternate Detroit.

"We're turning this area of Detroit into a car-free zone. We're lead front scavengers, looking to recycle any cars in our occupied territory into useful machines and products. We have a reprap to repurpose the materials. That's our job."

I didn't know what a reprap was. But even though things were hard on cars these days, you couldn't talk about turning Detroit into a car-free zone with a straight face.

These guys were nomadic extremist nuts of some sort.

"But what'll you do with the parts?" I asked. "What's the point?"

The guy grinned. "Oh, we'll put them to good use."

A pair of the crowd advanced on the back end of my car and smacked their axes into it.

"Hey!" I yelled, pointing my bat at them.

But the moment was past. They'd written me off as a threat and began tearing into the car with gusto.

So I grabbed the guy nearby with the axe and twisted it free. His friends hardly even noticed, too caught up in their fervor for car destruction.

I dragged the man, wrapping his cloth poncho around his neck and arms in a knot he struggled against, down to a set of steps away from the destruction.

"What...the hell?" he gasped.

Dramatic, yes. And yet, it got the attention I wanted. Now I had an axe. And a bat.

I held the axe up and looked at it. "What's your name?" I asked casually.

"Charles."

"Charles. Pleased to meet you. I'm Reginald." I loosened his poncho.

"That fascist bullshit doesn't fly, dragging me off like that," Charles spat.

Just like these other homeless, he was well-washed, well-shaved, with short-cropped hair.

I squatted in front of him. "Charles. I could care less. You chopped up the car I was renting. I have to think that violates my rental agreement. So you know who's going to get flack for that? Me. That puts me in a bad mood. And I'm the guy with the bat."

"And I'm the guy with some ten thousand other guys sitting just down the block," Charles said.

Fair enough.

I set the bat and axe down. "Okay." I pulled a chocolate bar out of my pocket and unwrapped it. "Just, explain to me what's going on." I waved my hand out at the camp, and the people on the side of the street.

Charles still sulked on the stairs.

I tried again. "You're all nomads, right, passing through Detroit?" Like Maggie, but in large tribes. Like locusts.

"Yeah, nomads. Low footprint nomads. We don't stress out the environment. Take what we need into recycling. Recycle what we have. We're here, but we're not part of the city, not part of the resources being sucked."

"So what are you doing with my car?"

"You ever ride a bike?" Charles asked me.

"Yeah. When I was a kid."

"It's a perfect technology. Ten to fifteen miles an hour for the energy required for a human to walk. And humans are good at walking," Charles said. "Evolutionarily, we're designed to just walk and walk and walk all day long. Eat some calories and watch us go. But look at this shithole."

He waved his hands around the street. "Not a bike-friendly city?" I hazarded.

"Fuck no! We're in the second century of having this perfect technology, but we kept focusing on something far less efficient. The streets aren't bike-friendly, the Wilds aren't friendly, Detroit and a lot of these other Midwest cities are throwing money at electric cars and power plants that run on coal, thinking that if they can just swap things out life can run right back on the course it did.

"Meanwhile, people run in gyms or just get fat because they keep using the lazy technology. At ten miles an hour, man, you can live within 15 miles of your workplace and still get in."

He had more, a complete rant, but I help up a hand. "My car, though."

Charles looked back at me. "People don't make voluntary changes, they just float downstream. Even when there's a freaking waterfall at the end."

"So you're going to make people swim upstream?"

"No." Charles laughed. "We're going to blow the river up. The car makers, their ghosts are still playing with the city. We're going to make it a carless city. Whether they like it or not."

I picked up the bat. Edgewater was dealing with ecoterrorists.

The last thing I wanted to do was get between the Eddies and these guys. Things got ugly, when you were dealing with people who'd already thought the world was ended, thanks to people like the Eddies.

No amount of lost love between authorities and eco-anarchists.

But I still wanted paid. And their little tent city under the bridge hid the lawyer.

I cradled my bat in my arms and left Charles on the steps. Around me people were dragging the remains of my rental off down the street in what seemed like thirty different directions for scrap. Or recycling. Or to whatever a reprap was.

I promised myself that I'd be out of the city before the crazy shit started happening.

But as I came out of the old, soot-stained brick buildings and looked out at the empty pavement and weeds in front of me, I wondered if I'd made an empty promise.

The entire tent city had disappeared.

A single, distant figure stood alone in the urban emptiness, as if just waiting for me.

I recognized the lawyer. Even in this distance.

The lawyer waited for me by his bike, both hands holding his briefcase in front of his waist.

"Mr. Stratton, you are a very persistent man."

I swung my bat up over my back, letting it hang loose, gripped by my right hand. I wasn't giving him a hand to shake. "Where'd they all go?"

"Staying in one place invites complacency, and authoritarian response. Takes time to muster the resources to evict a group of our size."

"But there were thousands of people here, with tents, and avenues between the tents," I protested. "They can't just evaporate in a morning when my back's turned."

"And yet they did."

I stood in the concrete emptiness, forced to concede his point. "A well-ordered army, then."

The lawyer smiled. "Now, Mr. Stratton, you're getting to the meat of it. Are you intrigued?"

"I want the rest of the money."

"I know. You willing to follow this all the way, then?"

I wasn't sure what he was getting at. But I nodded assent. "I want paid."

The lawyer leaned in with a tiny black wand, which he waved over my body. Around my collar it beeped, and the lawyer flicked a switch.

A tiny mote on my collar smoldered, then puffed smoke.

"Now that the Eddies can't follow you. I have a request," the lawyer said. He produced a dark blue hood.

I stared at the cloth. "You want me to wear that? You think the Eddies can't just patch into a satellite and find where your mob took off to?"

The lawyer sighed. "Granted. But where in the camp you are will be secret."

"Yeah, okay." Here we go. I pulled the hood on. "But I'm keeping the bat," I said, my voice muffled.

"Whatever you want, Mr. Stratton." The lawyer sounded bored. He pushed me forward. "There's a sidecar on my bike, please get in it."

Why hadn't he had me sit first before putting the hood on? To mess with my head? "So are you a part of all this, or are you just a turking lawyer?"

I could feel him climbing onto his bike. We jerked into motion. "I'm a part of the project."

"To destroy the auto-oriented world of Detroit?"

"Among other things, Mr. Stratton. The world cannot continue on its current path." The lawyer was huffing as he pedaled, getting us up to a quick clip. "We have returned almost to the time of city-states, like the Greeks. Each of these cities has a different past, and set of traditions and patterns set into its habits. Some of these habits have a fundamental impact, however, on citizens elsewhere. If you dump some form of pollution into the air from a smokestack somewhere, and people are affected hundreds of miles away, shouldn't they have some sort of say? It used to be there were country-wide principals and guidance, but in this day and age, it's city to city.

"Now, some of us don't have allegiances to any one city. Particularly those of us old enough to remember nationalism. You know what I'm talking about Stratton, you fought for country, once, not city."

"Didn't do much for me," I muttered. But I remember the days when bunting hung from porches and second floor windows.

"We have no allegiance to country, city, or company. We're neo-tribalists at best, but even then, not forming around any constitution or hierarchal structure. We're per-project affiliations, with reputation economics as our bond. Some of us stick from one project to another, others are committed to the larger plan of trying to create substantial memetic change to our urban environments."

"Like getting rid of cars."

"That's a sub-project, one that many have coalesced around. Some of the more enthusiastic, like those who recycled your car. Yes. But the energy use and issues of transportation are realistically a small segment of the greater issue of creating a city, or environment, that is carbon neutral and thus, sustainable. We're talking about the long term survival of the human species, Mr. Stratton, not just whether you recycle plastic and go to work in the approved transportational manner."

"I've been hearing doom and gloom for a long time," I grunted. "The end of the world's always just around the fucking corner."

"And you think it won't come?" The lawyer zigged through streets. Some alleys, too, I could tell by the echoes of our voices. "You think civilizations haven't collapsed? Someone, or something else will come along. They'll name some streets after us, maybe create a museum. We still find ancient cities by satellite, after the jungle or desert has long since over run them. Why'd they die off? Overuse of the soil, or whatever, or just plain bad planning when it came to picking neighbors. But the point is, their world ended. You can nuke a patch of ground, and the radiation will kill everything. Years later, nature comes back.

Generations later, some parts of it are livable. Still doesn't mean setting a nuclear bomb off in the middle of your living room's a good idea."

"Sounds like a lot of drama."

"We're sitting on an edge, Mr. Stratton. You've seen it all change in your life. The young around us, they've only known the slipping and scrabbling, watching energy prices spiral out of control. They're content to root around in their parents' and grandparents' trash to look for whatever they can recover. But you know better. You can feel it, that your life straddled the point where we hit the apex, and then started sliding. Remember when we used to *make* things."

I remembered the long factory lines, the smokestacks belching. The rows of gleaming product, sitting perched over enticing price tags, all packaged in sexy gleaming plastics. They *made* so much you just tossed it all when you were done, because they'd *make* more.

We descended down a ramp of some sort, and the world grew dark on the outside of my hood. The lawyer slowly came to a stop, and reached over to remove my hood.

"Don't ask where you are," he said. "I'm a delivery man, of sorts. Now that I'm here, I can't leave, but you may have to, and you can't know where this is. Most of the people in here don't know where it is. Keeps it safe."

I clambered out into the barely lit dimness of an industrial warehouse, the windows all blacked out. As my eyes adjusted I realized it was entirely empty.

Until the doors swung open. People wearing large datagoggles over their eyes walked in. I could see that none of them could see where they were, or what was in front of them. But they marched in, like robots, following invisible lines of information.

More came in, carrying chairs, some with desks, that they sat at predetermined points. They swarmed around each other like ants, following some larger pattern of commands.

Maybe hundreds of them had already swarmed in through the room, and most had gone.

Large industrial worklights lit up the inside of the warehouse, and an entire command center's worth of monitors had been strapped to a large metal trunk at the center, which had been quickly bolted onto the concrete floor.

Thick fiber optic cables ran all over the warehouse, terminating in a large trunk of bound cables that ran to a dish pointed out of one of the windows that had been pulled open.

The entire process had taken five very surreal minutes.

The crowds all evaporated, leaving ten individuals behind. One of them sat in a complex wheelchair that folded around him and held him up at eye-level. It whirred and balanced, and trailed cables behind it.

Inside the wheelchair, the gray-skinned man moved closer to me. Sunken eyesockets, lids stitched closed, and plastic-looking cheekbones. One missing arm, with what was left plugged into a socket on the chair. No legs; they were hidden in the depths of the chair.

One ear was missing as well, replaced with a metallic ovoid sitting over that with three blue lights steadily on.

"Mr. Stratton, I'm afraid we've been recruiting you," the man in front of me said. The wheelchair raised a bit higher so his face was level with mine. A small pair of cameras on his shoulder adjusted their focus with a faint whirr.

"Someone tipped off the Eddies that I was watching them. And someone didn't pay the other half of what I was expecting." For some reason, I'd been allowed to keep the bat. But bashing on a man with no legs, one arm, and no eyes was not going to be part of today's equation.

"Guilty as charged. Mr. Stratton, we're looking for a leader, someone who knows the area, and someone who has a good sense of the Edgewater contractors here. There are a number of candidates, but you're a service man with a record, and a good idea of what we'll be facing."

"Listen..." I wasn't sure how to ask after his name, so I floundered for a second.

"My tag is MockTurtle, the community moderator for this project." Mock Turtle. A little bit of this, and a little bit of that. An amusing name for a man who was as much machine. He saw my amusement through his camera and nodded. "Yes. I do find some humor in my situation. The alternative was despair."

"Okay, Mr. Turtle. The lawyer pitched me hard on your cause." I looked around the warehouse. "I'm not interested. If people want to bike and walk the town, that's their thing. I'm not getting involved in some riot."

The wheelchair backed away. "We're not, as such, asking you to volunteer. We're willing to pay for your services. And settle up on what you think we still owe you."

Now we were talking. "I'm listening."

"An apartment in downtown Detroit. Maybe even continuing work as security for it."

"A lease? How long, and how much?"

The ruin of a man in front of me chuckled. "You're not paying close enough attention, Mr. Stratton. See, at first, we weren't sure who we'd pick, or hire, to run the street side of this project. But then, you showed up, turking for us. It was a sign. Who better to run this than someone like you, down on your luck and needing the help? When you started snooping around, well, we had to bring you in. We're offering you an apartment. A whole apartment."

I stared. Like I said, there were some that would give their left nut for downtown space.

I included myself in that list.

"So you're going to riot to turn this into a car-free city. And you need my help." Too good to be true, it all was. And if there was one thing I learned in life, it was a little suspicion. "No way a downtown apartment's worth it for my help. You've already got an army, well-trained, you showed it off when you set all this up in here a few minutes ago."

The MockTurtle spread his one arm. I recognized what those scars came from: a landmine. Boston, or DC, I wondered. "You're right. It's not just the cars. That's a diversion. An important issue, yes. But we're involved in some urban renewal as well."

Which is where the apartment offer came from. They'd paid Maggie to try and overnight, I remembered. I could put a few things together. "You going to try to occupy the Slumps, are you?" All these nomads, they were going to settle in, try and reclaim some of these buildings.

I could have laughed.

"Not really, Mr. Stratton. It's...more complicated than that. We make no guarantees, but I will put a good faith payment up in escrow right...now. Consider it a down payment on the apartment. We need a dedicated team of protestors to keep the Edgewater contractors busy, but the protest cannot get to the size that the military is called in. You have to both keep the protest in line, and keep it out of the Edgewater's reach. It'll be a delicate balance. If it works, and if our project works in the meantime, you'll have an apartment of your own.

"If the project fails, you're one of several people offered large cash payouts for your services on the ground, rather than volunteering your time. You will still get an equivalent pay. We are fair people, we depend on our word and reputations."

Down the rabbit hole, off to meet the Mock Turtle, and now to engage in even more silliness.

But these mad hatters were certainly offering cold cash. I checked my phone, and the bank confirmed an escrow offer.

"The Edgewater guys, no deadly violence, right?"

"Yes."

"Then I'm your guy."

MockTurtle smiled. "Welcome aboard, Colonel Stratton."

I cringed. "That's why you came to me?"

"Of course. Welcome to Starship Detroit."

"You have a silly name," I said.

"You might not think so when we're done," said the strange man in the wheelchair.

I was in the heart of the sleeping dragon I'd sensed curled up in the darkness, the thing that S. Whatten feared.

I was deep into the crazy shit.

CMO S. Whatten, in his permanently wrinkle-free working suit, looked surprised. "Didn't think you'd show back up."

"Didn't think I'd be back." I handed him a receipt. "I refunded your payment. There'll be a claim on the car. It was wrecked."

Whatten took a sip of coffee, and looked down the street at the pair of men who'd biked me over to the compound. "Stratton. Colonel. I'm considering calling in reinforcements, or at least talking to the Edgewater board. I'm guessing that there are thousands of these people lurking around the city."

"I think you're overestimating," I replied. He wasn't, he was way, way underestimating.

"We tried to get satellite pictures of their camp from the other night, but someone has blocked it. A clever trick. I don't know the size of my enemy, or their nature. And now they have a known counter turk-army specialist. You spent years taking down networked insurgencies, Stratton. Overseas. Now, if I didn't know better, you seem to be working for one."

I leaned forward, until my face was just an inch from the chickenwire and bars. "They are eco-freaks, Whatten. They applied for a protest license."

"No one gets that anymore." The right to assemble and protest had long since been finessed into oblivion. Didn't stop them from happening, just meant you had no right to do it.

"I know. So they're going to go ahead with it anyway."

"And we'll have to stop it. I'll need reinforcements. Tell me why I shouldn't bump this up?"

"A gentlemen's agreement," I said. "I promise that the protest will not exceed a number. How many can the local Eddies and their compounds handle?"

Whatten chuckled. "I tell you that and you deploy a larger number and I'm up the creek." He sipped from his mug.

"Whatten, I shit you not, I'm trying to do you a favor. These are people who're going to do this one way or another, but they're scared of you. Remember fighting for country, the way things used to be? That's what they're after. The right to express dissatisfaction without getting a skull cracked. They hired me to keep it civil, keep things from getting crazy, because I have that expertise. Now, I could hire toughs to keep a barrier going between us, could get snipers up in the roofs, could make for some real ugly back and forths, but I just want to make an easy buck. We keep it small, balanced, and you get to round up some easy fines. They get to make their point. I get to make some serious cash from these hippies. One grunt to another, Whatten, let's make this easy."

I watched the gears turn. "You really think this'll go down that easy?"

"Do you want the board staring down too close into your operation? You want them calling in military? National coverage of the event? Serious battle?"

Whatten looked off in the distance. "Some of my men are a bit jumpy by now."

"Control them. Offer them bonuses for a calm day of rounding up these guys. Tell them chaos is not welcome. Tell them anything you want, but tell me what your threshold is for kicking the protest upstairs."

"I see more than three hundred people I'm calling in reinforcements," Whatten said.

"I'll keep it to half that."

"Half that?" Whatten looked incredulous. "It's not going to be a protest, it'll be a lunch date with a bad ending."

"Half. Thank you, Whatten."

"Call me Samuel. If it goes the way you say, I'll even shake your hand when it's all done. But Stratton...fellow grunt or not, we're going to round people up. And if it gets big, it's going to hit the fan. It isn't just my men who're jumpy. I'm getting it too. I'll call the second it looks odd."

"I know." I handed Samuel Whatten my phone number. "We'll keep in touch. Keep the lines open. The air clear. Just in case."

I walked back down the street, blinking in the morning sun. Charlie, the bike enthusiast, waited for me.

"So?"

"The Eddies can handle a hundred protestors."

"Damn it." Charlie hit his bike handles in frustration. "There is no way we can shut Detroit down with a hundred protestors."

I smiled. "We have an hour to do it, and then we have to keep doing it for twenty four hours. Come on Charlie, don't you believe in the vision enough to trust me?"

He just stared at me.

I laughed. "We'll need far more than a hundred people. We'll need thousands and thousands."

"But we're trying to avoid getting the military to come out after us," Charlie said.

"No more than a hundred can gather and protest. But the rest of the city is still a tool, Charlie. They still have eyes."

Charlie was frustrated that the citizens of the city wouldn't work to change their paradigms.

But they would.

You just had to turk them out in just the right way.

Detroit. Late morning. The first dry run I chose was near Grand Circus Park, a big intersection near a rundown, gothic-looking church. A set of roads ran semicircle around a portion of the intersection as well.

I sat, cross-legged, on top of a large stone block, in front of which was a statue of a sitting man.

It looked like Charlie's wet dream. One hundred bikes converged from four different directions. MockTurtle had given me a list of thousands of possibles, and I'd chosen the fittest, with the fastest bikes.

Speed would be an essential part of this equation.

A small smile quirked the side of my mouth, seeing the four sets of twenty-five bikers stream in at full tilt, pedaling away. They all braked to a sudden stop at the center of the intersection.

Now the chaos came. Cars with green lights braked, confused at the sudden clutter as the bikes made a barricade around the square of the intersection.

Waiting in electric utility vans was my support crew. I picked up my phone and selected the mailing list. "Roll out," I typed.

Fifty men leapt out from the backs of the vans. My heavies. Anyone with a self defense or military background. They lugged plastic cones, and began placing them around the edge of the bicycle barricade.

I slipped on a pair of shades and let them talk to my phone. I needed more screen real estate. Because now, things would get tricky.

The more practical drivers, realizing something was afoot, and not wanting to get caught up in the middle of some riot or demonstration, began to try and start turning their cars around.

Finally, the signs went up declaring the area a car free zone.

I could see Charlie standing with a bullhorn. Behold the rhetoric. Burn the gas-using relics of a failed era. Embrace the pedal-powered and walkable future.

All around the city I'd deployed bikes, messengers, and paid turks to call in the location of the Eddies. Small flags started popping up in my vision, on a map of Detroit via my heads up display glasses. Scrambling Eddies.

"Security out, ten to stay," I sent. And the heavies melted back into the vans, which pealed off, a handful remaining off to the sides.

The Eddies were ripping up Washington Boulevard toward us. When they crossed Michigan Avenue I tapped in the scatter signal.

Just as abruptly as they'd appeared the protestors scrambled onto their bikes and took off in every direction, leaving only the stalled and snarled traffic, the cones, and the signs.

I hopped off the public art and strolled down into the park, near the empty fountain, then turned back to watch as the Eddies waded into the mess we'd created.

Angry drivers, confused Eddies not sure if it wasn't the drivers somehow involved.

Some of them were. Paid to have trouble turning around, that was.

There was some small part of me inside chuckling. Being on the other side, there was a sort of beauty to this creative destruction. I'd always suspected there was.

Twenty Edgewater contractors, in full company uniform, were a bit frustrated.

I called a randomly selected heavy. "Atwater and Bates. Start forming it up." It was close to the tunnel to Canada, enough to really freak the Eddies out.

The fleeing bicyclists would find warehouses, shops, and eateries to duck into. Beta group was activated and ready to go.

An electric waited for me at the far end of the park. And hopefully Charlie and his pals would leave this one alone long enough for me to get through the day.

After swinging around the effects of jammed traffic I headed for a view of the next mess.

I found a spot a block away from the intersection and parked the car. Lit up my heads-up display glasses. The Eddies were chasing bicyclists. They'd captured a few, given the ten SOS flags I saw.

Time to send in the lawyers for them.

"Atwater and Bates: go," I ordered via my phone. The bicycles kicked into gear, and my heavies moved onto the scene to stand ready with cones and signs once more.

Since the turn of the century mobile networked insurgencies had been upsetting balance of force in urban environments for First World militaries.

Infrastructure, Stratton. Infrastructure.

As laws ate away at the rights to demonstrate, freeform riots had begun to grow, imitating the guerilla tactics abroad. Standing still for a protest didn't make any sense. Not when rioters would get classified as non-state terrorist entities when rounded up.

The trick was to control your membership. No violence. Which was hard to do when real insurgents waited in the wings to join protests as a cover for whatever they had in mind.

And when the Edgewater types paid turks to bring violence to a protest so that they could shut it down and levy massive fines for pure profit, one had to be quick on their feet.

Damn quick.

Even as my protestors set up, I saw Eddie flags popping up on my HUD map. They were reforming, dropping their chases, and coming my way.

Samuel Whatten was smart. Eyes on the ground reported a detachment of fifteen Eddies regrouping at Grand Circus Park.

"Security out," I ordered. And then as the Eddies approached I ordered half the protestors to evaporate ahead of the brunt.

The remaining fifty scattered tire-piercing jax with blue-tooth signals, giving up information about the negative effects of personal transportation as practiced by the city currently.

I was sure the drivers would be thrilled with that.

But the message delivered was this: today, any cars in the area defined by the river and Interstates 375, 75, and the Lodge Freeway, would be harassed. Charlie shouted it. Agents delivered messages to blogs, podcast hosts, old media outlets, and placed battery powered projectors on overpasses all around this section of Detroit we'd staked out for the protest.

Here be no cars welcome.

Of course, we couldn't shut down every street leading in. But if we caused enough trouble, and spread the word, enough people would get the idea and stay away because they didn't want to get caught up in an Edgewater round up and riot.

The effect would be the same.

And I had a few specific goals up my sleeve.

I ordered protestors to pedal out. We had a few more non-critical intersections to demonstrate at.

A few hackers under our pay tapping into Eddie radio chatter reported that the order was going out for all the compounds around Detroit to contribute extra contractors. All Detroit Eddies were getting yanked out of bed no matter their shift. Riot gear was being passed out.

Things were getting warm.

I yanked Charlie off the streets and had him chauffeur me around in my electric car. Things were getting complex enough I couldn't drive and coordinate at the same time.

Enough people had heard his talking points and been briefed. They were handed loudspeakers and told to carry on the crusade.

Plus, making pedal-powered Charlie drive me around appealed to me on a deep level.

"Spaceship Detroit," I asked him. "What do you know?"

"It's the higher level project," he said, from the front seat. He was doing his best to follow my orders, but not chat too much. Driving me around really had irked him.

It cheered me up.

"Urban renewal." I knew I was running a big diversion, and I wondered if true-believers like Charlie knew they were just turking out.

It was like one of those games-with-a-purpose you could play online.

You thought you were taking over the world in a digital simulation, but instead you were helping develop an algorithm for bottle-packing computers based on your reactions to certain variables.

I had to admit, I was enjoying myself a hell of a lot more than I was working as a bouncer just a few nights ago.

"It's noon," Charlie said.

"I know."

"So…"

"Give it a few minutes," I said. We passed by a series of office buildings. I could see faces in windows looking out. Word of a potential riot had gotten out. People were checking the streets before leaving for lunch.

We continued driving. As I drew more and more people into downtown, I wondered what would be happening in the Slumps.

Spaceship Detroit, huh?

I just hoped it wouldn't be a massive piece of multiplayer performance art, or something stupid. Maybe some of the rhetoric had stuck on me. It would, if people flung it at you long enough.

I would love a walking city, like those European ones, where they'd eased into post-auto societies due to their medieval city layouts and historically high gas prices. I'd visited them, on my way to the trouble spots.

A city where I didn't have to scrounge out in the Wilds, where the Slumps were utilized, and where it felt like there was action, and hope. I liked the sound of that.

"They're coming out now," Charlie said.

He was right. The lunch crowds were starting to form.

"Okay. Lunch time madness," I ordered via my phone.

Groups of twenty-five, in five different packs, descended outside popular restaurants, blocking off the roads to them with demonstrations. Again, jax, signs, and cones to muddy everything up.

Charlie's acolytes preached their slogans, and people did their best to get away from the traffic snarls. The Eddies, now out in patrols in full force, and having gotten a sense for the rough area we'd staked out, descended quickly. They'd spread out in a rough net, and were using their own information to quickly rally to a point.

Turks with live cams gave me feeds of each demonstration, as well as streamed them live to anyone who really cared. Already some people in the city were honking horns whenever they saw a pack of bicyclists going by. Drivers, sympathetic to the cause.

Funny.

In the middle of protest number three, my heavies dragged out a bicyclist from the middle of the group. Discreet, quick, they tossed him into the back of a van, and my phone rang.

"He didn't have an ID," they reported. Each official protestor had a small RFID tag that responded to a challenge/response query that the support team could broadcast via their phones.

"Try and work out who he's getting paid by," I said.

"He doesn't know. Just turking it," was the response.

"The Eddies are thinking quick. Take him out into the Slumps and dump him off."

Lunch had been successful. Late and annoyed business people, traffic tied up in all five locations. And we still were keeping just ahead of the increasingly frustrated Eddies.

A few of the protestors captured since the first demonstration had been shoved around a bit. But it was still civil.

"Lunch is over. Afternoon delight begins." I smiled.

For the next four hours they just kept shifting the fun around the city, frustrating the traffic and Eddies. Eating into rush hour traffic as everyone left just added to it. Drivers jumped at every little glitter on the road, imagining tire-piercing jax waiting for them.

Outraged bicyclists not associated with the riots were getting arrested throughout the city as they tried to get to buses or home. The temporary protests appeared, vanished, appeared, vanished, constantly moving about.

At this point some of them were riding in the vans, getting dropped off in locations faster than they could bike to. And to be honest, there were closer to five hundred bicyclists working for me, hidden all throughout downtown.

Even though the Eddies now had extras coming in from the Slumps and the Wilds, I was prepared to keep this up all through the night, when MockTurtle called.

"We have a problem," he said softly.

Outside, the sun was dipping over the skyline, the buildings throwing their long shadows down the streets.

"What kind of problem?"

"Edgewater is advancing on the project. They're liable to misinterpret what's going on."

"Well, what is going on?"

"Come and see."

And the directions to one of the skyscrapers in the Slumps popped up on my phone.

As we drove deep into the Slumps I realized why Edgewater might get nervous. As night fell thousands of people were crawling out of nooks and crannies.

Even as we drove, the streets were filling with people.

People were working on portable machine shops, or turning out parts via automated stamping machines. Others ran up and down the street with carts and toward the center of all the activity.

Spaceship Detroit. The skyscraper loomed over this section of the Slumps, where the buildings made perhaps fifteen stories at best.

Massive solar panels had already been mounted to the upper deck and outside the windows, jutting from the building like leaves from a demented, scrap metal tree. Charlie swore and stopped the car, and I got out.

Dump trucks of soil lined the block, the air hazy with dust as they dumped dirt onto conveyor belts leading into the building, where vacuum hoses and other contraptions moved the dirt elsewhere.

And everywhere, a swarm of humanity working furiously.

MockTurtle wove his way through the sidewalk, people blinded with their visors and tasks magically moving aside at the last second, a sea of humanity parting for him in his wheelchair.

"Welcome to the single most coordinated sudden attack of urban renewal ever witnessed," he proclaimed. "Two hundred thousand souls, dedicated to turning this building into a sustainable structure."

My knees were weak. "The Eddies are going to call in the military."

"Since dawn we've been quietly working on the infrastructure of the building inside, doing as much prep as we could. Parts have been manufactured off-site for months now. We've all been rehearsing on 3-d models in massive multiplayer online simulations for a year, since we identified the target. It's going to take eight more hours to get the soil in, and then finish the interior modifications once that's in place for the full occupation."

"But what is it?" Why did they need soil?

"People have been taking over unused buildings and repurposing them in decayed areas for as long as we've had cities. But what is the point in taking over structures like this, if we don't have any new paradigms to offer?" MockTurtle led me back toward the building. Inside the giant lobby people were working on a series of ponds. Sprinklers over my head went through a testing cycle, briefly dropping mist into the air.

My host continued. "It began in an online game that let people design homes. Many used it as a place to test how to make more efficient homes, or redesign existing homes in niches in cities. Eventually the designers realized we had the economy of a small country. And so they wondered how they could face some of these problems of how to be responsible dwellers. Out of that grew a community plan to create an embassy to the world."

We took a glass elevator up through the building's levels: I was seeing apple and orange trees, and rows of furrowed soil. I recognized all this. Farms. They were building farms. Like the skyscraper farms in New York. No need to worry about seasons. Much more efficient acreage. You could reuse the water as it filtered down via gravity.

"We used a squatter at first. That triggered a response from the Edgewater contractors here to evict that person. They have a contract to protect this building. Our hackers were able to then follow the report that Edgewater delivered about the incident back through several shell companies to the actual owner of this building."

We'd passed twenty rows of farms and garden, and now it turned into apartments and corridors.

"That information was made public, prompting liens and backtax collection actions against the owners which forced them into bankruptcy. Now we're claiming ownership, and offering to pay taxes and be good stewards. Under a subsidiary company based out of Turkey."

"Turkey?" I said. "Why Turkey?"

"We have allies at the top in America. Allies who want us to succeed, who played the simulations, who know what we planned. And from a simple financial point of view, if we own the building, we'll pay our taxes, raise the value of the building, and maybe even offer a plan to revitalize the Slumps. Since we put in a claim via a Turkish company to build an embassy, ostensibly for Turkey, we are technically on Turkish soil. They have a rule that says if you can build a building in a night where the owner doesn't notice it to try and stop it, then you can stay there.

"So we will be allowed to have this land if we can finish this project in one night. But the previous owners, under a reconstituted company, are counter-filing having the building taken away, and are trying to stop us by getting the Eddies over here, because we have no building permits and we're taking up the streets. It's all legal fictions and weirdness, but we need to stop the Eddies from coming over here."

He'd taken me to the top of the building, where a carefully landscaped set of gardens sat. With a waterfall trickling away already. I understood. Spaceship Detroit. A whole building that could sustain itself in all manners. This wasn't recycling our forefather's leftovers, or scrabbling about for what we could get today, this was its own direction. And it could be made right on the foundation of the existing.

"So how bad do you want that apartment? I could take you to see it, it's just under our feet. Recycled oak floors, two bedrooms…" I held up my hand to quiet him. We looked out over the twinkling skyline.

I'd had a feeling it would come to something like this. Riding the back of the tiger meant getting bashed up. It never came without consequences.

"I need three hundred very dedicated people," I said. "Not the cyclists. People ready to get hurt. Because the Eddies are not going to go easy."

"You can have thousands," MockTurtle said.

I shook my head. "Anymore than a few hundred is going to get the military involved. They'll be able to meddle with the project, easily enough. We want just the Eddies to stay involved and away from here."

"What are you going to do?"

I pointed off in the distance. "By the park, the Detroit Opera House. We take and hold it all night. It pushes over from nuisance into hostile, but with only three hundred of us, and them thinking it's today's protestors, they won't escalate this into a major emergency. But get your lawyers ready."

MockTurtle reached out with his good hand. "Thank you."

"Don't thank me yet." I looked out over the city with a sinking feeling in my stomach.

Was it just about the apartment now? Or had I gotten sick of skulking about in the Wilds by myself?

Or had a strong taste of the MockTurtle's kool aid gotten to me.

A little bit of all of the above, I figured.

We rushed the security guards quickly enough, and I set teams to boarding up the doors. Jax were scattered on the streets. Protest signs wavered on the walls outside, thanks to projectors dropped all over the street.

Charlie had stuck with me, and he looked at the team. "Not a lot of us here."

"Enough are," I said. "We have to hold out until we get the all clear from the Project or until we're all rounded up."

The Opera House was a recognizable building, a part of the history of the city. The Eddies would not ignore this.

Sure enough, my phone finally buzzed. CMO S. Whatten. "Stratton? I'm getting reports you're at the Opera House?"

"We're barring ourselves in for the night."

I could see on my heads up glasses that the Eddies were starting to stream this way.

"You sure about this?" Whatten asked. "We were just about to get a temporary city ban on bikes and end the whole protest. You want to take it up to this?"

"It's too late, Samuel," I looked around at the project volunteers. "We're here for the night."

The first Eddies were pulling up at the perimeter of our jax field.

But then, so were hundreds of people on bikes, and cars, and on foot, coming to see the latest star singer, sports player, or whoever they idolized.

Thanks to personal interest profiles, and thousands of turkers working to invite them down to the Detroit Opera House for a special showing of...whatever it was their interests indicated they would come down to see for a free showing.

These people weren't working for anyone, or getting paid. They wouldn't be classified as part of the protest.

But they were indirectly working for us.

The Eddies formed up, clearing away the jax. Their riot teams rolled up and out with battering rams to come in after us.

"Frustrated fans, execute," I ordered.

Outside, whisper campaigns started. The Eddies were here to take away the impromptu concerts being planned. They were here to ruin the fun.

Now this was incitement.

The project's lawyers were going to have to earn their money when I got bailed out later tonight.

My streaming video didn't show who threw the first bottle. But when it broke on the pavement, the Eddies moved their focus from the Opera House to the massive crowd outside.

Charlie, sitting next to me in one of the balcony seats, swore. He was looking at the streams on a small pad in his hands.

Outside erupted.

It was clear enough these weren't anti-car protestors. The Eddies had a two front war on their hands now. It bought us until just past midnight, as the Eddies had their backs to us to deal with the frustrated and unruly crowds trying to get in.

"You don't have room in your cells for us," I told Whatten when he called me again. "Why bother now?"

"We'll make do," he hissed. He sounded tired. The friendliness I'd found in him earlier had been wrung out.

"We have no weapons. We're just trying to make a point."

"You've well made it all day. *We're* going to make a point as well."

By one in the morning they had the whole outside of the Opera House surrounded, and they'd started smashing in one of the doors.

"Get up here," I ordered, moving to the location. We pushed our way forward with planks, doing our best to keep it reinforced.

They fired tear gas in, noxious smoke roiling through at us. We had masks for it and kept on pushing back at the splintered planks we'd nailed up, our shoes slipping on broken glass.

"Eddies're in the back," Charlie reported. And we split our forces.

But there were more Eddies. As each new breach appeared we split to deal with it.

At two in the morning I ordered the bulk of the project volunteers to fall back to the next floor. The volunteers at the doors faced the Eddies, who punched through and started dragging them away.

I left half of the remaining volunteers to hold upper floors, leaning against doors, or just forming human chains.

The rest of us, a hundred now, took to the roof. Barricading anything we found on the way up there, we had fewer doors to defend.

"They only can land a handful at a time by helicopter," I told a nervous Charlie. "And unlike the military during a riot, they're not going to shoot us, because that won't turn them a profit, will it?"

The hundred of us on the roof saw dawn break, helicopters hovering around the edges of the building, Eddies camped outside with fellow project members zip tied to each other and sitting outside in one long line.

When they got through, the Eddies kicked and beat us down. Making their point.

But by then, we really didn't care, did we?

MockTurtle himself came to spring us. "Are you ready to see your apartment?" he asked.

But I found that I didn't want it.

"What's the next project," I asked.

It was late in the morning, a year later.

I packed up my home, folding my tent back down. The skin-nable walls faded, their pictures and vistas disappearing as I shut the tent off.

I packed the trailer behind my bike, and as I locked it down, the rest of the city around me started to wake up. The smell of fresh coffee wafted over the neighborhood lines as slow wakers got stumbling.

Fresh bread, airshipped in from a vertical farm in Columbus, or so everyone said, also filled the air. But I was in a hurry, and had decided to skip breakfast.

Everything folded up and away, with a quick double check to make sure the chalked-off area of my lot for the night was clean, and I was off.

Friends from the last months of slow pedaling across the great American West waved at me as I cranked along through the streets of a tent city that had gone up overnight. Five thousand in this particular tribe.

I passed security along the edge and they let me through. Then it was out along the back roads and trails with my electric-assist trike, with the aerodynamic trailer behind me with all my belongings bumping along.

I had found, over the last year, that I didn't need much. I'd gotten rid of a lot of things as I'd moved my way West.

This last leg was easy, coming down out of the mountains. I passed a handful of other bicycles and small cars, a few gas-powered.

And there it was: Los Angeles.

I had two reasons for LA. For one, it was our next project. We had a new codename, didn't want the local Eddies to sniff us out ahead of time. We were trickling into LA a little bit at a time. Project Ceres had an ambitious hundred building goal, enough to completely feed the entire city, thus putting the project in the financial situation of becoming a major agribusiness and funding the formal creating of vertical farms anywhere it wanted. A different aim than the spaceship concept, but one I could still get behind.

We'd been perfecting our methods all throughout the center of the country, gaining recruits, resources, and abilities.

The second reason was Maggie.

She was out here in the city. With the Mock Turtle's resources, I'd found her.

I wanted to thank her.

It sounded ridiculous, but sometimes it took losing something important to you for you to shake yourself out of your old habits and seek out something new. Something different.

Sometimes, something better.

THE RED IN THE SKY IS OUR BLOOD

ELIZABETH BEAR

*Elizabeth Bear is having a heck of a year last year: Her short
story "Tideline" has racked up all sorts of awards, including a
Hugo Award, and she's also released a number of novels. She's
the Energizer Bunny of science fiction: She just keeps writing and
writing and writing. Fortunately, we all benefit from her output.*

*Bear's story here is excellent in its own right, but one thing
I'd like to point out is how it, with Tobias Buckell's "Stochasti-
City," is an excellent example of how the working relationship
among the writers of METATROPOLIS came into play. One of
the things we did as writers was to show each other our works
in progress, so we could see how others were solving the problems of fleshing out this world we created, and to make sure
that our own stories connected with the others.*

*In the case of Bear and Buckell, their two stories, both set
in Detroit, are an interesting and complementary set, and you
can hear how the two share story elements and themes, even
as their stories stand on their own. It's proof to me that the
idea of communal world building and individual story writing
can pay off in ways both expected and unexpected.*

Handlebars stung Cadie's palms as her front tire popped
off the curb and slammed cracked asphalt. Flexed elbows
absorbed the jolt, but she still felt the sting across her
shoulders. She skittered sideways between an autorickshaw and

two pedestrians, and entered the traffic flow. Detroit had never had much in the way of public transportation, and decayed infrastructure made the public streets practically impassable.

Cadie knew that. Knowing it didn't manage to lessen her irritation much when she had to stop on Randolph Street and dismount so she could lift her bike over a pothole that stretched the width of the road. Another day, she might have ridden over and popped the bike up the other side, but today she couldn't afford to risk a tire. She was already late and didn't have the spare cash for a new tube.

Heads turned as Cadie swung a leg over her machine again and rocked up onto the pedal, balancing on the scarred ball of her sneaker. She shook her dreads down over her shoulders, tossing back the one that always wanted to spring forward and sway like a pendulum in front of her right eye. Some yoob in a business suit turned around to stare at the stretch of her cargo pants as she kicked off and leaned forward. She could have flipped him off, but it was more fun to pump toward him, pedaling furiously, and tip his hat into the filthy street.

"Bitch!" he shouted after her as she vanished into the stream of rattling trucks and electric squirts. Then she did flip him off, without turning, the finger pointing down stiff and rigid beside her pumping haunches. Somebody else whooped laughter, a steel bracelet bright with rubber-edged jingling tags rattling on his wrist as he waved, but Cadie's antagonist shouted something she lost in a roar of giant wheels and the blare of her headphones as she slid in behind a truck. She was pretty sure it wasn't his phone number.

And if it was—she grinned as she pedaled down the echoing soot-blackened channel, anonymized by traffic—she had all the men in her life she needed.

Those wrist tags bugged her as she slid along through traffic, finally making better time now. Every counterculture has its recognition signals. Hanky codes and earrings. Slave rings and crossed wrists. Cryptic magnetic decals on the bumper of a car. Peace signs, band badges, piercings, dyed hair, long hair, cropped hair. Ankhs, safari vests, and Leathermans. Gang signs and team insignia. The colors of the tribe.

Every counterculture has its ways of keeping the gate. Some are secret for purposes of exclusion and control. Some are secret by force of necessity. Some flamboyantly broadcast their existence, but adopt impenetrable habits of speech. Some are driven underground at first, for centuries or decades, only to emerge when the conventions of society change.

But then they cease to be the counterculture; they lose their passcodes and secret handshakes; the recognition symbols that once served to discreetly identify them to friendly eyes become an open badge of membership. A Christian fish. A rainbow flag. Nuances of nonverbal communication are lost when it becomes safe to speak aloud.

Lately, Cadie had been noticing the tags. Rattling silvery metal, worn on a steel ball chain looped around throats under tailored sport coats, through the worn buttonholes of frayed denim jackets, hooked on a keychain carabiner. Sets of three or five or seven, once nine, always odd numbers, the thin sheets of metal rolled in colored rubber at the edges for safety and perforated like lacy antique punch cards. She hadn't gotten a good look at a set, but she thought there was some transparent, refractive material sandwiched between layers of metal, visible where the cutouts fell.

They weren't customary—she'd catch somebody with a set every couple of days, a few times a week. Once, she'd seen two in a day.

She wondered, sure. Googled around a little, checked a couple of trendy stores that sold fashion accessories. Found nothing. The thing that struck Cadie odd was that the tags—which looked more than anything else like miniature fine-jewelry replicas of dog tags—were the only thing the people wearing them seemed to have in common. She hadn't realized they were a recognition signal until she'd seen a bum in two pairs of too-short trousers, seven tags rattling against his filthy collarbones, nod in passing to a businesswoman walking between her bodyguards. A leather strap supporting a pilot electronics tote crossed the shoulder of her designer suit. Five tags swung freely from the strap loop.

The businesswoman had smiled faintly and nodded back.

By the concrete footing of a converted warehouse, Cadie locked her bike and set the zapper. Somebody had stenciled an outline of a grinning man smoking an upside-down pipe on the wall; whatever the encoded message was, Cadie didn't get it. She hustled up steps to a rusted steel door that had once been painted orange. Somebody had told her there was no word for the color "orange" in Hindi; there was only yellow and red, and whatever lay between them had to be assigned to one category or another. It seemed strange to think about at first, but then she realized that all the colors between blue and green didn't have their own names either. Just names by association, *teal* and *turquoise* and *aquamarine.* But weren't those colors just as real as blue or green? Didn't they have as much unique identity? Who was it that decided that they had to be one or the other?

So if you spoke another language and orange stopped being orange and became yellow, what then? Did the color itself change? Or was it just your perception of it?

Cadie nerved herself and tapped her code on the pad beside the door. Whoever was inside could see her on the cams. Facial recognition software had already identified her when the printreader on the keypad slid a bar of blue light along her fingertip. From its intensity, it seemed as if Cadie should be able to sense a chill.

Multiple system redundancy.

The battered door sagged against its hinges as remote locks slid back. Cadie squared her shoulders under her battered denim jacket, setting the fine swags of chain across the breast-pockets swinging, and stepped inside.

It was a long walk, past the guard's office with the door propped open by a chipped wooden wedge. The guard—a big warm man burdened with the parentally reprehensible name of Celsius Washington—waved at her as she passed, his Marine Corps ring and his shaved head catching bands of light. She waved back. With meaty lips and chipped white teeth, he grinned. "Your little girl is growing up fine, just like her mom."

Cadie rolled her eyes and flipped him off like the guy on the street, but when she gave Cel the bird it was a different gesture, with more English in it and framed with a smile.

More coded signals. Sometimes a *fuck you* was just a *fuck you*. And sometimes it was a whole bunch of other messages, and the *fuck you* was only the carrier wave.

Consider how Cel pressed both hands over his heart and leaned back in his chair, head tipped winningly to one side. Fatigued metal groaned under his shift of weight. She walked on past, leaving the finger behind, framed in the door until her arm dragged it after.

And heard him laughing all the way down the hall to reception.

Here, the character of the building changed. From reclaimed property and scarred tile to soft carpet in bright tertiary colors complementary to walls and furniture. The receptionist, James, had hung up his suit jacket and rolled up the sleeves of his immaculately pressed shirt, but his tie still snugged crisply below his Adam's apple and a semiautomatic pistol was clipped into a magnetic rig on his right hip. The reflected light from security monitors under the console wall gilded him blue.

"Hello, Ms. Grange," he said. He touched the control for his headset and announced her, indicating a chair by the next set of security doors. James held up a plastic envelope while she retrieved a butterfly knife with a pierced steel handle and a can of tear gas from her inside pocket. She dropped her weapons in and he bent the flap over, tucked it inside, and placed the resulting package in his top desk drawer, which he locked.

"I always expect you to swallow the key when you do that," Cadie said.

James tucked a coil of light brown hair behind his ear, a transparently flirtatious gesture. He had great big hazel eyes with heavy eyelashes, and was at least ten years too young for her.

And so what? "You're not staying long enough for that to be effective security."

She laughed and took the indicated chair, listening to the whisper of her metal fringe as she leaned her head back against the wall and closed her eyes. Too much work, not enough sleep. But there was no easy solution for that in her life, either.

After a suitable pause, James cleared his throat to draw her attention. She straightened, blinked, and was already rising when he said, "The staff will see you now, Ms. Grange."

The inner door swung open as she turned toward it. She passed within, was wanded, and walked through the imaging portal. The security staff were used to her jacket now, but they still gave it a thorough hand-examination. It was heavy in part because there were layers of body armor behind the swinging chains.

Nothing extravagant. Nothing she'd want to rely on to protect her from a gunshot. But a little extra edge, the sort sensible people acquired.

Cadie smiled when they gave her back her jacket. "How bad is the coffee today, Angelina?"

The woman with the wand, a broad-shouldered veteran whose straight black hair fell in a clipped line across her forehead, shrugged. "It's been on for a couple of hours. I'd see if it melts the spoon before I trusted it."

She winked and waved Cadie past. Cadie fluffed her dreadlocks back and decided she needed the coffee, for something to do with her hands if nothing else. And even burned, it was real coffee—a luxury not to be spurned. She filled a ceramic mug, added milk—organic, local farm, no BGH, from genetically random free-range cows—and decided it wasn't burned enough to really need the sugar.

It was a stalling tactic, she knew. Every time. She anticipated the visit all day, rushed to get here, and then it was all she could force herself to do, not to scramble back out the door without going in to spend her carefully allotted, scientifically calculated time with Firuza.

She turned and made herself face the one-way glass. Firuza, age five and a half, bent over a child-height table, her fingers and smock smeared with bright primary colors. A dab of yellow stood out against Firuza's cheek.

Cadie took a long drink of complex, slightly acrid coffee to brace herself, touched the biometric pad by the connecting door, and went in to her daughter. Firuza looked up as Cadie paused just inside, a sunny grin warming her expression. "Mom!"

The word was like a needle through her breastbone.

"Hey, kiddo," Cadie said. She dropped her jacket on the chair beside the door, crossed the room to Firuza, and buried her nose in the little girl's hair. She breathed deep, the clean tang of Ivory soap and the thick scent of gouache.

"Whatcha painting?"

Firuza wiggled blue-smeared fingers. "Clouds," she said.

Cadie dropped down beside her, bony knees pressing hard on the linoleum floor, and angled the paper a little so she could see better. Clouds, behind a tree, and the yellow sun. The tree was intact, regular, growing smoothly into the contours of a green fingersmudged hill. There was another one a little further away, a blurry brown animal which might have been a bear or a dog or a pony. "Who's this?" Cadie asked.

Firuza gave her the sort of look one normally reserved for mental midgets and random incompetents. "It's my dog Archie."

Cadie, wise to the ways of children, did not inform Firuza that she did not have a dog. There was a crèche dog, but his name was Rudolf, and he was a golden retriever, not a giant brown blurr of hair such as this appeared to be. "Your dog?"

Firuza nodded, solemnly. "The one we're gonna get when I can come live with you again," she said, and smeared blue paint all over Cadie's most rogue dreadlock.

Cadie stopped at James' desk on the way out to collect her effects and pay the bill. By the time she made it back down the corridor, the sky was periwinkle.

She leaned against the crèche's misleading facade and took a moment to reconstruct her own. The pause was more than a breather—it was her opportunity to observe her surroundings before descending to her bike.

No one in sight.

She unlocked her wheels and slung her leg over without incident. But as she was rolling down the sour-smelling alley to a cross street where evening traffic drifted past, a silhouette detached itself from the left wall and stepped gingerly towards her, both hands upraised beside its head.

Cadie hesitated, hip-shot, one leg stiff on the pedal as she coasted forward. Stay or go? She had the speed to jolt past him, knock him aside and go spinning out of the alley. Detroit had some little up and down, but nothing like when she'd lived in San Diego. He'd never catch her on foot—

Something jingled on the figure's wrist, casting rainbow sparks of light against the grubby walls. "Cadence Grange?" he said, and though his voice wasn't quite the same as when he'd been shouting after her, she recognized it.

Cadie stood on the foot brake, the bike wobbling slightly as she balanced it to a halt. "Who wants to know?"

He said his name was Homer, which—once they were ensconced in a booth in a greasy spoon—prompted Cadie to ask, "Who names their kid Homer anymore?"

"My parents were *Simpsons* fans." He took a bite of what passed for hamburger these days and wiped mayonnaise off his chin while Cadie studied him. He looked about mid-twenties, lightly freckled across the tops of his cheeks, his hair sticking out this way and that in tiny random twists about two inches long. His T-shirt bore a sweat stain around the collar, his forearms were tendon-cabled below the rolled-up cuffs of his cargo jacket, and a Marine Corps ring like a smaller cousin of the one Cel wore glinted heavily on his hand. Before he sat down, she'd noticed his boots were scarred across the toes, deep enough to show the steel caps in one or two places, and the laces were knotted together where they'd worn thin. Now she spotted the calluses on his hands, the chipped fingernails.

She asked, "What do you do?"

"Not, 'How do you know my name?' Or, 'What do you want from me?'" Another bite of hamburger. He was buying time. He pushed the paper basket of fries toward her while he chewed.

Hands folded around the water-dewed cup of iced tea he'd bought her, she frowned at the fries. Her stomach grumbled, but there was brown rice and beans at home, and if she was lucky the market she passed on the way would have the cheap bruised oranges from Florida she could almost afford. Beans and brown rice and oranges: not the best diet, but it wasn't missing anything you couldn't live without for a while. Sometimes, she scored greens as well, or a lemon or lime. She got by. Better than some people did.

"No thank you," she said. "I don't know where that's been."

He laughed, covering his mouth with a napkin. "I'm a blogger," he said.

"Huh." It seemed like he expected more, so she pressed her palms against the table and said "You make a living at that?"

He set the burger down—the smell wouldn't have been all that appetizing, even if she hadn't been able to see the gray interior, but it still made her swallow saliva—and wiped his hands before fiddling significantly with the frayed cuff of his cargo jacket. "I get by. Since we're playing first date, what do you do?"

The coincidence of phrasing made Cadie raise her eyebrows. *Screw it*, she thought. "Don't you already know?"

That could have been a wink, a flinch, or a nervous tic. Whatever it was, he eyed her steadily afterward, his impression sliding incrementally into a frown. He wanted her to break, she thought, to look down or glance aside. Instead, she tilted her chin up slightly and stared down her nose, matching him frown for frown.

Finally, he snorted laughter, rolled his eyes, and shook his head. "All right." He reached inside the jacket and palmed something from an inside pocket. Cadie's hand had already closed around her butterfly knife when he rotated his wrist and revealed a personal omnicommunications device. State of the art, metallic purple matte finish, with a strokable texture. He drew his thumb across it and it popped open, revealing a screen. Her own image slid into focus, digitally sharp, a flash of her downturned finger beside her butt cheek and below that, the registration plate on her bike. "See?" he said. "No mystery about it."

She relaxed, incrementally, but didn't take her hand off the knife. "And this is how you get a date?"

"No," he said. "This is how I make an offer. See, I know your name isn't Cadence Grange."

She thought she kept the reaction off her face. She'd practiced in the mirror. But the pierced handle of her knife left raised bumps in her palm as her fist clenched.

That was fine. Homer couldn't see her hand in her pocket, and the edge of the table would hide it if her forearm had bulged. "Really? That's news to me."

His grin broadened a little at her denial. "Now how did I know you were going to pull that bluff?"

He shook his head without taking his gaze off her, a cat intent at a crevice. Cadie wondered if he could hear the knocking of her heart, if he somehow knew about the cold sweat on her palms and the way her stomach twisted in nausea.

"All right, fine." He lowered his voice. "Cadence Grange wasn't *always* your name."

He reached for a fry while Cadie—despite herself—froze like a scared rabbit. He dipped the fry in ketchup, ate it, and made a face that made her wonder if he was mugging for his audience of one like a bad movie villain, or if he honestly thought he was funny. What kind of narcissism did it take, to try to entertain someone while you were leading her to the gallows?

He washed the mouthful down, rattling ice as he slurped, and said, "I know that people are looking for you and her. And it would be very bad for you both if they found you. Your real first name is Scarlet, like the color. You are technically still married to a foreign national, and not only is Firuza Grange also an assumed name—I assume because of her kidnapping risk—but she's also not your daughter. "

"Stop." She said it softly, but her voice brought him up short. *She is my daughter, asshole.*

The voice in her head that said it was answered by others, though, as always. The one that said, *Stepdaugher.* And the one that answered, *And if she is, why can't you stand to look at her?*

They sat in silence for a moment, staring at each other across the worn Formica tabletop, through air that stank of rapidly cooling grease and overcooked hamburger.

"What do you want?" Cadie asked, when she could gather herself to say anything.

Homer shook the ice against the sides of the paper cup. The gesture made the tags on his steel bracelet rattle. "I want to help."

Homer's ride was racked up outside the burger joint, where he must have left it when he came around the corner to fetch her. Cadie had inadvertently locked her own bike a few slots down and she rehearsed her options while she released it. She could make a break for it—no telling how good Homer was on his wheels, but almost nobody could keep up with Cadie through downtown if she really didn't want to be kept. But if she tried to ditch him, he had her registration, which meant he knew her address of record, and he would have no problem finding out who she ran packages for.

And he knew where Firuza was.

Cadie had plans for vanishing, like any good fugitive. But before she could use them, she'd have to shake Homer and get a message to the crèche—which had its own more than adequate security and evacuation policies, the reason Cadie had chosen it over any number of legitimate residential co-rearing facilities.

That, and Taras wouldn't get cooperation from the Detroit families, if he came looking. There weren't any favors there for him to collect, and enough bad blood—Cadie hoped—to make a smoke screen thick enough to conceal her and Firuza.

Homer might be decoying her someplace private to do her harm, but he hadn't made an aggressive move when they were alone in the alley outside the crèche, and she certainly hadn't grown less wary of him since. And if he *was* working for Taras, then Taras already knew where she was, and by the time she got back to the crèche, Firuza would be gone.

The possibility made her miskey the release. She dried her palms on her trousers before she tried a second time.

Taras, though. It would be like him to bring her back so he could make her regret the error of her ways specifically and in detail. But games of cat and mouse, wasting time distracting her, that *would* be out of character. He'd take her out and get what he had come for without unfortunate sentiment. He was efficient. Focused.

She'd found it attractive as hell once, before she'd learned what he was efficient and focused about. Before she'd had it demonstrated by way of Erzabet, Firuza's biological mother, that *efficient* and *focused* were only manifestations of ruthlessness.

When she'd confronted him on his affair, she hadn't expected his response to be her rival's corpse. He would have killed Firuza too, if she'd asked: she was sure of it.

Instead she'd asked for the little girl as a gift, and Taras—magnanimous as always, as long as you kept him pleased—had had his daughter delivered in a basket.

That was the day upon which Cadie began making her plans for escape.

No. If Homer were working for Taras, Cadie would already be as dead as Erzabet. Cadie wondered if there were a woman for whom her own murder would now serve as a gift. She wondered whether Taras' father had wooed his mother with similar offerings.

She couldn't trust Homer. She couldn't trust anyone—Taras had taught her that. But she could grit her teeth and pretend to trust Homer at least as far as she could throw him, at least as long as it took to learn what his game was.

Pretending to trust didn't mean being stupid, though. She triggered an emergency code on her omni as she slung one leg over her frame in unison with Homer's mount-up, and she felt the better for doing it. If it wasn't already too late, somebody would be getting Firuza out of harm's way even now. If the staff at the crèche hadn't been bought out. If—

—there were a lot of ifs to worry about.

When Homer pushed off, Cadie followed. They glided into moderate traffic like two fish entering the school. Homer's ride was as scarred as his shoes, gray-painted and dull looking, but Cadie knew a little about bikes, and the frame under that sloppy coat of primer was titanium alloy. She thought she could name the brand from the silhouette, if there were a sudden quiz.

Walking with a bike would have been awkward, but so was trying to talk while pedaling through city traffic. Conversation would have to wait for their destination. She still did pull up next to him in a lull in traffic and called, "Where are we going?"

"The secret clubhouse!" he called back.

Maybe that grin was intended to be encouraging, to make this all feel like an adventure. Maybe if she hadn't been shaking with adrenaline and doubt, she could have grinned back.

As it was, if she'd been carrying a stick, she would have spoked the motherfucker.

He only made her chase him for about ten kilometers by the odometer on her handlebars. Traffic, growing lighter in the dark, had all but dried up by the time they pulled in to the driveway of an unassuming, treeless ranch house with the interstate running through its back yard. A bike rack stood by the door, screened from the road by a piece of weathered stockade that looked like it had been assembled from salvaged fencing materials. Four bikes—none of them quite as battered or nondescript as Homer's ride—were already racked. Homer dropped his into the fifth slot and engaged the lock.

Cadie followed suit, but rather than locking in she just touched the key and let her hand slide off again. Sometimes, the option of a quick getaway was worth a little risk.

She took two deep breaths to slow her heart and put herself at Homer's shoulder as he centered before the door. The tags on his left wrist rattled when he reached for the handle. A biometric scanner concealed in the knob glowed blue through his palm for a moment before the lock clicked.

Homer swung the door open and stood aside. "Ladies first."

"Oh," Cadie said. "I don't think so."

How many women are injured or die because they're not willing to seem impolite?

She waited while Homer considered, nodded, and stepped in front of her. Sending him in first wasn't a lot of protection, but at least it meant he wouldn't be between her and the door if there were an ambush. She thought about trying to jam the lock as she passed through, but the attempt would be obvious and the chances of it working were small. She settled for leaving the door ajar, and was momentarily surprised that he didn't reach behind her to latch it.

The only person waiting inside the cozily-lit living room was a woman of average height, her gray hair pulled back in a bun and secured with chopsticks—a hairstyle Cadie wasn't sure she'd seen in over a decade. Not in America, anyway. Cadie knew her bias against men was unreasonable. She knew she shouldn't have felt a tickle of relief, but logic didn't enter into it. Women were comforting. They meant safety and allies.

"Please," the woman said. "Take a seat."

Cadie stayed beside the door, making no effort to conceal her assessment of the living room and its contents. A little box of a space, furnished in thrift-shop chic. The green velvet sofa was at least a hundred years old, and probably had not been reupholstered in half that. The wallpaper was peeling, and as Cadie's eyes adjusted, she realized that the lamps on the end tables generated their shimmering light from kerosene, not electricity.

"No, thank you." She wanted to fold her arms, but it was smarter to keep her hands free in case she needed them. "Who are you?"

The woman smiled, but did not rise. "Stephanie Shearer. Yes, before you ask, it's my real name."

Whatever that means. It sounded like the sort of name an unimaginative writing team would assign to a superhero's girlfriend.

Cadie said, "That's a precise but useless answer. What do you want from me?"

She felt Homer shift his balance slightly away. So he respected Shearer, and was possibly a little afraid of her response to Cadie's defiance. Either that, or he disapproved of the defiance itself, in isolation from Shearer's potential response.

Shearer pursed her lips. "You're Scarlet Boyko."

"I'd prefer," Cadie said, icily, "not to hear that name."

Shearer said, "So how did a nice California girl wind up married to the Russian mob?"

"It's a long story." Cadie could picture the conversation like intersecting fingers, locked at the base but pointing in incompatible directions, pushing against one another. They could fence forever, and get nowhere. "Look. Stephanie. You already have me at a disadvantage. You know who I am, what I'm worried about. You have to have a pretty good idea of what I can do for you, or you wouldn't have had Homer here contact me. You can't imagine that I'm going to hand you any additional advantages until you give me a corner to stand on, here. *What do you want from me?*"

Shearer's hands rippled on the arms of her worn cane chair. "Trust."

Cadie shook her head as if to clear her ears, but her understanding of the word still hanging almost visibly in the air between them didn't change. She had to restrain herself from glancing sideways at Homer, as if to share an eyeroll with him. Not that he was a likely source of solidarity, but—any port in a storm. "You're nuts."

"Not at all." Now Shearer stood, revealing herself to be of average height and build, and—by her movement—younger than she looked. Or perhaps she merely kept herself in excellent shape. She did limp heavily on one side, however, and Cadie wondered if it were a transitory or a permanent hurt. "Let me tell you about brand name loyalty."

This time, Cadie glanced at Homer before she could stop herself. He was regarding her with amusement, and she didn't think it was directed at Shearer. "You are deliberately wasting my time, Stephanie."

The irritation was a pose. The more of her time they wasted, the longer Cadie could stall, the more time the crèche had to spirit Firuza to safety. A first-class evacuation protocol was one of the reasons Cadie paid such a premium for Firuza's registration there.

"Brand names," Shearer said as if she had not heard Cadie's challenge, "represent a particularly successful exploit of basic human psychology. They work because of the metrics humans use to assign trust."

"Trust."

"You distrust me now because you don't know me. But in general, when you do begin to trust a person, it is because you know them, or you know people who know them, and can vouch for them. And you trust the word of certain people more than others, because you know them to be ethical, or well-informed. It's a reputation economy."

Cadie caught herself leaning forward a little. "I'm listening."

"So a brand name is in essence a fake person you can feel like you know. The psychology is pretty simple."

Homer cleared his throat and added, "And totally cynical, in application, because there is no person back there. No reputation to rely on. No sense of ethics. A corporate board, which has the same sense of morals as a stiff dick."

Cadie leaned against the doorframe, careful not to nudge the door itself shut. This time, she let herself fold her arms, needing the sense of support. "I'm really not following why you are telling me this." *At length*, but she kept that part to herself. She didn't need to antagonize these people.

"It's a philosophy," Shearer said. "We want you to understand why we've approached you and why it is that you should help us. We've approached you because of reputation. Your personal reputation. Because you were willing to go up against Taras Boyko to protect the life of a child to whom you have no biological connection, and against whom you have reason to harbor a good deal of resentment."

"She's a *child*—"

"Nonetheless," Shearer said. "Nonetheless."

"You want something from me."

She shrugged, a fatalistic gesture that Cadie took as confirmation of her—Cadie's—grasp of the obvious. Nearer by, however, Cadie saw the corner of Homer's mouth twitch. "We want you to do something for us. Something dangerous."

"Or else you'll hand me—or Firuza?—back to Taras?"

"Ms. Grange," Homer said, sounding tired. "We are the good guys."

Good guys. Sorry. Right. But Cadie didn't say that either. "Then stop yanking my chain, please. Or my leg. Or whatever it is you're pulling until it's about to come off with a pop. What do you want, and why should I help you?"

Shearer wasn't done with Cadie that easily, though. She smiled and glanced at Homer, who shook his head. "I always forget what it's like, dealing with people who've been living outside for too long. Cadence, who do you think your crèche turns to in order to evacuate threatened children? Who do you think is most interested in raising children away from government programming? We know you can barely afford the residential program Firuza is registered for."

She couldn't stop the nervous scrape of tongue and teeth across her lips, and cursed herself for how much it gave away. "What do you want with my daughter?"

"She's not your daughter."

"Stepdaughter."

"Interesting philosophical question," Homer said. "Is your spouse's bastard child still technically your stepchild? Or is it some other kind of nonbiological relationship?"

The sharp chill along Cadie's spine intensified. She was good at keeping her expression impassive—a skill she'd perfected while living in Taras's house—but apparently her poker face wasn't good enough this time, because Homer and Shearer shared a significant glance, and Shearer said, "We're not going to hold her hostage. We'll help you take care of her whether you assist us or not."

Rather than easing the tension across her shoulders and neck, the nonchalance in his statement brought it into sharp focus. "You're giving me my child back. Just like that. What if I tell you I don't want your help?"

"We'll try to convince you otherwise." Homer shrugged. "We don't operate that way."

"But—why not?"

Shearer smiled. "We're the good guys." She limped a few steps away, as if giving Cadie room to think clearly. But once she got there she turned back and twisted her hands together earnestly. "And we want you to be one of the good guys too. Human neural hardwiring is deeply tribal, at the bottom of it. One builds trust by mutual cooperation. It's like branding, only there are real people standing behind it." She jingled her tags, a shimmer of sound like a glass wind chime. "To want to help us, you have to trust us. To build that trust, we offer you help, first. I realize we have some work to do with you—"

Cadie grimaced. "I mistakenly married a Ukrainian mobster," she said. "He killed his mistress while we were married, and claimed he'd done it as a gift to me. It's *not* the sort of mistake you want to make twice in a lifetime."

"No," Shearer said. "I imagine not."

Homer shifted his feet. "You know, when Bluebeard tells you not to look in that little room under the stairs…"

It shocked Cadie into laughing. When she finished, she reached for the chair beside the door, the one she had been standing next to. She turned it slightly so it faced Shearer—the scrape of its legs on the gritty floor set her teeth on edge—and dropped into it, decisively. "—It's time to ask for a divorce, yes. Are you going to tell me what you want from me?"

They looked at each other again. Homer shrugged. "You have a route out of eastern Europe," Shearer said. "One Taras Boyko obviously does not know about, or know how to monitor. And if he doesn't, it's a safe bet that nobody in government does either. We need it. There are people there who want to join us. You're our hope of getting them out."

"Oh," Cadie said, when the silence had gone on long enough to make her shift from buttock to buttock with discomfort. "I see what you mean about dangerous, now."

Scarlet. In Russian, the word for "red" was the same as the word for "beautiful," as Taras has more than once reminded her. Another reason Cadie had been only too eager to leave her name behind. Not just because it was also his name, but because he had managed to ruin the part that wasn't.

Shearer paused to pull a cane out of the stand beside the door, and then gestured Cadie and Homer after her as she led them down the short hall toward the back of the ratty little house. As she followed past the rear rooms of the house, Cadie made herself breathe evenly and calmly, and keep her hand from knotting around the butterfly knife in her pocket. She didn't need any more dents in her hand.

Cadie asked, "So, do you live here? In this house? It's a sort of safe house?"

She thought of terrorist cells, pallets on tile floors six to a room.

Homer shrugged. "Who lives anywhere, anymore? We're digital nomads." When he patted the omni on his belt, his tags jingled. "Where my data is, that's my home. *Stuff* is just stuff. Almost anything can be replaced, or rented."

A lesson Cadie had learned hard and well. When it's time to run, you run, and don't worry about your suitcase. Still she said, "You've given me a lot of ammunition. It makes me wonder how you're lying to me."

She wasn't sure why she gave them that. Frustration. The urge to provoke. The hope that if she made Shearer and Homer angry, one of them would let something slip past the facade.

Whatever response she anticipated, it wasn't that Shearer would snicker behind her hand. "Honestly," Shearer said, as if speaking to a ridiculous ten year old, "What do you expect anyone could do to us? Confiscate our goods? We don't own any. Send us to jail? We're not doing anything illegal, short of a little trespassing, although I suppose they could legislate against us. But if that happens, we just move on. We're pioneers, Miss Grange. We're leaving your stratified society behind and building something new."

Shearer shifted her weight entirely to her crutch on the left side, and with her other hand threw open the door at the end of the hall. Wet, warm air and green light enveloped Cadie, as if that door led into a jungle. She half-expected birdsong.

Shearer ushered her forward. Framed in the door, Cadie stopped short, one foot still raised. Slowly, she put it down. The walls of what must have once been the master bedroom had been torn off, the spaces between the framing replaced

with heavy billows of translucent plastic and glass walls con-
structed of a mosaic of car windows fixed together with lath-
ing and caulk. Just within those stood tall racks, reaching from
floor to ceiling, that looked as if they had been assembled from
old car bumpers.

The racks were full of tanks, and the tanks were full of plants.
Tomatoes, cucumbers, gourds, melons. Things Cadie didn't at
first glance recognize. The air smelled green and sharp, fecund.
She breathed deeply by reflex, and had to remind herself not to
enjoy it. "A garden?"

When she looked over, Homer was grinning. "Distributed
resources," he said. "There are a lot of abandoned homes in
Detroit. Some of them are petroleum farms, some are food
farms. All salvaged materials. We have our own network. All
salvaged materials."

"Salvaged?" The planters were old-fashioned plastic gallon
milk jugs. Cadie reached out and touched the nearest, setting it
swinging slightly. Moisture dewed her fingertip. She rubbed the
pads together, thinking she would like to taste it.

"Landfills are essentially giant plastic mines," Homer said.

"All you need to live," said Shearer. "Food, water, a place to
sleep, protection from the elements, connectivity. Exploitation
of natural resources, manufacturing—*stuff*—is a dead technology, Miss Grange. The world needs to invent something new.
New ways to live. We've proven that upsizing and globalization
really don't work as well as we'd hoped. Economies of scale
make stuff cheaper, but they also demand that we move stuff
from place to place, and create demand for stuff that's really not
needed. And so rapid growth may lead to rapid collapse. With
modern communications, you don't need to be *big* anymore to
be diversified."

"And you think *these* are the first steps towards inventing it?"

"More than the first steps," she said. "The federal government has been manufacturing petroleum in landfills for years,
by seeding them with bacteria that consume organic material—
but manufacturing synthetic oil doesn't help address issues of

carbon load and climate change. And burning those hydrocarbons returns carbon load to the atmosphere that was previously trapped in discarded consumer goods. Growing carbon-negative crops and processing those into synthetic petroleum may be more helpful, but surely it's even more helpful to stop shipping your food from Costa Rica?"

Cadie thought of the oranges at the market, trucked from Florida at perfectly daunting prices. She touched a broad-leafed plant by the greenhouse door. "This is a banana."

"It is," Shearer confirmed.

Cadie said, "You really are trusting of somebody you just met."

"We know you very well." Shearer folded both hands together on the handle of her prop. "Besides, what are you going to do to us? Tell your ex-husband that we plan to smuggle a few random Ukrainians out of Kiev? I don't think so. Inform the authorities? You're no more a threat to us than a knife is to water, Miss Grange."

It was just like Kiev. When order crumbled, something rose to fill the vacuum. Something like Taras.

Or maybe something else?

Cadie thought of people trapped where she had been trapped, without the resources she'd had. At least she'd had money. Taras had never minded if she spent *money*. Giving her things was a way to keep her dependent, to ensure loyalty. She touched the shiny leaves of the banana again. "So you want to use me as a tool."

"No," Homer said. "We want you to be an ally. Come on, we've got something else to show you. We need to take a little drive."

"I need my bike—"

"Your bike will still be here when you get back, if you decide you need it."

The other presumed bicyclists had never materialized, though their rigs were still by the back door. However, out of deference to Shearer's infirmity, when Cadie and the others left the little house with a freeway in its yard, they took a tiny hybrid car with Homer driving and Cadie scrunched into the backseat, pondering.

Perhaps it indicated a lack of imagination on her part, but she was having a hell of a time figuring out the catch. And like the feral animal she'd become, that in itself made her wary. If you couldn't see the trap, it still stood to reason that there might be one.

She had ceased to worry about simple abduction or a hit, at least. If they wanted her, they'd had her the second she walked into that weird gutted house that grew like a leaf off the dying stem of I-75. There was no reason to string her along like this, except for a con, and a con would have been appealing to her greed or vanity by now. Of course, there was always the possibility that they were exactly as they seemed...

Unlikelier things had happened.

Cadie folded her hands in her lap and resigned herself to wait. Wait, and ask questions, as Detroit purred past outside the hybrid's windows. The little car only made louder sounds when it struck rutted pavement. Cadie wondered how it stood up to the mess of Detroit's alleged streets.

"What makes you think Firuza's not perfectly safe where she is?"

Homer didn't glance away from the windshield. "We found her." A flat informative answer, and a very good point.

Cadie settled against the back of the chair, folding her arms over the safety belt. Her butterfly knife gouged her hip.

"You haven't explained yet how you live without...stuff," she said. "Everybody needs stuff. Clothes, cooking utensils. Sheets and blankets. Vacuum cleaners. Lawn mowers."

Shearer rummaged in her purse. "How often do you mow your lawn?"

"Excuse me?"

"Your lawn." She craned her neck so she could look at Cadie over her shoulder, frowning. "How often do you mow it?"

"Right now, I don't have a lawn."

"Fine. And if you did?"

Cadie paused, thinking back to Taras, his house, the staff and the manicured lawns. Just picturing the place—a dacha, by which he meant palace—had her swallowing nausea. *He's on the other side of the world,* she lectured herself. *He can't get to you here.*

Except if she did what these weird people wanted her to do, she might be leading him right to her.

Anyway, regular people probably didn't mow as often as Taras' gardeners did. "Once a week," she said, trying to sound like she wasn't guessing.

"So what do you do with the lawnmower the other 167 hours of the week?"

"Oh. So you only need one lawn mower for 168 houses?"

"Well, no," Shearer said. "Because sometimes people want to mow their lawn at the same time—everybody on Sunday afternoon, right? And sometimes it's dark out. But you can have one lawn mower for ten houses. Or fifteen. Or you can all chip in for a lawnmower and then take turns mowing all the lawns. Say you have one lawnmower and ten yards. You mow five lawns Saturday, your neighbor mows five lawns Sunday, and then both of you are off the hook for a month. And collectively, you have saved the price—and the resource drain—of nine lawnmowers. I mean, it would be more sensible not to mow the lawn at all, but people like short cropped grass. You have to work within the sacrifices people are willing to make, and take it slow. Once they realize how much cheaper it is to share equipment, living space, and so on—a lot of them come around. We're really a quite communal species, the last couple of hundred years excepted. We've built bridges and mills and fences and barns as a team for centuries. When we've become conscious of the advertising messages that surround us constantly, exhorting us to own things—the shinier and more expensive the better—we adapt remarkably well to sharing. Collective child-rearing is already making a comeback; it's just too hard to bring a baby up alone. Here."

She thrust her hand into the back seat. A metal circle like a medieval seneschal's key ring dangled from her fingers, a single pierced silvery tag swinging from it. "Take this."

"What is it?"

"It entitles you to access our resources—as an apprentice, in a limited way. More tags are awarded for contributions. It's a means of keeping the unscrupulous from gaming the system. And of rewarding labor, which is one of the problems Utopian communities have traditionally had. Well, that and attempting to move urban people into a rural lifestyle without the proper training or technology, so they more or less had nothing to do but starve and quarrel...but then, we're a practical community rather than a Utopian one."

Shearer paused, as if she was considering saying more. And then she shook her head and turned her face back to the road ahead, which now wound pockmarked and undermaintained through the sort of suburban war zones that had become unsupportable in the oil crunch. As they ventured deep into the Wilds, Cadie found herself watching carefully, as if spotting a potential threat along the side of the road would help them avoid it. There were gangs out here, packs of the disenfranchised, squatters and petty warlords. Nobody went out of the city if they could help it.

Certainly, nobody took surface roads.

Cadie slid a little lower in her seat, half-expecting a roadblock or a group of armed men to materialize in front of them. She'd heard stories of cars stripped, of office buildings and grocery stores and homes sacked and occupied. *Very small city-states*, she thought, swallowing a nervous giggle.

Shearer's voice interrupted her reverie. "Go ahead and put it on."

"Hm?"

"The tag."

Dubiously, Cadie fastened the ring around her wrist and shook it so the lone tag made a shimmering sound against the band. It sounded pretty. "And are you taking me to your community?"

Homer took a hand off the wheel to gesture. "Our community is everywhere. A core is easy to uproot. A distributed model—"

"Like water to a knife, right." Cadie meant to sound ironic and arch, but it didn't quite come out that way. These people were so obviously true believers, fanatics. Adrenaline chilled her as a sickening suspicion took hold. "You guys aren't the ones who commandeered that skyscraper, are you?"

But Shearer snorted with such obvious dismissal that Cadie instantly felt like an idiot for asking. And then felt like an idiot for feeling like an idiot, because what was to stop Shearer from lying to her until she gave them what they wanted?

"We salvage," Shearer said. "We don't steal."

Homer caught Cadie's eye in the mirror. "We come or go, more or less as we please. Some of us hold down outside jobs, like Stephanie." He shrugged. "Some of us do not."

Cadie scrunched her legs around behind his seat, trying to encourage blood flow. The bracelet was a weight on her wrist; it seemed like she could hear the tag shimmer every time she so much as took a breath. The sound made her as conscious of every tiny motion as if a predator watched her. "How much longer?"

Homer pulled the car onto a narrow road that wound through a heavy copse of trees. An ivy-covered sign, unreadable, made Cadie think this must be the remains of an abandoned office park. Somebody had laid truckloads of gravel over the ruined asphalt, so the driveway was smoother than the municipal road that led to it.

"To see your lawnmower," he said.

"Like industrialization and the black satanic mills, globalization is a failed model that nevertheless we have to pass through to invent the next modality." Even holding the car door for Cadie, Shearer was still lecturing. And Cadie was still listening, though she was starting to find some intelligent questions.

"So who makes the stuff you can't salvage?" she asked. "The stuff you hold in common? Does your society work without an industrial society to...to parasitize?"

Shearer grinned. "Maybe not. But industrial society has it coming. Allez-oop." Propped on the open door, she offered Cadie a hand, and Cadie—despite her better judgment regarding Shearer's frailty—accepted it. She tried to use the frame of the auto as her primary source of lift for standing, but the older woman's strength surprised her. In reflected light, Cadie could see where parking lots had once been. Now, the rustle of tall corn filled the night.

Here, there were people. Men and women moved along pathways lit by solar-powered LED lamps stuck on spikes into the grass, so Cadie had very little sense of their faces, forms, or how they were dressed. But she heard the click of high heels and the rubbery thud of heavy boots, the scuff of sneakers. And the light high tinkerbell shimmer of tags ringing on each other as their wearers moved.

Everyone seemed casually busy and a few were far more intent—obviously in a hurry. But some passers-by still glanced at Cadie and her escorts, and several greeted Shearer and Homer with a word or a wave. Cadie found herself hiding half-behind Homer, sticking close to his heels like an uncertain dog or a child.

"I'm going to let Homer take you around," Shearer said. "My hip has had enough."

Homer studied her with a concerned expression, but his only response was a nod. "I'll meet you in the lounge."

Shearer winked before she turned away. "Make sure you take her up to the roof."

Inside, they paused in a glass-roofed atrium full of potted chest-tall fruit trees. The heavy scent of oranges filled the air, sharp enough to wrinkle Cadie's nose. The space was not brightly lit; instead, strands of fairy-light LEDs strung overhead gave illumination enough to walk by. And as with outside, there were people walking. A woman in blue jeans and a flannel shirt with the sleeves rolled up tended the orange and lime trees, dropping fruit into a basket that curved around her hip. A man surrounded by six or seven school-age children climbed the wide stair to the mezzanine level, and a security guard or receptionist or both looked up from behind the desk beside the doors. Her entire head and body except her face was enveloped in a hijab and chador, but based on her gimlet-eyed appraisal of them as they entered, Cadie did not think the concealing garments would slow her down at all. After her inspection, she nodded, though Cadie caught her rechecking Cadie's wrist for the bracelet before she looked down.

When Cadie stuffed her hand into her pocket the tag caught on the fabric, keeping her from reaching easily to the bottom. She was still following Homer like a duckling, head down so her dreads hid her expression, but she had to steal glances at the flock of children climbing the stairs and Homer caught her.

She imagined Firuza laughing with these children, flocking with them like so many noisy starlings. Her own childhood had been play groups and educational trips and team sports in the summertime, and she wondered what it was like to grow up surrounded by foster siblings. Did their caretakers watch them? Make sure nobody got bullied, that the little ones got their fair share?

Everybody in San Diego must think she was dead by now. She wondered what they had done, when the emails and phone calls had stopped coming. Had they worried?

Had her sister said to her mother, *Mama, I told her so?*

You did. You did, Ruby. You did.

"You have your own crèche?" she asked, as they reached the bottom of the flight themselves. The kids and their minder vanished through a door at the top of the stairs.

"School," he said. "Not crèche. They stay with their guardians at night. Guardians or parents," he amended. "They're probably on their way home now. Distributed model also makes child rearing that much easier."

She watched his shoulders rise and fall, and suffered a realization. "You have kids."

"Had." He paused at the top of the stair and waited, looking down at her until she caught him. "You'll discover that a lot of people find us out of some kind of life trauma."

"Oh," she said. "I'm sorry."

This time, the shrug came with wide-spread hands. He looked at her, really looked at her, and she looked back just as hard. What she saw was a skinny sallow-skinned person with acne scars across the tops of his cheeks, one who didn't look down when she stared right at him. *It's about people, too,* she realized. *You can't do what they want to do without people.*

And then, like a tripping cat, the realization. *I'm people.*

"It is what it is," Homer said. "Come on."

A bank of elevators waited silent immediately before them, but two had the buttons taped over, and the third bore a hand-lettered sign that read **ARE YOU SURE?** Cadie found the implied faith in personal judgment refreshing, and was about to say so to Homer, but he was already vanishing up a stair. He paused just inside to hold the door for her, and she ran a couple of steps to catch up.

"Farther up and further in," she said, but Homer looked at her blankly. "Nevermind," she finished with a wince.

He didn't seem concerned about it anyway. He led her up three flights at a trot that made her glad of the time she spent in a bicycle saddle, and then out into a corridor that connected on either end to a broad open space broken up by partial-height walls. "A cube farm?" Cadie asked.

"Former cube farm," he said, and led her out into the walk-ways between the once-beige fabric walls.

Somebody with little concern for corporate image had been at them with fabric paints and glitter glue, illuminating the cubes with vivid primitive paintings of macaws and monkeys, sea turtles and sloths. Even in the LED fairylight, the colors were stunning enough that Cadie wished she were seeing them by daylight. Curtains—repurposed blankets, draperies, and shower curtains—hung across the doorway of each cube, and from inside some of them Cadie could hear the click of keypads or the rustle of cloth. One or two stood open, empty, revealing futon mattresses with neatly folded bedclothes, plastic crates set beside them to serve as storage and tables.

"Dormitories," she said.

Homer cocked his finger like a gun and made an approving click. "Yours if you want to use them. First-come, first-served, though it becomes possible to make reservations with enough history of service. But as you can see, we're rarely full."

There were plants here too, racked in front of the floor to ceiling windows where they would break up the glare of the light. Cadie recognized potted strawberries, thyme, basil, rosemary, and sage.

"Clover?" she asked, pointing. "What for?"

Homer followed her line. "Wood sorrel," he said, "It grows like a weed, and it's tasty and full of vitamin C. We toss it in soup. Might as well. Here, follow me."

He led her to another stair, this one in the corner of the building and boasting an old FIRE EXIT sign. Again, she climbed behind him, this time hearing the giggles of children echoing down the glass and cement stairwell. She was not sure if she wanted to catch them, or if what she really wanted was to clap her hands over her ears and block the sound away.

Whatever her conscious mind thought, her subconscious was sure. She only caught herself walking faster when she almost trod on Homer's heels. "The person who painted the murals," she said, when Homer turned back to see what the rush was. "Did she—he?—earn more tags for doing that?"

"Not just for that," Homer said. "She's kind of a polymath. But yes, that's one of her contributions."

"Okay," Cadie said. "So really, it's not all that different from anything else. Except instead of money, you get tags...."

"Except, instead of contributing to an exploitative economy designed to line the pockets of the top capital holders, we're contributing to a collective economy in which people know one another by reputation."

"Until it gets too big."

"Then we split up," Homer said. "Subdivide until we reach a sustainable level. Growth—getting as big as possible as fast as possible—is not the only way to survive. Think about dinosaurs and mammals."

His grin was infectious. He pushed open the roof door and she followed him, surprised by the springiness of turf under her feet, and the sweetness of cool night air. She had, perhaps subconsciously, been expecting gravel and the reek of rubber roofing after a long day baking in the sun.

"Green roof," she said, an exclamation of surprise, and felt Homer's smug pleasure beside her.

"This is all ancient technology," he said. "From turf roofs to cooperative agriculture. It's just that for a while we got confused about progress, and hooked on the idea that it *also* means giving up what *works*."

As they moved out into the darkness and Cadie's eyes adjusted, she could make out the silhouettes of other people. First, the children she'd glimpsed earlier, not giggling and shoving now but standing in a close and cheerful huddle, gathered around something illuminated by the LED flashlight in their crouching instructor's hand. Beyond them, a couple pulled each other close, watching the crescent moon rise over trees, the taller man's head leaned on top of his lover's.

Cadie stepped away from Homer, towards the huddle of children gathered around the puddle of bright green light. The instructor glanced up as she came close, registering her approach, but didn't otherwise acknowledge her. Since he also made no move to exclude her, she rose up on tiptoe to see over the heads of the kids. They were gathered around an unprepossessing black beetle the size of a kidney bean, and as Cadie was wondering what, exactly, the point of the exercise was, the instructor took his thumb off the button on the LED flash and the light went out.

Her eyes took a moment to adjust to blackness and moonlight, the silver-limned figures of the hunched-over children and the high block wall of the roof edge beyond. Moonlight, she remembered from somewhere, is comprised of parallel rays, because it is reflected as if by a giant mirror. It's cold—reflected light is cold—and it casts perfect sharp-edged shadows, because it does not scatter the way sunlight does. It turned each blade of grass into a slender knife of frost, and the pools of shadow under the children into bottomless wells. Twinkling green fairy lights flickered on and off overhead, casting no appreciable illumination, unlike the LED chains in the lobby.

That's what Cadie thought, at least, until at the center of their gathering, a sharp signal flickered, a cold chemical light as green as the doused LED answering the flashes overhead. "Firefly," she breathed, understanding, and bit her lip just in time to keep from embarrassing herself by saying it out loud.

"The female stays on the ground," the instructor said. "Until she finds a male that flashes fast and bright enough to interest her. When that happens, she flashes back, to show him where to find her. Until she does that, the male doesn't even know she's there."

"But then why don't all the bad flashers get bred out?" It was a girl who asked the question, Cadie thought, though it was hard to tell from the voices in the dark. She wondered if Firuza had ever seen a firefly.

"That's a really good question, Sabrina. See, there are other males, who aren't such good flashers, and sometimes they wait until a female flashes at a male who is bright, and then try to get to her first and fool her. So they can pass on their genes by being tricky. Salazar, here, pick out a male, one of the flying ones. Take the LED and see if you can imitate the flashes well enough to get him to come down to you—"

In the intermittent backglow of the LED, Cadie could make out Salazar's face. He might have been eight or nine years old, and as he looked up his expression was as perfectly intent as any scientist's as he tried to pick one male firefly's flash pattern out of the holding pattern overhead.

Cadie only realized she was holding her breath when Salazar's silent concentration imploded around the sudden, unmistakable hail-pelting rattle of gunfire.

She hit the ground—or the roof—intuitively, sweeping Salazar and one of the other children into her arms and covering them with her body. Homer hit the turf beside her as the instructor began snapping orders to his charges, quick commands that spoke of faithful drill. As they all dropped to a crouch and began moving quickly and in good order towards the roof door, Cadie rolled to let the children she'd shielded scramble alongside their classmates. At the edge, the two men who had been watching the moonrise both went to their knees, peering over the wall like archers over a battlement. One—the shorter one—touched his headset. Cadie saw the blue light flicker live as he began to speak into it.

Homer touched her arm. "Follow the kids. Ernie will take care of you."

"Homer, this might be about me—"

"Miss Grange," he said. "Not everything is about you. Go with the nice man."

Cadie thought about arguing, but Homer was already moving away from her while Ernie—Ernie must be the instructor—shooed eight-year-olds down the stairs single file, counting each child with a tap on the head as he or she passed. Cadie, bent double with her knees against her chest, ran to meet him.

"Homer says you'll take care of me," she said, when Ernie looked at her with elevated eyebrows. He'd doused the light inside the stairwell, but she could see his expression plainly by moonlight. She bit her lip and said "Sorry. I'm new."

It was the first real notion she'd had that Homer and Shearer's hard sell was working. Ernie studied her for a second, dark thick hair falling in a wing across his forehead until he shook it back irritably. "Right," he said. "Sorry. Didn't mean to be an asshole. Come with me."

Down the stairs in the dark, without even the light of the LED flashlights to guide them. Only one floor, because this stairwell was at the corner of the building, and they would have been visible and vulnerable through the glass if anyone had cared to look up. The children stayed close to the center of the staircase, heads ducked, shoulders hunched as they crabbed down the flight. Cadie mimicked them, protecting the ones closest to her with her body as much as she could. The descent gave her a strobe-image series of glimpses of the firefight below, muzzle-flash and then a shuddering roar of water as defenders within and atop the besieged office building opened up with firehoses. Searchlights flooded the lawn and crop fields with light. Rows of corn shook with the passage of running bodies, like something out of a horror movie.

A child at the front of the file pressed her tags to a control panel by the door on the landing, and it slid open with a whisper of complaint. The kids ducked through, Ernie pausing to usher Cadie through, and then he sealed the door behind.

Once the solid door was shut, the kids straightened up. Cadie tried to emulate them, fighting a contraction of her abdominal muscles as if someone had fastened her lower ribs to her pelvis with giant hog-nosed staples. By placing one hand on the wall and pushing against it, she managed to stand up tall, though she thought Ernie and all the kids could see her shoulders and knees shaking.

"It's better than being shot at for real," Ernie said, with a wink, and slapped her on the shoulder. "Come on, the panic room's not far. Come on, kids, look sharp!"

Doors had closed across the corridors like airlocks, breaking each one into defensible segments, and Ernie opened each one with his tag and cleared the other side like a pro before he let them pass each one. He urged them into a trot, using his voice like a border collie's bark to keep them both moving and close. Cadie was pretty sure herding children wasn't supposed to be that easy.

Given the circumstances, she was happy to be herded as well. It's easy to give up authority in crisis. Easy to do what you're told. Easy to follow orders and let somebody else take responsibility. Easy to pretend you didn't know what was going on.

It's not the same thing as trust, but it's like trust.

She reached into her pocket and palmed her butterfly knife right-handed, slipped the pepper spray into the left. Caught the glance across the children's heads that told her Ernie had seen her do it, and nodded agreement when the quick jerk of his head sent her up to the front of the line. She flipped the knife open, hiding it from the kids with her body. The motion made her tag ring on her bracelet with a clear sharp chime.

"Open the door," Ernie said when they came to the next lock. Cadie brushed her tag against it and pushed it open with her shoulder, telling herself to be ready for whatever was on the other side.

Nothing, and the sharp beat of her heart left the taste of rotting metal in her mouth as she turned left, then right, and made doubly sure. Her pulse ratcheted down a half notch, and she was just about to slink forward and clear the offices opening off both sides when the door to the nearer one flipped back and she found herself face to face with a man with a gun.

She reacted almost without knowing it, taking in so many details in an instant—the stubble on his cheek, the way his gun shook in his hand. It was just adrenaline. She didn't think for a moment that he would hesitate to shoot her.

Her left hand came up and she maced him in the face. His gun went off; the head-spinning boom almost blinded her. But he'd flinched, and the first bullet must have missed her, because she didn't feel it hit. She stepped forward, the knife rising from her fist like a scorpion's sting, and punched him under the ribs. Hard, something shoving her hand down. Thunder against the side of her head, a blow as if somebody had struck her on the ear with a cymbal. Hot air kicked against her cheek as the gun fired again and he staggered into her. The knife driving down her fist because he leaned against it, and how was she on her knees? How had that happened? He slumped on top of her, everything slippy and wet, his shirt tearing away from the knife blade so she could see the dark ink of the tattoos across his chest. Should his skin be that white under the red? Maybe all the blood was on the outside now. She fell under his weight, hard thump as her head hit the floor.

Her strength all swirled out of her like somebody had pulled a cork on a string.

She woke briefly at the bounce of the gurney as paramedics lifted her into place, woke again as they slid the trolley into the elevator—*Are you sure?* Cadie thought, unironically—and felt herself going under, swept along a tumble of semiconsciousness and battered on its rocks. "I need my daughter sent them," she said, or tried to say, but there was something over her nose and mouth and the paramedics looked at her as uncomprehendingly as farm animals.

She would have panicked—she tried to panic—but even the adrenaline could not keep her above water when the tide of exhaustion swept over her again.

The next awakening was gentler. Gray, soft, in cool sheets. Someone beside her, because Cadie could hear the breathing. She turned her head and opened her eyes, and found herself face to face with Stephanie Shearer.

The rustle of sheets must have alerted Shearer, because she looked up from her omni—opened flat in reader mode—and smiled. "Awake pretty fast," she said, and folded the omni away.

Cadie made a noise that she meant to be a word, but it game out as more of a wheeze.

"Sorry," said Shearer. "I can't give you a drink. The bullet perforated your intestine. But it's all fixed now, and you can have a swab. Will that help?"

Helplessly, Cadie nodded. She managed to raise a hand to take the soaked sponge on a stick that Shearer handed her. There wasn't enough water in it, but it did ease the stickiness on her tongue and palate. A few moments later, she managed to croak, "What happened?"

Shearer took the swab away. "You got shot. And then managed to knife the shooter fatally. Don't worry, we have very good lawyers, and you're unlikely to be charged."

"Firuza," Cadie said. She tried to make it sound like a question, but she couldn't get her voice to lift at the end.

"Safe in the Cascades. We have a place there." Shearer smiled, dunking the swab in the water glass again. "Distributed living. You can go see her as soon as you're well enough. I mean, assuming you want to stay with us."

Cadie wasn't ready to think about that yet. So she said, "You were the artist."

"Artist?"

"On the cubicles." Her voice was coming back. "You painted the cubicles in the dormitory."

"Busted," Shearer said, smiling. "You saw me coming. I thought they needed something to make them feel like home." She rummaged in her pocket, came up with something, and laid it on the bedside table with a soft chime.

Cadie lifted her head to look, aware now of the tug of needles in her left hand. It was the circular bracelet, and now—she saw—there were three tags on it. "Is that mine?"

"Can't keep you on probation when you've gotten shot defending us," Shearer said. "What do you say?"

"Your people. In Ukraine. You still need help?"

Shearer nodded.

So did Cadie, though it made her head spin. "All right." Then she pressed her head back into the pillow and closed her eyes against the dizziness. "I'll do it. You know the thing about your Utopia—"

She didn't open her eyes to look at Shearer, but she felt the tension, heard the creak of her chair as she leaned forward.

Shearer said, "It's not a Utopia. It's just maybe something that sucks a little less. And it's not mine."

"Yeah," Cadie said. "Whatever." It took a minute for her to gather her strength. "This will never work."

A longer silence this time, until Shearer said, "It's hope. Even if it fails. It's hope. We need hope. We need to learn to trust the people we *ought* to trust again."

"Yeah." Cadie swallowed. Her throat still ached with dryness. She wondered if she had enough strength to ask for the swab again. "I can't argue with that."

UTERE NIHIL NON EXTRA QUIRITATIONEM SUIS

JOHN SCALZI

Now we come to my story, and to explain my story, I need to expand a little on what I saw as my role as during the creation of METATROPOLIS. As I've mentioned, I was the editor of the project, which meant that in the early stages I needed to help direct the world building conversations and move them toward a workable plan. Later, when the stories came in, I gave feedback to the other authors about what needed to be tweaked in their stories. The good news in both cases was that I was working with really smart, really talented and experienced writers and creators, so in that respect my responsibilities were very easy and simple. Go me.

But I was an author here as well as an editor, and the editor in me decreed that the author in me would be the "spackle" of the anthology—that is, if after all the stories were in there was some aspect of this shared world still left unexplored, that I would go in and cover that hole. And as it turned out, there was one small hole: The stories of METATROPOLIS were indeed meta—that is, they looked beyond cities in interesting and fascinating ways. However, that meant to me that there needed to be a story actually situated inside a city, from the point of view of someone for whom the cities were simply "home." So that's the story I assigned to myself.

And because I'm dumb, I gave it a title in Latin that I can barely pronounce. Shhh. Don't tell.

When people look at my wedding photos, they often wonder what the pig is doing in the wedding party. Well, let me tell you.

It all began, like so many things do, on a Monday.

The first thing I remember is my little sister Syndee poking me in the cheek.

"Mom says it's time to get up," she said.

I swatted at her with my eyes closed. "It's too early to get up," I said.

"It's nine thirty," Syndee said. "Says so right on your alarm clock."

"The clock lies," I said.

Syndee started poking me in the face again. "Mom told me to tell you if you missed your placement appointment that she would make you regret it."

"I'll be up in a minute," I said, and then rolled over and tried to go back to sleep. I could hear Syndee stomp off, calling for mom. A couple minutes later, I heard someone come back in the room.

"Benjamin," said a lower voice than my sister's. It was mom. "You have your placement appointment in an hour. Time to get up."

"I'm up," I said.

"There is no definition of 'up' that includes lying in bed with your eyes closed," mom said.

"Five more minutes," I said. "I swear I'll be up then."

"Oh, I know you will be," mom said, and that's when she poured a pitcher of water onto my head. I tried to jump out of bed and got tangled in my blankets, and fell head first onto the rug.

"That's better," mom said.

. I rubbed my head. "That wasn't necessary," I told mom.

"No," mom agreed. "I could have poured hot coffee in your lap instead. But either way, you're out of bed. Now you get into the shower. You have five minutes for that. After that I switch the shower over to greywater, and I know how much you hate that."

I pulled myself off the floor and stomped over to the bathroom. Mom was right; greywater sucked. Technically it was filtered to be just as clean as regular water. Psychologically I didn't want to bathe in water one filtering process away from someone's kidneys.

"Five minutes," mom said again. "And don't think I'm not paying attention. You're not going to *miss* this appointment, Benji."

"I'm not going to miss it," I said, starting the water.

"I know," mom said. "Because I'll drag you there by the hair if I have to." She walked off. As she walked off I saw Syndee smirking at me.

"Should have got up when I said to," she said.

"Piss off," I said. She smirked some more and flounced off. I stripped out of my underwear and stepped into the shower and stayed in it until that sulfur smell told me mom had switched the tank over to greywater. Then I soaped up, rinsed off and got out.

Ten minutes later I was standing on the curb, waiting for at least one other person to come out of the complex and rideshare. You can take a pod by yourself if you have to, but it comes out of your overall household energy budget, and we were already splurging on the standard water for showering. If I solo'd a pod to my appointment, mom really would drop hot coffee into my lap. So I stood there for a few minutes waiting to see who would come by.

"Hey, look," someone said, behind me, stepping into the pod queue. "If it isn't Benji."

I turned and saw Will Rosen, one of my least favorite humans, and Leah Benson, who was one of my favorites. Sadly, Leah and Will were a couple, so spending time with Leah meant having to tolerate Will, and him having to tolerate me. So I didn't see Leah all that much.

"Hello, Benji," Leah said.

"Hi, Le," I said, and smiled, and then glanced over next to her. "Will," I said.

"You're up early," Will said. "It's not even noon."

On cue, a pod swung up on the track and opened the door to let us in. I considered telling them I was waiting for Syndee and taking the next pod.

"Coming, Benji?" Leah said.

I climbed in.

"Parker Tower," Will said to the destination panel. He was off to work.

"Kent Tower," Leah said. She was off to work, too.

"City Administration," I said.

"Running an errand for your mom?" Will said, as we started moving.

"No," I said, more defensively than I intended. "I've got a placement appointment."

Will feigned a heart attack. "I don't believe it," he said. "That means you actually *took* your Aptitudes."

"Yeah," I said, and looked out the window. I was trying to avoid this conversation.

"Miracles do happen," Will said.

"Will," Leah said.

"Benji knows I'm kidding," Will said, the same way he always did when he was doing some serious knife twisting work. "And anyway I think it's great. He's the last of our class to do it. He always did things on his own schedule, but I was beginning to wonder how close he was planning to cut it."

"Now you know," I said.

"Well, congratulations," Will said. "It'll be nice to know you're part of the contributing part of society now. That you're not just relying on your mom to get you through."

That was when I decided I'd had just about enough of Will. "Thanks, Will," I said, and shifted position. "So, how's your brother these days?"

Will got a look that I guessed you might get if you had something very cold and hard suddenly thrust up your ass. I treasured that look.

"He's fine," Will said. "So far as I know."

"Really," I said. "That's great. I always liked him. The next time you see him, you tell him I said hello."

Leah shot me a look that said *stop that*. I just smiled pleasantly as pie for the next couple of minutes, until the pod slowed down, came to a stop, and then opened to let Will out. He was still sitting there, glaring at me.

"Your stop," I said.

Will snapped out of it, gave Leah a quick kiss, and hustled himself out the door of the pod.

"That wasn't very nice," Leah said to me, as we started moving again.

"Well, he asked for it," I said, and motioned back to the platform where Will had gotten off. "You saw it. He was crapping all over me in that 'I'm just kidding' condescending way of his. Like he always does. Tell me he wasn't trying to push my buttons. Like he always does."

"He was trying to push your buttons," Leah said, agreeing with me. "But you don't do much to stop him, Benji."

"I think asking him about his brother stopped him pretty well," I said.

"There are better ways," Leah said.

"Are there?" I asked. "Leah, you know I love you, dearly, but the guy you're dating is kind of an asshole. Why are you still with him?"

"You mean, why am I still with him, and not you?" Leah said.

"It's crossed my mind," I said.

"I remember trying that," Leah said. "I don't remember it working out very well."

"I was young and stupid," I said, and gave her a smile. "I got over it. Really."

Leah smiled, which was something I liked to see, and looked out the pod window for a moment. "Benji, you were always very cute," she said. "But as much as you'd hate to admit it, Will has a point. You've been taking longer to grow up than the rest of us did. When the rest of us finished our studies, we took the Aptitudes and got jobs. You spent your time sleeping in and screwing around. Will's right that you're the last one in our class to take your Aptitudes and to get placement."

"That's not true," I said. "There's Taylor White."

Leah fixed me with a look. "You're really going to compare yourself with a guy who was eating crayons until he was fifteen," she said.

"That's a rumor," I said.

"It's not a rumor," Leah said. "I saw him do it. Art class. It was a green pastel. He nibbled it, Benji. And then he put it back. I had to share the pastel box with him. It was disgusting."

"Nibbling's not the same as *eating*," I said.

"Does it really matter?" Leah said. "Taylor's a sweet guy, but we both know he's going into the assisted job track. You don't have that excuse. You're two months off from being twenty, Benji. That really is cutting it close."

"I don't know what that has to do with you going out with Will and not me," I said. We were coming into Leah's stop.

"I know, Benji," she said. "That's sort of the problem."

The door slid open. Leah reached over and kissed my cheek. "Good luck today, Benji," she said.

"Thanks," I said. Leah slipped out of the pod. "Hey," I said. She turned back to look at me. "Even if you're not going to date me, you could still do better."

Leah looked like she might say something to that, but the pod door slid shut.

And so I landed in the office of Charmaine Lo, Public Assignment Officer for the city of New St. Louis.

"Ah, Mr. Washington," she said, from her desk, as I walked in. Behind her was a large monitor that took nearly the entire back wall of her office. "Why don't you come and have a seat."

"Thanks," I said, and admired the monitor. Lo followed my gaze to the monitor and then looked back at me.

"It's a monitor," she said.

"I know," I said. "It's nice. I need to get one of those for my bedroom."

"Not unless you have a special dispensation from the energy board," she said. She was looking down now at the tablet monitor that held my case file.

"I'll have to talk to my mom about that," I said, trying to make it sound like a joke.

Lo looked up at this with a look that told me I had failed, badly. "Oh, that's right," she said. "You're the son of Josephine Washington."

"I am," I said.

"Must be nice having your mother on the executive board of the city," Lo said.

"It's not too bad," I said.

"I voted for your mother in the last election," Lo said.

"I'll tell her that when I get home," I said.

"I hope you understand, Mr. Washington, that your mother's stature and influence won't help you here," Lo said. "Job assignments in the city are based on merit, not nepotism."

"I know," I said. "Sorry. About the monitor thing, I mean. I was trying to make a joke."

Lo looked at me for a moment. I decided not to make any more jokes. "Sorry," I said again.

"Well, then, let's get to it," she said, and tapped her tablet. The wall monitor sprang to life with thousands of boxes, each with text in them. She pointed at the wall, and looked back at me. "Do you know what this is?" she asked.

"No," I said.

"This is a representation of every single job that is available right now in New St. Louis," Lo said. "Everything from neurosurgeon right down to janitorial systems maintenance crew. Roughly about one thousand jobs, at the moment. This is a live feed, so you'll see some jobs disappear as they are filled, and new ones show up as they come online."

I looked up again and took a closer look. She was right about it being a live feed; while I watched, one of the text boxes winked out of existence. Somewhere in New St. Louis, someone had a new job as a crèche supervisor, watching bunches of hyperactive two-year-olds while their parents were off at their jobs.

"As your mother has no doubt told you, New St. Louis has a managed employment economy," Lo said. "Every adult who lives in NSL is required to work, and all vacancies are filled internally whenever possible. Each new entrant into the NSL workforce, whether through immigration or through graduation from the NSL school system, is required to take a series of aptitude tests that help us place that person into their initial job."

"Right," I said, and remembered the Aptitudes. How I hated them.

First off, they took two days out of your life, after you've already gotten your education certificate. In other places in other times, a high school diploma was all you needed for a job—not especially good jobs, my mom would point out, but even so—but here in New St. Louis, all your education certificate meant was that you were allowed to take your Aptitudes.

So, two days. The first day was a recap of math, science, history, literature and other school subjects. Which to me seemed a waste of time, these days. Yes, it's nice to remember all this stuff in your head. But the fact of the matter was even if you didn't, everything you had to know about anything was a database search away and had been for decades, and out in the real world the chance that you would need to know when New St. Louis was founded or the intricacies of the city's "zero-footprint" ecological and economic philosophy—and would not have a mini-terminal in your pocket— approached zero.

You know, I think of myself as a practical person, and in practice, all this the memorization just seemed like busy work to me. I know I can find out anything with a query; worrying about stuffing things into my head seems too much.

That said, I wasn't completely stupid. I did spend a little time reviewing the basics before my Aptitudes. And because I didn't want to stress myself overly, I also made sure to have a good time a night before. I think that being relaxed is key. My mother might disagree. So might Leah.

If the first day was annoying the second day was just mystifying: a series of conversations with a rotating pack of NSL city workers about completely pointless subjects that really had nothing to do anything as far as I could tell. Sometimes I didn't understand my home town's job protocol.

"I notice you took your Aptitudes at the last possible opportunity to do so," Lo said.

"I'm sure a lot of people do it that way," I said.

"No, not really," Lo said. "Most kids do them right after their schooling is completed, so everything is still fresh in their heads. Most of them are also eager to start contributing to the well-being of NSL as soon as possible—and to start their career paths."

I shrugged. After I'd gotten my education certificate schooling, I decided to travel to some of the other cities that shared "open borders" with New St. Louis: The Portland Arcologies and other parts of Cascadia, the Malibu Enclave, Singapore and Hong Kong and the new Helsinki Collective. They kept me busy for a few months, and in a good way, I thought. Travel broadens the mind, and all that.

Mom wasn't very happy about this, but I had promised her I'd take the Aptitudes the next time they were offered once I got back. And I did try, but things kept getting in the way. I finally took them because I was coming up on my twentieth birthday, and here in New St. Louis they had a word for twenty-year-olds who hadn't taken their Aptitudes to get assigned a job: evicted. Even New Louies who went to university outside the city had to take their Aptitudes before their twentieth; they took them remotely and had their scores filed away for later. Miss them, though, and out you go.

That's what happened to Will's brother Marcus. He missed his last chance to take the Aptitudes five years ago, and the City showed up at the door with his Document of Removal, escorted him to the city border, placed a credit card worth sixteen ounces of gold into his hands and waved goodbye. Now Marcus was living outside, in the banged-up ring of suburbs around St. Louis, new and old, that we referred to as "the wilds," doing whatever the hell it was people in the wilds did with their time. I suspected he was scrounging and gardening, not necessarily in that order. And now you know why Will would have been happy to stab me for mentioning his brother.

Marcus could get back in one day...maybe. People who'd been booted out of NSL for missing their Aptitudes could get back in only once they'd taken a new set of tests and waited to see if there was a job that no one in the city wanted. And even then they'd have to wait in line, because the list went New Louies first, citizens of other "open border" cities next, and then finally the rest of the world. You skip your last chance at the Aptitudes, it might be years before you get your citizenship back.

Now you know why I didn't miss that last Aptitudes testing day. I try to imagine what mom would do if the City showed up at the door to boot me out and my brain just shuts down. On that path lies madness. I shivered just thinking about it.

Lo noticed. "Cold?" she asked.

"No, sorry," I said. "Just thinking about something." I motioned toward the board. "So, what now? Do I pick one of these jobs?"

"Not quite," Lo said. "I'm showing you all of these jobs so you have an idea of the scope of the city's need for labor."

"Okay, I get it," I said.

"Good," Lo said. "Now, what I'm going to do next is plug in your aptitude test results into this matrix of job openings, and see which ones they qualify you for. First, the results from your first day of testing—the recap of your knowledge from your education." Lo tapped her tablet screen.

I watched as roughly ninety percent of the job openings disappeared from the wall. I spent the next minute or so opening and closing my mouth to no real good effect.

"I think there's something wrong with your wall display," I said, finally.

"The wall display is fine," Lo said. "The problem is that over-all you scored in the 35th percentile for your aptitudes. Look." She held up her tablet display and showed it to me. My test scores were on a trio of lines, showing my ranking relative to others who had taken the test the same days I did, in the same year as I had, and since the beginning of the tests, just a few years after the founding of New St. Louis.

"Actually, the 35th percentile is for the historical chart," Lo said, pointing. "You scored lower among the people who took it with you, and who have taken it in the last year. And most of the people who did worse than you were people who were taking the Aptitudes from outside the city."

"Maybe there was a mistake in the scoring," I said.

"Probably not," Lo said. "The tests are triple-scored by machine to catch errors. You're more likely to get hit by light-ning than suffer an incorrect Aptitudes score."

"I can take them again," I said.

"You *could have* taken them again if you had taken them ear-lier," Lo said. "But the next set of Aptitudes isn't scheduled until after your twentieth birthday. So for the purposes of your first job, you're stuck with these scores, Mr. Washington."

I slumped back into the chair. Mom was going to kill me. Lo looked at me curiously. I began to resent her, or at least what I figured she thought of me. "I'm not stupid, you know," I said.

"You don't appear stupid, no," Lo said, agreeing. "But I'd be willing to bet you didn't pay very close attention in school, and taking time off before you took your Aptitudes certainly didn't help either."

Okay, that sounded exactly like something mom would say. And like with mom, I really didn't want to have that discussion right now. "Fine, whatever," I said, and pointed at the wall. "So now I pick from these jobs?"

"Not yet," Lo said. "Because now I have to plug in the results from your second day of testing: the evaluator's reviews of your attitude and psychological fitness. The good news here is that a good score can put back on the board some of the jobs that you might have lost before. There are a lot of jobs that the city feels a motivated worker could do even if they don't have the academic Aptitude test scores."

"Okay, good," I said. I felt slightly encouraged by that; I think I'm a pretty personable guy.

"Here we go," Lo said, and tapped her tablet again.

All but three jobs disappeared from the board.

"Oh, come *on!*" I yelled. "That *can't* be right!"

"Apparently it is," Lo said. She gave her tablet to me. I took it and looked at it. "You scored even lower on the evaluator's reports than you did on the academic testing. It says there that you struck them as arrogant, bored, and defensive. One of them actually called you 'a bit of an asshole.'"

I looked up from the tablet for that one, appalled at what I was hearing. "You can't say that on an official report," I said.

"They can say whatever they want," Lo said. "They're trained to evaluate everyone's fitness as an employee and they're required by law to write their honest impressions. If one of them called you a bit of an asshole, it's because that's what you are. Or at least what you come across as."

"I'm not an asshole," I said, thrusting the tablet back at Lo.

Lo shrugged. "You came in *here* with some attitude, didn't you?" she said, taking the tablet. "That 'joke' about the monitor and your mom, for example."

"I really did mean it as a joke," I said.

"Maybe you did," Lo said. "But it comes off like you're just dropping your mom's name to hint to me that you should be given a cushy job. Whether you mean it that way or not, that's how you present. And it is more than a little annoying. I can believe you came across as an asshole in your testing. And I can believe you probably weren't even aware of it at the time."

"Can we talk about something else, please?" I said. This was not a good day so far. "Like what jobs are available?"

"Okay," Lo said. She tapped her tablet. The three tiny squares remaining on the wall disappeared, replaced by three very large job listings.

"The general feeling about you is that you're best off not working a job that requires any interaction with the public, or that requires a great deal of technical competence," Lo said. "So basically we're talking some form of back-end job with a heavy physical component. And among those types of jobs we have three openings: Assistant Greensperson at park tower number six, Composting Engineer, trainee level, at the East End waste transformation plant, and Biological Systems Interface Manger at the Arnold Tower."

"'Composting Engineer'?" I said, leaning forward in my seat.

"That's what it says," Lo said. "It's a polite way of saying you'll be shoveling shit. Although as I'm sure you remember from your studies, there's more to industrial scale composting than just shit."

"I'm not doing that," I said, recoiling a bit.

"Well, you have to do something," Lo said. "If you hit your twentieth without a job, you lose your citizenship, and not even your mom will be able to help you then."

I was beginning to get annoyed at her bringing up mom all the time. "'Assistant Greensperson' doesn't sound so bad," I said.

"That would be my choice," Lo said. "The park towers are nice. I go to the one down the street here on my lunch break sometimes. The greens keepers are always tending to the trees and flower and bees. It's physical work, but at least you'll be in pretty surroundings. And remember, this is only a first job. If it's not to your liking, you can always get more training and education, and try for a different sort of job. The important thing is you have a job."

"Fine," I said. "I'll take that one."

"Good," Lo said. We both looked up at the listing.

It disappeared.

"Whoops," Lo said.

"'Whoops?'" I said. "What 'whoops?'"

Lo accessed her tablet. "Looks like someone else just took the job. It's gone."

"That's totally not fair," I said.

"Other people are having their assignment sessions just like you are," Lo said. "If you had taken the job first, someone else would be saying 'no fair' right now. So now we're down to two jobs: Composting Engineer, trainee level, and Biological Systems Interface Manager. Pick one. I'd suggest you pick quickly."

I looked up at the wall and my two remaining choices. Composting Engineer just sounded vile; I wanted no part of it. I had no idea what "Biological Systems Interface Management" meant, but, you know, if it was management, that probably meant a good chance that I wouldn't be hunched over with a shovel or tiller in my hard, aerating solid waste and food scraps.

"Mr. Washington," Lo said.

Oh, who cares anyway, I thought. *I'll talk to mom about this and get it all sorted out.* Because while mom was a hardass about me taking a job, I was willing to bet there was almost no chance that Josephine Washington, executive council member, would let her only son spend any significant amount of time doing menial labor. She expected better of me, and I thought she'd help me live up to her expectations.

"Biological Systems Interface Manager," I said.

Lo smiled. "Excellent choice," she said, tapping her tablet and securing the job. "I think you'll be perfect for it."

"What is the job?" I asked.

She told me, and then laughed when she saw the expression on my face.

"So, let's recap," mom said to me at dinner. I'd explained my situation without quite telling her the job that I'd gotten. "You want me, a member of New St. Louis' executive board, a highly visible public servant, to pull strings for you so you can get a better job than the one you're qualified for."

"Come on, mom," I said. "You know I'm qualified for lots of jobs."

"Do I?" mom said. "I know *you* didn't read your Aptitude scores when they came in, Benji, but *I* did. I know what you got. I know you spent most of your education screwing off and screwing up because you didn't think any of it mattered. I told you to do better, but you were happy just to do well enough."

Oh, God, I thought. *Here we go again.*

"Look, mom," said Syndee. "Benji's got his 'I'm not listening anymore' face on."

"Shut up, Syndee," I said.

"Well, you do," Syndee said.

"Kiss ass," I said. She was sixteen and a model student, and a little too smug about it for my taste.

"Benjamin," mom said.

"Sorry," I said, shooting a look at Syndee. "And anyway, mom, I'm listening to you. Really."

"Good," mom said. "Then you'll hear me fine this time: I'm not going to lift a finger to get you another job."

"Why not?" I said. It came out more of a whine than I would have preferred.

"First off, because the last thing I need right now is for the news blogs to be talking about how I used my influence to get my son a job. Honestly, now, Benji. You think people wouldn't notice? This isn't like me asking the school to switch your class schedule around, and you remember how much crap I got for that."

I looked at her blankly.

"Or maybe you don't," mom said.

"I do," Syndee said.

"Hush, Syndee," mom said. "That was bad enough. Actually yanking you out of the assignments queue and handing you a job you don't qualify for is the sort of thing that will get me kicked off the executive board. It's an election year, Benji, and

I've already got a fight on my hand because I'm for technology outreach. You know how many New Louies hate that idea."

"I don't like it either," I said. "Technology Outreach" was a plan for NSL to help the people in the wilds by offering them some of the city's technology and support. It amounted to basically helping a bunch of people who had intentionally gone out of their way to fail in creating a sustainable civilization. "I think it's a dumb idea."

"Of course you do," mom said, acidly. "You don't want us to share technology with the folks in the wilds because then we wouldn't have something over them. And then you wouldn't be a precious little snowflake, like all the other smug precious little snowflakes in here. Keeping technology bottled up isn't why New St. Louis was founded. Quite the opposite, in fact. And these days it's more important than ever. Cascadopolis had the right idea: Develop useful technology, send it out into the world."

"Look where it got Cascadopolis," I said. "It doesn't even exist anymore."

"You spent too much time with those idiot cousins of yours in the Portland Arcology," Mrs. Washington said.

"Whatever, mom," I said. My cousins weren't idiots, even if they were snobbish enough that even I noticed it. "I just don't see what it has to do with you helping me."

"That's my point," mom said. "You don't appreciate what the consequences of my 'helping' you like that would be. All you know is that you don't want the job you've been assigned. What job have you been assigned anyway?" Mrs. Washington reached for her iced tea.

I shrugged. No point keeping it from her now. "Biological Systems Interface Manager at Arnold Tower," he said.

Mom choked on her tea.

"Mom, tea just came out your *nose*," Syndee said.

"I'm fine, baby," mom said, and reached down into her lap for her napkin.

"See," I said, accusingly. "Now you know why I want another job."

"There's nothing wrong with the job," Mom said.

"You just spit tea everywhere when I told you what it was," I said.

"I was just a little surprised, is all," mom said.

"Come on, mom," I said. "There's got to be something else out there. Something better than this," I said.

"The job is fine," mom said, and pounded her chest to get the remaining tea out of her lungs. "In fact, I think the job will be great for you."

"Well, great," I said, throwing up my hands. "Just what I need. A learning experience."

"That's right," mom said. "You do need a learning experience. To get back to the list of reasons why I won't help you change your job, the second reason is that you need to understand the consequences of your choices, Benji," Mom said. She dropped her napkin back into her lap. "Somewhere along the way you decided that you didn't need to work all that hard for things, because you figured that I would always be there to bail you out, and that my stature would help you get the things you wanted."

"That's not true at all," I said.

"Please, Benji," mom said. "I know you like to think it's not true, but you need to be honest with yourself. Think back on all the times you've asked for my help. Think back on all the times you've given just a little less effort to things because you knew I could back you up or put in a good word for you. If you're honest about it, you'll recognize you've relied on me a lot."

I opened my mouth to complain and then flashed back to Will in the pod, telling me how "happy" he was that I wasn't going to rely on my mom to get me through things. I shut my mouth and stared down at the table.

"It's not all your fault," mom said, gently. "I've been always telling you to do things for yourself, but when it came down to it, I let you slide and I bailed you out of a lot of things. But that has to change. You're an adult now, Benji. You need to be responsible for your actions. And now you're learning that the actions and choices you made before make a difference in your life now. I kept telling you about this, and you kept not listening to me. Well, now you have to deal with it, so deal with it."

"You could have told me a little harder," I said, and poked at my dinner.

Mom sighed. "Benji, sweetheart, I told you almost every single day of your life. And you did that smile and nod thing you do when you decide you're hearing something that doesn't apply to you. You can't tell someone something if they don't want to listen."

"Uh-huh," I said.

"Look, mom," Syndee said. "He's got that face on again."

On the way to the Arnold Tower the next day, to start the first job of the rest of my life, I saw what looked like a protest at one of the entrance gates to New St. Louis.

"Do you know what that's about?" I asked my podmate, an older man.

He looked over at the protest as we glided by and then shrugged. "Some of the folks in The Wilds have been demanding we help them out with their food crisis," he said.

"There's a food crisis?" I asked.

The guy looked over to me. "It's been in the news lately," he said, pointedly.

"You got me," I said. "I haven't been watching the news."

The guy motioned out toward where the protest had been. "The drought is bad this year. Worse than usual. Outside of The Cities, there's been a run on staples and prices are up. Someone's been telling the folks in The Wild that we've got food surpluses, and technology to increase food yields, which is how we got the surpluses. So we get protests every morning."

"Do we have food surpluses?" I asked.

"No idea," the man said, and went back to his reading. I looked back in the direction of where I saw the protest and wondered what it was the protesters were doing—or not doing—that they could take time out of their work schedules to protest on a daily basis. About two seconds after that, I recognized the irony of me, who was going to his first job more than a year after most of my class had gotten their first jobs, wondering how other people could be slackers.

A minute later I was at the Arnold Tower. I walked over to the receptionist.

"Benjamin Washingon," I said. "I'm here to start work."

The receptionist eyed me up and down. "Oh, honey," she said. "You shouldn't have worn good clothes." She shooed me away to sit down and picked up her phone. Shortly thereafter a door opened and a very dirty man came out of it. He looked around until he saw me.

"You Washington?" He said.

"Yeah," I said.

"Come on, then," he said. I got up and followed him. He smelled terrible.

"Nicols," he said as we walked down the corridor, by way of introduction. He glanced at my clothes. "Tomorrow you should probably dress more casual," he said.

"I thought we might have uniforms," I said, nodding at Nicols' blue uniform. I was trying to keep my distance from Nicols. He was beginning to make me gag.

"We have coveralls," he said, "but the smell still gets into everything.. You don't want to be wearing anything nice around here." He glanced down. "You'll probably want to get boots, too."

"Boots, casual clothes, got it," I said. We approached a pair of doors. "Anything else?"

"Yeah," Nichols said. "Noseplugs."

He opened the doors and a wave of stink rolled over me and I very nearly threw up my breakfast. Instead of retching, I looked out into the vast room to doors opened on to. There were pigs on almost every square inch of it. Pigs eating. Pigs sleeping. Pigs milling about. Pigs farting. Pigs pooping. Pigs generally making astounding amounts of stink.

And my job was to look after them. That's what Biological Systems Integration Manager meant: Pig farmer.

"Welcome to your new job, kid," Nichols said to me. "You're going to love it here."

"I kind of doubt that," I said.

"You're stuck here," Nichols said. "You might as well learn to enjoy it. Now come on. It's time to get you set up, and to take you to meet the boss."

Lou Barnes, my new boss, pointed at a carved plaque on his wall. "Do you know what means?" he asked me.

I looked at the sign, which read *Utere nihil non extra quiritationem suis.* "I don't know Spanish," I said.

"It's Latin," Barnes said. "It means 'use everything but the squeal.' People used to say about pigs that you could eat every part of them but the squeal." He waved toward the plate glass window that overlooked an entire different floor of pigs than I saw earlier; Arnold Tower had twenty stories, and every story had thousands of pigs in it, or so Nichols told me on the way up to Barnes' office. "The pigs you see here are a fundamental part of the zero-footprint ecological ethos of New St. Louis. When you toss your dinner leftovers into the food recycling chute, they're sterilized, fortified and brought here as part of the pigs' diet. In return, we get manure, which we send to the agricultural towers and to the test gardens on the top of the tower. We get methane, which we collect and use for fuel. We get urea from the pig's urine, which we use to make plastics. We recycle the plastics when we're done with them. Around and around it goes."

"We make plastic from pig pee?" I said. I knew about manure and methane, but this was a new one on me.

"Urea's a bulking agent," Barnes said, and when I gave him a look that indicated I hadn't the slightest idea what he was talking about, changed tracks. "Yes. Plastic from pig pee. You got it."

"I suppose we get pork chops from them as well," I said.

Barnes made a face. "No," he said. "Not these pigs." He waved out at the floor again. "These pigs are genetically engineered to maximize output of end products."

I tried not to go to the next logical place and just couldn't avoid it. "You've produced prodigiously pooptastic pigs," I said, with as straight a face as possible.

Barnes gave me a tight-lipped smile. "Laugh it up, Washington," he said. "And while you're laughing it up remember that all this pig shit and pig piss is part of the reason New St. Louis isn't on the verge of economic collapse or starvation, like most of what's left of our suburbs. And Missouri. And Illinois."

I thought back on the protest I saw outside my pod window on the way in and sobered up a little.

Barnes seemed to approve. "Look, Washington, I know why you're here," he said. "You screwed around in school, got crappy Aptitude scores and this wound up being the only job you could get. Am I right about that?"

"Sort of," I said.

"'Sort of,'" Barnes repeated. "I know you think this is a dead-end job, below your dignity. But what you need to understand, Washington, is that if anything, it's *you* who have to step up." He jerked a thumb back to the pigs. "I don't suppose you know that those pigs are part of the Technology Outreach program your mother and some others on the council are trying to push through."

"Pigs count as technology?" I said.

"*These* pigs do," Barnes said. "The same genetic improvements you are joking about are what make them valuable. They're *exceptionally* efficient processors of urea and other valuable elements, and we've improved their already considerable intelligence enough that they actually know where to go to get rid of their waste."

It took me a minute to process this. "You mean they're potty trained?"

Barnes motioned to the window. "Look for yourself," he said.

179

I walked over to the window and stared out at the pigs. At first I had no idea what I was looking at, except for lots of pigs wandering around. But then I started to see it: trickles of pigs flowing into marked-off areas with grated floors. When they got there, they would let fly, and then wander back out when they were done.

"Does someone have to teach them to do that?" I asked.

"At first someone did," Barnes said. "But these days they teach each other."

I looked back at him. "They've teaching each other things?" I looked back at the pigs. "And you're not worried about a piggy revolution or anything."

"It's not *Animal Farm*," Barnes said. "And it's not like they're teaching each other calculus. But now you understand why these pigs are valuable."

"What do you think of my mom's Technology Outreach thing?" I asked Barnes. I know you're not supposed to talk politics with your boss, much less on your first day on the job, but I was curious.

Barnes shrugged. "I'm sympathetic," he said. "People out there aren't starving yet, but they're getting close. No one's going to eat these pigs—they shouldn't, at least—but they can help with crop production and the production of biodegradable plastics. *But,*" And here Barnes looked at me significantly, "the reason it works here in NSL is that we actively manage it. It's a closed loop. Zero-footprint. Everything gets recycled, nothing gets wasted."

"We use everything but the squeal," I said.

"That's right," Barnes said, approvingly. "Not just here but all over New St. Louis. Now, you give the same technology to people who aren't managing their system—who don't believe in that sort of zero-footprint philosophy—and all you're going to do is make things worse." He nodded out to the pigs again. "These guys are great for us, but they're like any crop or animal that humans have messed with, either by old-fashioned domestication or modern genetic-engineering. They have to be managed. Put a bunch of pigs designed for high outputs of urea and nitrates into an open system, with their waste flowing into streams and seeping into groundwater, and you'll have a goddamn mess on your hands. Your mother is right, Washington: We need to help the people outside of the city. But we have to do it right, because they've already messed things up badly enough that they can't afford another screw-up. And neither can we. That's why we haven't given the technology to anyone else yet. The genetics of these pigs is still a state secret. Which is another thing you need to know."

"And here I thought I was just going to be a high-tech pig farmer," I said.

"Well, you are," Barnes said. "Make no mistake about that, Washington. It's just that pig farming is a lot more important than you thought it was. And that's why I'm hoping your shitty Aptitude scores are more of a reflection of you farting around than you actually being stupid. If you're an idiot, I can find jobs for you to do. But if you're not an idiot, I can actually use you."

"I'm not an idiot," I said.

"I'd like to believe that," Barnes said. "We'll see. In the meantime, we'll start you on vacuum detail."

"It's simple," said Lucius Jeffers, who was the head of the four man work detail I was assigned to, on the fifth floor of Arnold Tower. "Whenever you see some shit or piss on the floor, you suck it up with this." He waved the business end of a vacuum tube at me. "The mess goes into the tub here, and when the tub is full, you drag it over to a waste port at either end of the floor." He motioned to one of the waste ports, which looked a little like the fire hydrants I saw in old children's books. "Attach the tube to the waste port, switch the unit from the 'vacuum' to the 'expel' setting and let it empty out. Lather, rinse, repeat."

I looked at the vacuum unit doubtfully. "I thought these pigs were toilet-trained," I said.

"They are," Jeffers said. "But they're also *pigs*, you know? Sometimes they just let fly. We've tried training them to use the vacuum to pick up after themselves. It didn't work."

"You really tried that?" I said.

Jeffers smiled. "You're going to be a lot of fun, Washington. I can tell that already. All right, off to work with you. You can start with that pile of crap over there." He pointed to a fresh leaving on the floor. "Try to get to them before the other pigs start walking through them," he said, and left. And then off I went, sucking up crap.

After an hour or so of doing this, I noticed that one of the pigs was following me around, usually about five feet behind me wherever I went. The porker was on the smallish side, and seemed to be grinning at me whenever I looked at it. I asked Jeffers about it at lunch time.

"Yeah, they do that sometimes," Jeffers said. "The biologists made them smarter than the average pig, so now they're a little curious about us. Pinter here," Jeffers pointed at one of the other guys on the crew, "he had a sow follow him around for months. I think she was in love."

"It wasn't love," Pinter said, between sandwich bites. "We were just good friends."

"Yeah, right," Jeffers laughed, and turned back to me. "The sow was probably just looking for a little action. They don't let these pigs breed normally."

"What do you mean?" I asked.

"You'll find out after lunch," Jeffers said.

After lunch I was taken to the Love Lounge, filled with silicone pig-sized objects.

I looked at Pinter, who had taken me to the Lounge. "Tell me these aren't what I think they are."

"They are *exactly* what you think they are," Pinter said. "We bring in a bunch of male pigs, fill the air with Scent of a Sow—" he pointed at what looked like a fire sprinkler on the ceiling "—and then the boys go to town. After they're done we suck out the leavings, send them down to cryo for storage, and then clean out the love toys with an injection of soap and hot water."

"You have got to be kidding," I said. "I just ate."

"It's not so bad," Pinter said. "Come on, get into the control booth. You don't want to be in here when the boys come in. Once they get the sow scent into their nose, they're not exactly discriminating."

I got into the control booth as quickly as I could. "Okay," Pinter said. "Ready?" He pressed a button, and the sprinkler fizzed to life, coating the love dolls. Then the far door slid open, and a small pack of randy pigs trotted in.

"Oh, God," I said, a minute later. "That is so *not* right."

"Makin' bacon," Pinter said, and looked at me. "Well, half of it, anyway. What would that be? 'Bac'? Or 'con'?"

"I think there's something wrong with you," I said.

Pinter shrugged. "You get used this place after a while. And it's not so bad working here once you do. I listen to my husband complain about his work day every single damn night. He complains about work, about his co-workers, and about his boss. I'm about ready to strangle him." Pinter pointed out to the pigs, who were now winding down; they were not the long-lasting sort, apparently. "I wouldn't say this job is glamorous—"

"That's a good thing," I said.

"—But on the other hand I don't have to go home and whine to him about my day at work, either. Pigs are easy. People are hard. You learn to appreciate it after a while."

"I'm not entirely sure about that," I said.

"Well, if you don't like it, you can always take your Aptitudes again and do something else with your time," Pinter said, as the door to the Love Lounge opened and the pigs trotted out. "I like it fine. Now come on. We've got to collect this stuff while it's still hot."

I swear to you, I never thought I would be so glad to get back to vacuuming up pig crap. And sure enough, once I started up again, there was the little pig again, trotting behind me.

"Hello," I said, finally, when I stopped to drain the vacuum, and the pig parked itself to watch. "I think I'll call you Hammy. Or how about Pork Chop? Or maybe Mr. Bacon. Or just plain Lunch. What do you think about that?"

The pig snorted at me, as if acknowledging my choices.

"Great," I said. "The first day on the job and I'm already talking to the pigs. Shoot me now."

Lunch snorted again.

The vacuum suddenly chugged to a stop.

"What the hell?" I said. The vacuum was still half full. I pulled my phone from my coverall pocket and called the Arnold Tower number for Jeffers. "Something's wrong with my vacuum unit," I said. "It stopped working and it's half full."

"Let me check on this end," Jeffers said. "It's not your vacuum unit," he said after a minute. "You've got an embargo situation."

"What the hell is an embargo situation?" I said.

"It means there's some sort of clog in the piping," Jeffers said. "Your vacuum unit shut down because if it didn't, you'd be spilling pig shit all over yourself right about now."

"What do I do now?" I asked.

"I'm going to need you to do a diagnostic on that particular drainage tube," Jeffers said. "There's a diagnostic panel for the tube hardwired into its terminus, which is in the Tower sub-basement C."

"Why can't I access the panel on my phone?" I said. "Why can't you?"

"This is an old building, kid," Jeffers said. "One of the first built in New St. Louis. The diagnostic system is a legacy system from back in the day. Just go down there and check it out, okay? Go to the lobby and switch elevators. You have to take a special elevator down to the sublevels."

Five minutes and one elevator transfer later, I was in sub-basement C. Even after a full day of walking around pigs and their smell, the fumes down there were something special. On a shelf facing the elevator were a set of breathing masks. YOU

NEED THIS, said a weathered sign, followed by another equally weathered sign with the fine print about why the masks were needed. I didn't need the fine print; I was getting near woozy from the fumes even before I slipped the mask over my head.

After a couple of deep breaths my head cleared and I walked into the sub-basement, which seemed to be the top floor for several massive conduits, into which the drainage tubes from all the various floors of the Arnold Tower drained.

"You're going to want to open the access port to conduit 2," Jeffers said. "Don't worry, it's automatic. No heavy lifting. Just walk on top of the conduit and hit the 'open' switch."

"There's going to be a river of crap in there," I said.

"No there's not," Jeffers said. "Whenever there's an embargo situation all the other drainage tubes freeze and the conduit empties out, because they know someone has to go and check out the diagnostic panel. It's going to smell like hell, but you have your mask on right?"

I got to the access port, and lugged the switch over to "open." "I want to talk to whoever designed this system."

"It's been decades, kid," Jeffers said. "The person who designed it is probably dead by now. Come on, Washington. Crap is piling up. We don't have all day."

I carefully put myself on the access ladder coming down from the port and stepped down. There was recessed, sealed-off lighting at the top of the conduit, so at least I could see. The conduit itself wasn't exactly clean, but it was drained as promised. Despite that, the residue on the curved floor of the consuit made me be careful how I placed my steps.

"Where am I going?" I asked.

"You're looking for the third...no, wait, fourth tube junction on your left," Jeffers said.

I counted off the tube junctions and then stood in front of the fourth one on the left. "Where's this diagnostic panel?" I asked.

"It should be there," Jeffers said. "They're small. It might be covered in gunk. Stand closer."

"I am closer," I said. "I'm standing right in front of the tube, and I'm not seeing anything."

"You're sure you're in front of the right tube?" Jeffers asked.

"I can count," I said.

"Hey, Washington," Jeffers said.

"What?" I said.

"Embargo lifted," he said.

Then I heard the rumbling. And the laughter from the other end of the phone.

I looked at the tube and had just enough time to think *oh, shit* before what I thought became a reality.

Ten minutes later I was in the Arnold Tower locker room, standing under a shower head, fully clothed, glowering at Jeffers, Pinter, and the other members of my work detail, who were mostly on the floor, laughing so hard that they couldn't breathe.

"I will remember this," I said.

"We know!" Jeffers said, and hooted so long he fell off the locker room bench.

Around this time Lou Barnes strolled through the locker room and stopped to get a look at me.

"Don't tell me," he said. "You fell for the embargo trick."

"Oh, God, Oh, God," Pinter said. "Please don't make me laugh anymore. Please, God, no." And then he laughed some more.

"You know they do this to everyone the first day," Barnes said. "Think of it like a baptism."

"Praise the Lord!" Jeffers said, from the floor.

"It just means you're one of us now," Barnes said.

"Great," I said.

"It's an honor, if you think about it," Barnes said. "Really." And then he busted out laughing, too. Which made all the rest of them laugh some more.

"I *will* remember this," I said to Jeffers, once he finally managed to peel himself off the floor.

"Oh, kid," Jeffers said, wiping a laugh tear from his eye. "We wouldn't have it any other way."

I noticed a funny thing on the pod ride back home, which was that someone would get in the pod I with me, and then get off a stop later. This happened three times before the door slid open and Leah popped her head in.

"Trust me, Leah, you want to take the next pod," I said.

"What's that smell?" she said.

"It's my job," I said. "It stinks."

"Hey, you have a job!" she said, and came in to give me a hug. The door slid closed behind her.

"Now you're in for it," I said.

"I think I can handle the smell of an honest day's work," she said, and then gave her destination to the pod. We started off. "I mean, I hope you won't smell like this at the end of every day. But first days are always stressful. What's the new job?"

"Pig farmer," I said.

"Normally I'd tell you to stop kidding around, but given how you smell at the moment, I'm willing to believe it," Leah said.

"Oh, believe it," I said. I told her about my day.

"It could be a positive," Leah said. "It's like an initiation rite into the tribe. If they didn't like you, they would have just said good night to you at the end of your shift."

"So, when you started your job, did your co-workers do something like this?" I said.

"No," Leah admitted. "They took me out for a drink. But they don't have access to pig droppings, either."

"I'm not sure I agree 100% with your tribe initiation theory," I said.

"In that case, stick with it and get them back," Leah said. We were coming up to our stop. "Because you now have access to pig droppings, too."

"That's a very good point," I said. "And here all this time I was thinking you were a nice girl, Leah."

"I *am* a nice girl," Leah said. "I'm just not a pushover."

Later at home, mom opened the door a crack while I was in the shower. I was using the graywater because I was wanting a real long soak and after my day, whining about graywater just seemed kind of stupid.

"Syndee told me about your day at work," mom said, through the door.

"Did she tell you I rubbed her face in my shirt after she called me a 'stinkpig'?" I asked.

"That was how I found out," mom said. "I told her I was going to let it slide this time. Do you want to have me talk to your supervisor about it?"

"Since my supervisor was one of the people laughing his ass off about it, I don't think it would do much good," I said.

"Well, then, his supervisor," mom said.

"I thought you said you weren't going to fight my battle for me anymore," I said.

"Having your kid drenched in pig shit changes things," mom said, and I realized she must really be pissed, because she hardly ever swore in front of me or Syndee. I laughed. "What's so funny?" mom asked.

"Never mind," I said. I turned off the shower and grabbed a towel and wrapped it around my waist. Then I opened the door all the way and have my mom a big sloppy hug.

"Damn it, Benji, my blouse," mom said.

"Sorry," I said. "And thanks for wanting to stick up for me. But you said it yourself. I'm an adult now. I can handle this on my own. Okay?"

"You sure?" mom said.

"Oh, I'm sure," I said.

And so the days and weeks started to go by.

At work, I still did menial vacuuming and Love Lounge duties, as did everyone else. But slowly I was shown the other parts of the pig trade, from handling feed and water trade to helping the Arnold Tower vets with the vaccinations and their medical rounds. I also learned how to handle Arnold Towers securities and diagnostic systems—which, in fact, could be handled remotely by phone once I was given my access codes. I proved to be a quick study with the computer systems, and because of it I was put in the rotation for late night shifts, when it was just me, a couple of members of the administrative area janitorial staff, and thousands upon thousands of sleeping pigs. Late night shift workers were exempt from the solo surcharge on the pod system and sometimes I took advantage of that to take the long way around New St. Louis, cruising over the streets at night, watching my hometown slide by silently.

Outside the city, the drought that threatened in the early months of the year delivered with a vengeance, drying up croplands all over the American Midwest and in the lower part of the Canadian corn belt. Mom was having a difficult time selling the rest of the NSL council on Technology Outreach but managed to convince them to make an emergency release of food surpluses to the surrounding suburbs and The Wilds. The generosity of the gesture seemed to be lost on the people in The Wilds, since NSL was accused of holding back on what it could have given, and the protests on our doorsteps got bigger and louder. This frustrated mom and enraged a fair share of New Louies. I was annoyed myself.

About ten weeks after I had my "embargo" event, Jeffers and Pinter were preparing to herd their boys into another session in the Love Lounge when an apparently random computer glitch locked them out of the control room and then cycled through the session, spraying them with swine-tuned aphrodisiac just as the door slid open to admit a fine selection of very horny pigs. If the door to the control room hadn't randomly unlatched a couple of minutes in to the session, Jeffers and Pinter might have found themselves porked into oblivion. A routine check of the systems after the event found no tampering and no reason why the system would have behaved like that. Barnes ordered the software reloaded and everyone was given new security codes into the system.

A week after that, protests at the city border finally turned bloody, as a small group of Wilds folks attacked the NSL police force, seriously wounding one of them when a rock dented his skull. I saw this particular protest from above as I slid into work; if it wasn't an actual riot it was practicing to become one. The NSLPD told the executive council it didn't have enough officers to handle the growing crowds. The council, over the strenuous objections of my mother, contracted with Edgewater for border control. After that the protest crowds got larger but they also stayed mostly under control. The rumor was that the Eddies got paid bonuses on a quota basis, and were just looking for some-one—anyone—to get out of line. I asked my mom if the quota bonus rumor was true. She looked at me and told me that now would be a great time to change the subject.

Shortly thereafter Syndee completed all her education requirements, got her certificate, and took her Aptitudes. She scored high enough on them that she qualified for New St. Louis' executive training, which meant she was now on a fast track to be an administrator either here or in another city we shared "open borders" with. Despite myself, I was really proud of her.

As for me, I got a promotion, of sorts: Arnold Tower had a lorry it used to transfer pigs or other things from our tower to Wilber Tower or Pippo Tower, the other two non-meat pig tow-ers in New St. Louis, and the driver of the lorry had slipped while stepping out of the cab and broken his leg. While he was on desk duty, I was assigned temporary driver. I spent part of my day on the actual roads of the city, which beat vacuuming up shit. One day as I was driving along I saw Leah and Will stand-ing on the street corner, waiting to cross. I honked as I went past, which delighted Leah and confused Will, which seemed about right in both cases. Sometimes I took Lunch with me on the trips; he sat up front with me. He seemed to enjoy the ride.

As bad as the protests where we lived were, they were worse in other places. In California, the Malibu Enclave was nearly burned to ground when protestors there started fires in the canyons and pushed the fire line right to the border of the enclave. A lucky shift of the wind let firefighters save the enclave; other parts of Malibu were not as lucky. When the protestors came back, they put the blame for the fires on the Enclave. Edgewater, which had a contract with Malibu just like it did with New St. Louis, saw a lot of its people get bonuses that night. The protesters saw their people go into the Eddie's holding cells or the hospital.

Despite the rising tensions, mom kept hammering away at her Technology Outreach program, trying to convince the other executive board members that time was running out. It was already too late to have the outreach be any use for this year, she said, but next year we're going to see the same thing happen again, and the year after that, and the year after that. But it wasn't doing her any good. Opinions were hardening against The Wilds, which looked more like anarchy than anything else these days.

Eventually even mom gave up and tabled the outreach program until after the elections. Her opponent, who as it turned out was distantly related to Will's dad, had been gaining ground on her, mostly by hammering on her for wanting to do outreach to the same people who were rioting on our borders. He didn't seem to have any other platform, but at the moment he really didn't need any other platform. Mom looked at what her support for Technology Outreach was costing her and had to dump it. And even though I'd been opposed to it, I was sorry for my mother that something she cared so much about couldn't get a fair hearing.

At the end of summer, my work group had a classic cinema movie night, which included *Babe*, *Deliverance* and *Mad Max Beyond Thunderdome*. When I saw the latter, I finally got the "embargo" reference.

On the first day of autumn, as I pulled a night shift, I invited Leah to the experimental gardens on the roof. We brought Lunch along for security purposes.

"It's beautiful up here," Leah said.

"I'm glad you like it," I said. "I thought you might want to see it before all the leaves fell off."

"Why are they called the experimental gardens?"she asked.

"The plants up here are genetically engineered," I said. "The botanists share the genetics lab with the geneticists who work on the pigs. The lab takes up the whole twentieth floor, actually. Common rabble like us aren't allowed in there, but they let us come up here on our breaks and during lunch. I come up here with Lunch all the time. Lunch, the pig, I mean. For lunch. You know. I think I'll stop talking now."

Leah smiled, which was a pretty thing in the moonlight. "I think it's adorable you have a pet pig," she said.

"I wouldn't use the word 'pet' around him," I said. "He's his own pig. We just happen to be friends."

"Well, fine," Leah said. "I think it's adorable you have a pig for a friend. Are you happy now?"

"I'm getting there," I said, and even in the moonlight, I could sense her blushing a little. Leah was still with Will, and she wasn't the sort of girl would let something like that slide, even for a minute. But it wasn't a secret to her that I still wished she was with me. And I didn't see much point in pretending that I felt any other than I did. You can let people know how you feel about them without seeming desperate, or at least, that was what I was hoping.

"I like where you work, Benji," Leah said, after a minute.

"You're only saying that because I haven't taken you to sub-basement C," I said. "Let me give you the embargo treatment and we'll see what you think then."

Leah laughed. "I think I'll pass on that," she said.

"Chicken," I said. She smiled again and reached down to pet Lunch. He snuffled at her.

One of our phones rang. It was Leah. She stepped away and took the call. A minute later, she came back, holding the phone in front of her. "Here," she said. "It's for you."

I took the phone. "Hello?" I said.

"Benji," Will said, on the other end of the line. "I have a favor to ask of you. A real big favor."

"It's Marcus," Will said, when I met him and Leah for lunch the next day. "I haven't seen him in nearly three years. We email a little, and talk about what's going on, but he's always somewhere that's nowhere near here. Then he calls yesterday—actually calls—and tells me he's in St. Charles and he wants to see me. He said there's a rave he'll be at out there tomorrow and gave me directions and the time. So I know where he'll be and when he'll be there. I just don't have a way to get there."

I squirmed in my seat. Will asking me to take the Arnold Tower lorry to drive him to see his brother out in the wilds was bad enough, but asking me to take it to a rave edged on the insane. "I don't understand," I said. "Just requisition a car from the city. It'll put a hole in your energy budget for the month, but it's your brother. He's worth it."

"I *tried* that," Will said, and he let his irritation creep into his voice. "Maybe you're not keeping up with current events, Benji, but we've got a daily near-riot right outside the city. The city's not letting people take their ground cars out into that; they'd get stripped before they got to the Interstate. Jesus, you're clueless sometimes."

"Will," Leah said.

Will held a hand up. "I know. I'm sorry, Benji. It's just that I haven't seen Marcus in so long, and I have no idea when I'm going to get to see him again. You know how important he is to me."

The hell of it was, I did know. Long ago, before we decided we actually really didn't like each other, Will and I were friends, and I hung out with his family. Will idolized his older brother. He was crushed when Marcus blew off his Aptitudes and ended up out of the City. It was why I knew how to poke him in that particular soft spot whenever I felt like he had gone too far with his belittling of me.

"Look, Benji," Will said. "I know we haven't been friends in a long time. I know we don't get along. I know you resent me—," he stopped before he could actually say *for being with Leah*, and chose something else instead, "I know you resent me for a lot of things. And I know I've treated you like crap. If you said no to this, no one would say I didn't deserve it. But I'm asking you, just this once, for a favor. I can't get a car to get out to St. Charles. But you can. Your lorry can get through the gates and get back. You don't even have to stop at the gates like regular cars do because the lorry has a signature transponder in it, right?"

"You've thought this through, Will," I said.

"It's my *brother*, Benji," Will said. "I want to see him. Help me. Please."

I looked at Will and then I looked over at Leah, who was keeping a very carefully neutral expression on her face. But I knew what she wanted me to say, and I know what I was going to say because I knew what Leah would want.

It takes a special kind of pathetic loser to help someone you hate just to make his girlfriend happy, I thought. There was more to it than that, I knew. But at the moment that's exactly what it felt like.

"Let me see what I can do," I said. "I can't promise anything. The same restrictions that are out there for groundcars might be there for city lorries, too. And if there are, I'm not stretching my neck out for you, Will. It's not like I have a whole lot of job options available to me at this point. Okay?"

"Okay," Will said, and looked like he was going to cry. "Thank you, Benji. Really. I'm not going to forget this."

"Thank you, Benji," Leah said.

"You're welcome," I said, looking at her, and then looking at him. "You're both welcome."

"Here's the deal with the lorry," Barnes said, to me. "I'm not saying yes, but I'm not officially saying no. All of us have unofficially 'borrowed' that truck from time to time. As far as I'm concerned it's one of the perks of the job; a little something to make up for having to work in pig crap all day long. That said, if you take it out and something happens to it, then officially you're screwed and there's nothing I'm going to be able to do to dig you out of that hole. So don't run it into a tree or hit a deer or let anyone set fire to it. Got it?"

"I got it," I said.

"What do you need it for, anyway?" Barnes asked.

"I'm taking someone to see his long lost brother in St. Charles," I said.

"That's not a trip I'd want to take these days," Barnes said. "That must be some friend."

"It's not a friend, actually," I said.

"I'm confused," Barnes said.

"His girlfriend," I said. "My ex. Still hold a candle. And so on."

"Ah," Barnes. "Well, and I hope you don't mind me saying this, but that's got to suck for you."

"It really sort of does," I said. Barnes clapped me on my back and headed off.

The next night, late, Will and Leah and I rolled out of New St. Louis and took the bumpy city streets of old St. Louis until we found a suitable onramp to Interstate 70, heading west. The Interstate was not exactly in what you would call brilliant condition these days—the US federal government's list of priorities was getting smaller and smaller, and the Interstate system had clearly not made the most recent cut—but it was workable as long as you didn't go too fast, and the traffic out to St. Charles from NSL was pretty much non-existent.

"So you actually have directions to where we're going, right, Will?" I said. I had gotten to the I-70 on my own, and Will had been silent for all of the ride so far.

Will pulled something out of his coat pocket and handed it to me. "Here," he said.

I took it. It was a pair of goofy-looking glasses. "What the hell are these?" I said.

"Marcus had them sent to me," Will said. "He had me stand at one of the gates where there wasn't a protest, and someone came up and gave them to me."

"Who gave them to you?" I asked.

"It was just some guy," Will said. "He said he'd been paid to turk the package. Put them on."

I put them on; the lenses were clear and non-correcting. "Do these do anything but make me look stupid?" I asked

"You have to turn them on," Will said. "There's a power switch on the rim of the lens."

I fumbled with the glasses with one hand until I found a slightly raised ridge. I pressed it.

There was suddenly a bright orange three-dimensional arrow in my field of view, pointing down the Interstate.

"Whoa," I said.

"The lenses are supposed to superimpose images over the real world," Will said.

"Well, it works," I said.

"Marcus said they're from company out of Switzerland. He said they're going to be huge in a few years," Will said.

"That's great," I said. "But am I supposed to follow this arrow or what?"

I was. When the arrow turned, I turned. 45 minutes later, we rolled up to what looked like it used to be a city park, which had gone to pot sometime in the not-too-distant past. In the middle of the park lights flashed and music pulsed. We were at our rave.

"What now?" I asked, once we'd gotten out of the lorry and I'd clicked on the security settings.

"Do you still have an arrow in your glasses?" Will asked.

"Yeah," I said.

"Let's follow it," Will said.

We wandered through the crowd for a few minutes, pushing our way through clots of dancers. From time to time I saw faces I recognized; there were a lot of New Louies at this particular rave in the Wilds. I wondered how they found out about it, and how they got there, but before I got to spend any real amount of time on it, the arrow in my glasses suddenly changed orientation and hovered directly over someone.

"I think I found Marcus," I said to Will, but he was already pushing past me to hug his brother. Leah trailed behind him. I stood in the middle of a bunch of dancers with a pair of incredibly dorky glasses on my head.

"So, okay, then," I said, to no one in particular. "You're welcome. No, no. Happy to help. No thanks necessary." I sighed and took off the glasses.

When I looked up again Leah was standing in front of me. "Come on," she said. "Marcus is asking for you." She held out her hand. I took it.

As a kid, I remember Marcus towering over both me and Will. He was still as imposing as I remembered him.

"Benjamin Washington," Marcus said, and extended his hand. I shook it and compared my grip to his, despite myself. "I remember you very well. You were not quite so tall the last time I saw you."

"I was fourteen the last time you saw me," I said.

"True enough," Marcus said. We were standing in a rest area at the rave, with card tables and folding chairs around us. He motioned for the three of us to sit. We did. I could tell that Will was a little puzzled why his brother wanted to talk to me when he was around. I was wondering that myself.

"Will tells me you waited until the last minute to take your Aptitudes," Marcus said.

I glanced over at Will. "That sounds like something Will would tell you," I said.

"I was curious why you waited," Marcus asked.

I shrugged. "I wanted to see some of the rest of the world first," I said.

Marcus smiled. "And did you? See the rest of the world?"

"Some of it," I said, and listed the places I had traveled.

"Ah," Marcus said. "I see. You did see the world—but just the safe parts."

"I don't know what you mean," I said.

"You went to all the other hermetically sealed places on the map," Marcus said. "All the other cities like New St. Louis. The zero-footprint, low-impact, archipelago of new-age city states that dot the globe. The ones that have cut themselves off from the rest of the world and think themselves virtuous for doing so. Do you think they are virtuous?"

"I don't know about virtuous," I said. I had no idea where Marcus was going with any of this. "I think right about now we're trying not to starve like everyone else is about to."

Marcus tilted his head at this. "You New Louies could help everyone not starve, if you wanted to," he said. "If I hear correctly, your mother tried to get New St. Louis to share some its technology, but no one else was buying the argument. Why was that?"

"I think all the protests began to piss people off," I said. "My mom got the city to give up some of its food surplus and no one seemed grateful. I think that pissed people off, too."

"It pissed *me* off," Will said, trying to get into the conversation. Leah was silent, watching the three of us.

Marcus smiled over at his brother but kept talking to me. "I think what bothered people about that was the New St. Louis was giving The Wilds a fish, rather than teaching them how to fish."

"I don't follow you," I said.

"'Give a man a fish, and you feed him for a day,'" Marcus intoned. "'Teach a man how to fish, and you feed him for life.' Surely you've heard this saying. I'm saying that the people in the Wilds know the different between a fish and being taught how to fish. They resent being given the one, when they need the other."

"But the city didn't have to give them a fish at all," I said.

"Of course not," Marcus said. "That's the advantage of being a zero-footprint paradise, isn't it? You're whole unto yourselves. You can keep your own clockwork ticking while all the world is running down around you. But it's a lie. John Donne had the right of it when he said that no man is an island. No city is, either, Benjamin. Your mother recognizes this, at the very least; it's why she's trying to pass that outreach of hers. Or tried, anyway, until she realized she had an election she needed to win. I recognized it. It's why I never bothered to take my Aptitudes. It's why I let them come to my family's apartment, serve me that silly court order, walk me to the city gate and shove that ridiculous credit card in my hand. They thought I was being expelled from paradise; I knew I was gaining my freedom. I wondered if you might have recognized it, too, Benjamin." Marcus cocked his head again. "But now I'm not so sure. And I wonder if that's not a pity."

I sat there for a second and then stood up. "I think I'm keeping you from catching up with your brother," I said, and then nodded to both Marcus and Will, and walked off.

Leah followed behind me a few seconds later. "What was that all about?" she asked.

"I swear to you I have no earthly idea," I said.

"I think Marcus was trying to tell you something," Leah said.

"I know he was trying to tell me something," I said. "I just don't know what it is. And I think it's pissing me off."

Leah looked like she was about to say something else, but then both she and I heard screaming coming from the dance area of the rave. She and I both looked over and saw what looked to be a really active mosh pit in the middle of it. Then a girl came weaving out into the light, holding her head while blood was gushing from a scalp wound, and I realized it wasn't a mosh pit after all.

I pushed Leah back toward Will and Marcus. "Go get Will," I said. "Tell him we're leaving now." Leah stumbled back toward her boyfriend and I turned back just in time to see two very large and scary looking dudes coming right for me. I tried to wheel back and run, but one of them grabbed me and pushed me down. I cracked my skull on the ground.

Things went real fuzzy after that. At some point I felt someone turn me over and take out of my back pocket the case I had my ID in. If they were looking for money they were going to be disappointed. I didn't have cash, I had an energy budget. I tried laughing at that and it hurt so much I passed out.

Some indeterminate time later someone hauled me up from the ground. "Name," they said.

I looked around for who was talking to me. "What?" I said.

"Your name," they said—he said, actually, since now I could tell it was a man.

"Benji Washington," I said.

"You're fine," he said. "If you can remember your name, you're gonna live. Are you missing anything? You have your wallet?"

I fished in my back pocket and found the case I carried my NSL ID in. It was still there. Start fob to the lorry was still there too. I must have hallucinated the theft. I looked over to who was talking to me and realized that he was an Eddie—an Edgewater guard. One of the guys who the city was hiring to keep the protestors out. "What happened?" I said.

The guard snorted. "You got beat on is what happened. You New Louies are dumb as hell, you know that? Go out to a rave in the middle of The Wilds, and then you're surprised when the kids out here start taking a crowbar to your heads. Let me give you a little tip, townie: The kids out here in The Wilds, they don't like you. If you give them a chance to crack open your skull, they're going to do it. You got it?"

"I got it," I said. I felt like I was going to throw up.

"Good," the guard said. "You're lucky we got tipped off to this thing or you'd probably be in the hospital by now. How old are you?"

"Twenty," I said.

"Then you're an adult and I don't have to drag your ass back into NSL," he said. "Go home, kid. Stay home." He wandered off. I bent over at the waist and threw up. Then I went looking for Will and Leah.

I found them by the lorry. Leah came running up to me to check my head; I tried to wave her off.

"You look like hell," Will said.

"Thanks, Will," I said. "I can always count on you for a good word. How's the lorry?"

"What do you mean?" Will said.

"I mean did anyone smash it during the riot?" I said.

Will checked. "It looks fine," he said.

"Great," I said, hobbling over to it. "Then we're going."

"I still have to look for Marcus," Will said.

"Will, he's gone," Leah said. "He disappeared as soon as the Eddies showed up."

"He's still around here somewhere," Will said. "I'm not going anywhere without him."

"You can stay, Will," I said. "But I'm leaving now and I'm taking the lorry with me. If you don't want to walk all the way back to town, you better get in the truck."

"Come on, Will," Leah said. "It's time to go."

Will looked extremely unhappy but got into the truck cab. Leah followed. I hauled myself up into the cab and nearly threw up again doing so. I drove twenty-five miles an hour on the Interstate all the way back.

The battle of New St. Louis took place a week later.

The protestors at the gates of the city had a problem: They couldn't get into New St. Louis. The city was sealed in like a medieval fortress, with only a few entrances, all guarded. Try to get through a gate without an ID with a transponder chip, and you weren't going to go anywhere. Lose your ID, you were in a world of pain. I lost my ID once and I had to sit through a battery of identification tests even though my mother was on the executive board. The instant the city knew the ID was missing, they voided the transponder signal, so if anyone tried to sneak into NSL using that ID, they'd be immediately tagged as a criminal. It was a problem: if you weren't a New Louie, you couldn't get into the city without an ID. And if you stole an ID and tried to sneak in, they'd catch you. So if you wanted to sneak into New St. Louis, how would you do it?

It turned out, by not stealing the IDs—just the information in them.

The rave had been the honeytrap, an attractive place for bored young New Louies to be lured to, out beyond the safe walls of the city. The rave allowed the conspirators close contacts with the city kids—close enough contact that the recording devices they carried could read and clone the New Louie's ID transponder signals. The riot afterward was an opportunity to crack heads...but also to snatch the ID information from a few extra people, like me. Since no physical IDs were stolen, no one reported any stolen identities.

This made it easy for several dozen unauthorized people to walk right through the gates of New St. Louis. The conspirators were chosen to more or less resemble the people whose identities they had stolen, so if the gate guards were to glance down at their screens, they wouldn't notice anything out of the usual. But since the gate guards were busy dealing with the exceptionally heavy crowds of protestors that day, apparently no one really bothered to look. The IDs checked out as the people walked through; what else was needed?

After the First World War (I learned this later, after the Battle of NSL) the French, fearing another attack by the Germans, built a massive set of fortifications called the Maginot line, which would form an impenetrable line which the Germans would not be able to cross. The French were so confident in the Maginot line that when they placed their big guns into it facing out toward Germany, they never considered the idea that at some point, those guns might need to face in the other direction, toward France. This became a problem when the Germans invaded France by pouring through a gap in the Maginot line and then were suddenly behind it, and on their way to Paris.

New St. Louis was built the same way: It was focused on keeping people out, not dealing with what happened when they got in anyway. This was why the city was not prepared when the attack came, from behind, inside the city walls.

The attackers were smart; they didn't bother to attack the city's main gates, the ones with the biggest number of protestors,

NSL cops and Edgewater guards. Instead they picked one of the small, quiet entrances, one small enough to be quickly closed and sealed at the first sign of unrest by just a couple of guards—and therefore only covered by a couple of guards, who are easily dealt with by a couple dozen determined conspirators. With the guards taken care of, it was simply a matter of opening the doors and letting in the hundreds of people hiding outside.

These hundreds were on the scene to do one thing and one thing only: Trash New St. Louis as hard and as fast as they could, in order to draw the police and the Edgewater guards to them as quickly and as brutally as possible. They set to this work with a will, armed with bats, sledgehammers and Molotov cocktails, setting fires and causing the sort of property damage that's not easily fixed. It worked; within minutes of the destruction beginning, the police and Edgewater were swinging clubs and firing electric bolts and trying—and failing—to close the open gate that hundreds more were now pouring through.

This was a feint, a distraction to keep the authorities occupied away from the real goal of the riot. And that was the agricultural towers, which by their very nature were open to the elements and undefended. Into these towers went dozens of invaders, intent not on filling their stomachs but their gene samplers and seed bags, detailing a whole Eden of genetically improved, quick-growing, high-yield fruits and vegetables.

Once these invaders had breached the agricultural towers, they were under no impression, even with the help of the staged riot, that they would make it out of the towers with their seeds and samples. Instead they moved their way up the towers, sampling as they went, until they stood in the roof gardens of the towers. There, they welded the access doors shut, pulled open their backpacks, and clicked together the tiny remote controlled airplanes they carried with them. Then they shoved their samples into the even tinier cargo holds and tossed the planes into the sky, carrying their trove of genes out past the city walls and into the waiting hands and sequencers of their compatriots on the other side.

That done, the invaders sat down in the roof gardens and waited to see how long it would take for the few police and Edgewater guards who could be spared to deal with them to figure out they weren't actually planning to come down and make an escape.

It took them a long time. More than enough time for the mastermind of the entire attack to get what he came for, completely unnoticed by law enforcement.

I was working the night shift in Arnold Tower when my phone rang and Lou Barnes was on the other end, telling me to lock everything down because New St. Louis was under attack. I did what I was told and threw the switched that closed up the Tower to everyone but qualified personnel and vehicles. If Barnes wanted to come in and take over, that would have been all right by me. I called the NSL police and reported the lockdown; the dispatcher on the other end asked me if anyone was attacking the building. I said no; she said I was on my own for the evening and hung up.

Thirty minutes later the security system pinged me that the garage entrance was opening to let in the Arnold Tower lorry. I stared at this for a moment because I knew exactly where the Lorry was parked. I flipped the security monitor over to the garage camera and saw no lorry, but instead four people walking down the parking garage ramp. Two were carrying bags; one was dragging another along. I looked at the two of them for a minute before I recognized who both of them were.

I got very upset. And started thinking very fast, as fast as I ever had in my life.

My phone rang. I picked it up.

"I know by this time you can see me in your security cameras," Marcus Rosen said. "And so you know by this time who I have with me."

"I can see her," I said, looking at Leah.

"Good," Marcus said. "Will told me that you still had a thing for her, and I suspect he was right. So I thought she might be a useful motivator. Now listen to me, Benjamin. I'm sorry you're the one I'm having to deal with right now, but that's just the way things are. If you cooperate, we can get through this quickly. I'm coming for some genetic samples of your pigs. That's all I want. We don't have to hurt them, all we have to do is take skin samples. It'll be simple, quick, painless, and at the end of it you'll have your friend Leah back. Does this sound like a good deal to you?"

"It does," I said.

"Good," Marcus said, again. "Then here's the plan. I'm going to stay down here in the garage while my two friends here come up to where you are. You're going to take them to where they can get some samples. And then they're going to come back down. When they come back down, I'm going to let go of Leah. Do you think you can handle that?"

"I can," I said.

"I'm glad we're handling this rationally," Marcus said. "All right. I'm sending my friends up."

"I'm unlocking the garage door," I said. "Have them give me a couple of minutes, and then they can take the elevator to the fifth floor. I'll meet them in the floor lobby."

"They're going in now," Marcus said.

Five minutes later the elevator doors opened and two men got out.

"Hi," I said.

"Take us to the pig floor," one of them said.

"No," I said. The two looked at each other and then at me, unamused. I held up a hand. "There's an entire floor of sleeping pigs in there," I said. "If you startle or surprise them, they're going to come out of sleep freaked out, and then every pig around them is going to freak out, and then that's a few thousand pigs in a frenzy. I don't want to be responsible for you getting trampled." I pointed to a door at the far end of the lobby. "We have an examination room over there. I've already got some pigs for you. They're already awake. Fewer pigs means less hassle for all of us. All right?"

The two of them looked at each other.

"Come on, guys," I said. "I just want to get my friend back."

"Fine," one of them said, and walked with me into the room.

"What are these things?" one of them asked, pointing at the pig-shaped forms.

"And where are the pigs?" the other asked.

"Those are the examination tables," I said, moving into the control room. "Pigs hate to get picked up, so we just have them lean up against these instead. And they're behind that door there because before they come in, I want to spray some disinfectant in the room. Helps keep infection down. No, you two stay in there. You need to be disinfected, too."

"We just need skin samples," one of them said.

"I understand," I said. "But you break the skin while getting the samples, these pigs are highly susceptible to infection, and then that will catch to the other pigs. I'm already in enough trouble. This will only take a couple of seconds." I pressed a button, and liquid spritzed out of a sprinkler-like attachment in the ceiling.

"Okay," I said. "Here come the pigs." The two started unzipping their bags to take samples as I slid open the door to let the pigs in.

Two minutes (or so) later, I called Marcus. "We have a problem," I said.

"What is it?" Marcus said.

"I don't know how you told these guys to take samples, but however you told them, the pigs didn't like it," I said, and then held up the phone so Marcus could hear the screams and squeals. After a minute of that I got back on the phone. "I could open up the video feed," I said. "But I don't think you'd like that."

There was silence on the other end of the phone. Then, "I don't think you appreciate the seriousness of the situation," Marcus said.

"It's not my fault," I said. "You asked me to help them get genetic samples. I did exactly what you asked. It's *your* guys who are fucking around here."

"Get them out of there," Marcus said to me.

"It's not safe," I said, truthfully. "I think the pigs will eventually wear themselves out, but I'm not going anywhere near them until then."

"I still need a sample," Marcus said, after a minute. His ability to write off his two assistants was almost admirable, in its way.

"I can get you a sample," I said.

"I need it from more than one pig," Marcus said.

"I can give you samples from as many pigs as you need," I said.

"You need to come to me," Marcus said.

"I can't do that," I said. "The pigs won't exactly follow me."

"Considering what just happened, I'm not going to come up to you," Marcus said. "And let me remind you your friend Leah is still with me. And I still have a gun on her."

"Okay," I said. "I will come to you, but then you'll need to come with me. Give me a minute. I know where we can go to get your samples."

"Here," I said, handing them both gas masks and taking one for myself. "It's like the sign says. You're going to need this." I fit mine on myself and waited for the other two to fit theirs on. "Come on." I started walking toward conduit 2.

"Where are we?" Marcus said, through his mask.

"Why are you doing this, Marcus?" I asked him, as we walked out over conduit 2. "Last week you talked to me about the problems of a zero-footprint paradise and how we're cutting ourselves off from the rest of the world, but I get the feeling you're not doing this for the good of humanity."

"No," Marcus said.

"Then why all the talk?" I asked.

"I needed to see what was going to work on you," Marcus said. "Will told me in email that you got a job here in the Arnold Tower. I had a client who has been very interested in getting the genetics of these pigs for a while now. I saw an opportunity. I knew your mother was pushing for technology outreach, so if you were of the same mind as her, I might have been able to get you to play along. But it doesn't seem like your thing, so I went with your friend here."

"I'll have to thank Will for that," I said.

"He doesn't know," Marcus said. "You can't blame him."

"Nice of you to treat your brother that way," I said.

I could see Marcus shrug, briefly. "It's the real world out there, Benjamin. Some places still use money, not energy budgets. I have a living to make."

"So all of this—attacking New St. Louis—is just another day on the job," I said. We'd reached the access port. I bent down to open it up.

"That was going to happen anyway," Marcus said. "New St. Louis and the other cities are too closed off from everything around them. The people in The Wilds were already planning something. I don't care about it one way or the other, really, but it was useful cover for what I needed to do. So I provided the logistics. I borrowed the basic battle plan from a similar action in Detroit a couple years back. They used a fake riot to build an agricultural tower. We're using a real riot to steal from one."

"And they signed off on this, too, I suppose," I said.

"They don't know anything about this," Marcus said. "As far as they're concerned, the big event is gathering seeds from the agricultural towers. They're going to sequence those genomes and put them out for everyone to use. That's admirable, in its way, but my client has other plans for the pig genes."

The access port was fully opened. "After you," I said.

"I don't think so," Marcus said. "After *you*." I shrugged and went into the conduit. Marcus kept a bead on Leah as they she stepped down the ladder. Finally he stepped down.

"Where the hell are we?" Marcus said again.

"What does your client want with the pig genes?" I asked.

"I'm paid not to ask," Marcus said. "But I think he wants what the people in The Wilds want: the benefit of someone else's work. Having this genome means he has to do lot less work to make the next set of improvements."

"My mom was planning to make this part of the Technology Outreach," I said. "He could have just waited. *He* didn't have to start all this. *You* didn't have to start all this."

"I don't think my client believes having this genome be open source technology is in anyone's best interest," Marcus said. "And personally, I just want to get paid. Now. Enough. Give me the samples."

I looked over at Leah. "You remember when we were on the roof, and I talked about being here," I said.

"I do," she said.

"I'm sorry you're getting the embargo treatment," I said.

"It's all right," Leah said.

"Benjamin," Marcus said.

I reached down and flipped open my phone.

"My samples, please," Marcus said.

"'Embargo lifted,'" I said into the phone. I looked at Marcus as the rumbling started. "Here they come now," I said.

Leah reached up and pulled the gas mask off Marcus' face just as the first of the samples blew out of the pipes. He caught a load in the face and went down sputtering. Leah and I bolted for the ladder, her first, me following. As I cycled the access port shut, I could see Marcus trying to get a grip on the ladder. I think he might have gotten up the first step before the port sealed shut.

"The human body is simply not designed to swallow that much pig shit," is what Lou Barnes told me the next day. Nevertheless Marcus Rosen survived, although not well, and faced with the prospect of a life watching the world go by in a cell, lawyered up, cut a deal and brought down some industrialist from the Portland Ecologies—or, well, would have, if the fellow hadn't permanently relocated to Turkey. It's my understanding that he's not going to be very happy if he ever steps onto North America again.

Will took the fall of his brother badly, and the fact that his brother had betrayed his emails and idol worship even worse. Leah never blamed Will for any of it, but Will blamed himself and eventually that was the excuse he needed to break up with Leah and leave New St. Louis entirely. He settled in Vancouver eventually and is doing quite well. He and his wife send holiday cards.

The Technology Outreach program took a hell of a hit in the aftermath of the Battle of New St. Louis, not in the least because so much of the biotechnology that mom would have used for outreach flew over the wall in tiny planes. But mom, who won her election, rolled with the changes, and rather than trying to prosecute those who stole from the agricultural towers, the executive council gave them amnesty and open sourced the genome maps of the plants that were taken, making everyone's lives easier. And after a few decades of sitting behind its wall, New St. Louis is beginning to open up to The Wilds and the people there. They're nowhere close to being zero-footprint beyond the border, but they're starting, and that's something.

After the Battle of New St. Louis, my mother offered to find me a new job if I wanted it; her thinking was the man who caught the mastermind behind the attack should be able to get any damn job he wanted, even if he was her son.

I thanked her but I told her no. I still work at Arnold Tower. And more than that: Leah and I were married there, up on the experimental rooftop garden, with Barnes, Jeffers and Pinter as my groomsmen, Syndee as my "Best Sis," and Lunch as ring bearer. He seemed quite pleased with the job. We were quite pleased to have him.

And that's how a pig got into our wedding party.

It's a good story, right?

TO HIE FROM FAR CILENIA

KARL SCHROEDER

Although I am the editor of METATROPOLIS—the mayor, as it were—to a very real extent you could consider Karl Schroeder METATROPOLIS' "Founding Father"—he was the one that got the ball rolling by proposing the idea of cities of the future, and did much of the heavy conceptual lifting for the project, not because no one else would do it—really, thinking up cool ideas was not a problem with this bunch—but because he thought it was fun and because he had so many cool ideas that sometimes it was all the rest of us could do to keep up. The guy's amazing that way, folks.

And so it's fitting that his story not only closes out our anthology but also in its way opens the door for yet another kind of "metatropolis"—yet another way for societies to create themselves and build and thrive and compete. I'll talk no more about that, since I don't want to spoil the pleasure you'll get from hearing this story. Suffice to say that if your brain hasn't already been blown by now, it's going to get cracked wide open here. And I think you're going to like the sensation.

Sixteen plastic-wrapped, frozen reindeer made a forest of jutting legs and antlers in the back of the transport truck. Gennady Malianov raised his flashlight to peer down the length of the cargo container. He checked his Geiger counter, then said, "It's them, all right."

"You're sure?" asked the Swedish cop. Hidden in his rain gear, he was all slick surfaces under the midnight drizzle. The mountain road stretching out behind him shone silver on black, dazzled here and there by the red and blue lights of a dozen emergency vehicles.

Gennady climbed down. "Officer, if you think there might be other trucks on this road loaded with radioactive reindeer, I think I need to know."

The cop didn't smile; his breath fogged the air. "It's all about jurisdiction," he said. "If they were just smuggling meat...but this is terrorism."

"Still," mused Gennady; the cop had been turning away but stopped. Gennady glanced back at the contorted, freezer-burned carcasses, and shrugged awkwardly. "I never thought I'd get to see them."

"See who?"

Embarrassed now, Gennady nodded to the truck. "The famous Reindeer," he said. "I never thought I'd get to see them."

"Spöklik," muttered the cop as he walked away. Gennady glanced in the truck once more, then walked toward his car, shoulders hunched. A little light on its dashboard was flashing, telling him he'd gone over the time he'd booked it for. Traffic on the E18 had proven heavier than expected, due to the rain and the fact that the police had shut down the whole road at Arjang. He was mentally subtracting the extra car-sharing fees from what they'd pay him for this very short adventure, when someone shouted, "Malianov?"

"What now?" He shielded his eyes with his hand. Two men were walking up the narrow shoulder from the emergency vehicles. Immediately behind them was a van without a flashing light—a big, black and sinister shape that reminded him of some of the paralegal police vans in Ukraine. The men had the burly look of plainclothes policemen.

"Are you Gennady Malianov?" asked the first, in English. Rain was beading on his bald skull. Gennady nodded.

"You're with the IAEA?" the man went on. "You're an arms inspector?"

"I've done that," said Gennady neutrally.

"Lane Hitchens," said the bald man, sticking out his beefy hand for Gennady to shake. "Interpol."

"Is this about the reindeer?"

"What reindeer?" said Hitchens. Gennady snatched his hand back.

"*This*," he said, waving at the checkpoint, the flashing lights, the bowed heads of the suspects in the back of the paddy wagon. "You're not here about all this?"

Hitchens shook his head. "Look, I was just told you'd be here, so we came. We need to talk to you."

Gennady didn't move. "About what?"

"We need your help, damn it. Now come on!"

Some third person was opening the back of the big van. It still reminded Gennady of an abduction truck, but the prospect of work kept him walking. He needed the cash, even for an hour's consultation at the side of a Swedish road.

Hitchens gestured for Gennady to climb into the van. "Reindeer?" he suddenly said with a grin.

"You ever heard of the Becqurel Reindeer?" said Gennady. "No? Well—very famous among us radiation hunters."

The transport truck was pinioned in spotlights now as men in hazmat suits walked clumsily toward it. That was serious overkill, of course; Gennady grinned as he watched the spectacle.

"After Chernobyl a whole herd of Swedish reindeer got contaminated with cesium-137," he said. "Fifty times the allowable dose. Tonnes of reindeer meat had already entered the processing plants before they realized. All those reindeer ended up in a meat locker outside Stockholm where they've been sitting ever since. Cooling off, you know?

"Well, yesterday somebody broke into the locker and stole some of the carcasses. I think the plan was to get the meat into shops somehow, then cause a big scandal. A sort of dirty-bomb effect."

The man with Hitchens swore. "That's awful!"

Gennady laughed. "And stupid," he said. "One look at what's left and nobody in their right mind would buy it. But we caught them anyway, though you know the Norwegian border's only a few kilometers that way…"

"And *you* tracked them down?" Hitchens sounded impressed. Gennady shrugged; he had something of a reputation as an adventurer these days, and it would be embarrassing to admit that he hadn't been brought into this case because of his near-legendary exploits in Pripyat or Azerbaijan. No, the Swedes had tapped Gennady because, a couple of years ago, he'd spent some time in China shooting radioactive camels.

Casually, he said, "This is a paid consultation, right?"

Hitchens just nodded at the van again. Gennady sighed and climbed in.

At least it was dry in there. The back of the van had benches along its sides, a partition separating it from the cab, and a narrow table down its middle. A surveillance truck, then. A man and a woman were sitting on one bench, so Gennady slid in across from them. His stomach tightened with sudden anxiety; he forced himself to say "Hello." Meeting anybody new, particularly in a professional capacity, always filled him with an awkward dread.

Hitchens and his companion heaved themselves in and slammed the van's doors. Gennady felt somebody climb into the cab and heard its door shut.

"My car," said Gennady.

Hitchens glanced at the other man. "Jack, could you clear Mr. Malianov's account? We'll get somebody to return it," he said to Gennady. Then as the van began to move he turned to the other two passengers.

"This is Gennady Malianov," he said to them. "He's our nuclear expert."

"Can you give me some idea what this is all about?" asked Gennady.

"Stolen plutonium," said Hitchens blandly. "Twelve kilos. A bigger deal than your reindeer, huh?"

"Reindeer?" said the woman. Gennady smiled at her. She looked a bit out of place in here. She was in her mid-thirties, with heavy-framed glasses over her gray eyes and brown hair tightly clawed back on her skull. Her high-collared white blouse was fringed with lace. She looked like the cliché schoolmarm.

Around her neck was hung a heavy-looking brass pocket-watch.

"Gennady, this is Miranda Veen," said Hitchens. Veen nodded. "And this," continued Hitchens, "is Fraction."

The man was wedged into one corner of the van. He glanced sidelong at Gennady, but seemed distracted by something else. He was considerably younger than Veen, maybe in his early twenties. He wore glasses similar to hers, but the lenses of his glowed faintly. With a start Gennady realized they were an augmented reality rig; they were miniature transparent computer screens, and some other scene was being overlaid on top of what he saw through them.

Veen's were clear, which meant hers were probably turned off right now.

"Miranda's our cultural anthropologist," said Hitchens. "You're going to be working with her more than the rest of us. She actually came to us a few weeks ago with a problem of her own—"

"And got no help at all," said Veen, "until this other thing came up."

"A possible connection with the plutonium," said Hitchens, nodding significantly at Fraction. "Tell Gennady where you're from," he said to the young man.

Fraction nodded and suddenly smiled. "I hie," he said, "from far Cilenia."

Gennady squinted at him. His accent had sounded American. "Silesia?" asked Gennady. "Are you Czech?"

Miranda Veen shook her head. She was wearing little round earrings, he noticed. "*Cilenia*, not Silesia," she said. "Cilenia's also a woman's name, but in this case it's a place. A nation."

Gennady frowned. "It is? Where is it?"

"That," said Lane Hitchens, "is one of the things we want you to find out."

The van headed east to Stockholm. All sorts of obvious questions occurred to Gennady, such as, "If you want to know where Cilenia is, why don't you just ask Fraction, here?"—but Lane Hitchens seemed uninterested in answering them. "Miranda will explain," was all he said.

Instead, Hitchens began to talk about the plutonium, which had apparently been stolen many years ago. "It kept being sold," Hitchens said with an ironic grimace. "And so it kept being smuggled from one place to another. But after the Americans took their hit everybody started getting better and better detection devices on ports and borders. The plutonium was originally in four big slugs, but the buyers and sellers started dividing it up and moving the pieces separately. They kept selling it as one unit, which is the only reason we can still track it. But it got sliced into smaller and smaller chunks, staying just ahead of the detection technology of the day. We caught Fraction here moving one of them; but he's just a mule, and has agreed to cooperate.

"Now there's well over a hundred pieces, and a new buyer who wants to collect them all in one place. They're on the move, but we can now detect a gram hidden in a tonne of lead. It's gotten very difficult for the couriers."

Gennady nodded, thinking about it. They only had to successfully track one of the packets, of course, to find the buyer. He glanced at Fraction again. The meaning of the man's odd name was obvious now. "So, buyers are from this mythical Cilenia?" he said.

Hitchens shrugged. "Maybe."

"Then I ask again, why does Fraction here not tell us where that is, if he is so cooperative? Or, why have those American men who are not supposed to exist, not dragged him away to be questioned somewhere?"

Hitchens laughed drily. "That would not be so easy," he said. "Fraction, could you lean forward a bit?" The young man obliged. "Turn your head?" asked Hitchens. Now Gennady could see the earbuds in Fraction's ears.

"The man sitting across from you is a low-functioning autistic named Danail Gavrilov," said Hitchens. "He doesn't speak English. He is, however, extremely good at parroting what he hears, and somebody's trained him to interpret a language of visual and aural cues so he can parrot gestures and motions, even complex ones."

"Fraction," said Fraction, "is not in this van."

Gennady's hackles rose. He found himself suddenly reluctant to look into the faintly glowing lenses of Danail Gavrilov's glasses. "Cameras in the glasses," he stammered, "of course, yes; and they're miked...Can't you trace the signal?" he asked Hitchens. The Interpol man shook his head.

"It goes two or three steps through the normal networks then jumps into a maze of anonymized botnets." Gennady nodded thoughtfully; he'd seen that kind of thing before and knew how hard it would be to follow the packet streams in and out of Fraction's head. Whoever was riding Danail Gavrilov was, at least for the moment, invulnerable.

While they'd been driving, the rain clouds had cleared away and, visible through the van's back windows, was a pale sky still, near midnight, touched with amber and pink.

"Do you have any immediate commitments?" asked Hitchens. Gennady eyed him.

"This is likely to be a long job, I guess?"

"I hope not. We need to find that plutonium. But we don't know how long Fraction will be willing to help us. He could disappear at any moment...so if you could start tonight...?"

Gennady shrugged. "I have no cat to feed, or...other people. I'm used to fieldwork, but—" he cast about for some disarming joke he could make, "I've never before had an anthropologist watching me work."

Veen drummed her fingers on the narrow tabletop. "I don't mean to be impolite," she said, "but you have to understand: I'm not here for your plutonium. I admit its importance," she added quickly, holding up one hand. "I just think you should know I'm after something else."

He shrugged. "Okay. What?"

"My son."

Gennady stared at her and, at a loss for what to say, finally just shrugged and smiled. Veen started to talk but at that point the van rolled to a stop outside one of the better hotels in Stockholm.

The rest of the night consisted of a lot of running around and arrangement-making, as Gennady was run across town to collect his bags from his own modest lodgings. They put him up on the same floor as Veen and Hitchens, though where Fraction stayed, or whether he even slept, Gennady didn't know.

Gennady was too agitated to sleep, so he spent a long time surfing the net, trying to find references to his reindeer and the incident on the road that evening. So far, there was nothing, and eventually he grew truly tired and slept.

Hitchens knocked on Gennady's door at eight o'clock. He, Veen and Fraction were tucking into a fine breakfast in the suite across the hall. Fraction looked up as Gennady entered.

"Good morning," he said. "I trust you slept well."

The American term 'creeped out' came to Gennady's mind as he mumbled some platitude in reply. Fraction smiled—except of course, it was Danail Gavrilov doing the actual smiling. Gennady wondered whether he took any notice at all of the social interactions going on around him, or whether he'd merely discovered that following his rider's commands was the easiest way to navigate the bewildering complexities of human society.

Before going to sleep last night Gennady had looked up Fraction's arrangement with Gavrilov. Gavrilov was something Stanley Milgram had dubbed a 'cyranoid'—after Cyrano de Bergerac. He was much more than a puppet, and much less than an actor. Whatever he was, he was clearly enjoying his eggs Benedict.

"What are we doing today?" Gennady asked Hitchens.

"We're going to start as soon as you've eaten and freshened up."

Gennady frowned at Veen. "Start? Where is it that we start?"

Veen and Hitchens exchanged a look. Fraction smiled; had somebody in some other time zone just commanded him to do that?

Gennady wasn't in the best of moods, since he kept expecting to remember some detail from last night that made sense of everything. Though the coffee was kicking in, nothing was coming to him. Plus, he was itching to check the news in case they were talking about his reindeer.

Miranda suddenly said, "Hitchens has told you about his problem. Maybe it's time I told you about mine." She reached into a bag at her feet and dropped an ebook on the table. This was of the quarto type, with three hundred pages of flexible e-paper, each of which could take the impressions of whatever pages you wanted. As she flipped through it, Gennady could see that she had filled its pages with hand-written notes, photos and web pages, all of which bled off the edges of the e-paper. At any readable scale, the virtual pages were much bigger than the physical window you looked at them through, a fact she demonstrated as she flipped to one page and, dragging her fingers across it, shoved its news articles off into limbo. Words and pictures rolled by until she planted her finger again to stop the motion. "Here." She held out the book to Gennady.

Centered in the page was the familiar format of an email.

Mom...(it said) *I know you warned me against leaving the protection of Cascadia, but Europe's so amazing! Everywhere I've been, they've respected our citizenship. And you know I love the countryside. I've met a lot of people who're fascinated with how I grew up.*

Gennady looked up. "You're from the Cities?"

She nodded. Whatever Miranda Veen's original nationality, she had adopted citizenship in a pan-global urban network whose cities were, taken together, more powerful than the nations where they were situated. Her son might have been born somewhere in the Vancouver-Portland-Seattle corridor—now known simply as Cascadia—or in Shanghai. It didn't matter; he'd grown up with the right to walk and live in either megacity—and in many others—with equal ease. But the email suggested that his mother had neglected to register his birth in any of the nations that the cities were supposedly a part of.

Gennady read a little further. *Anyway,* (it said) *I met this guy yesterday, a backpacker, calls himself Dodger. He said he had no citizenship other than the ARG he's part of. I went sure, yeah, whatever, so he mailed me a path link. I've been follow-ing it around Rome and, well, it's amazing so far. Here's some shots.* Following were a number of fairly mundane images of old Roman streets.

Gennady looked up, puzzled. Alternate Reality Games—ARG's—were as common as mud; millions of kids around the world put virtual overlays and geographical positioning infor-mation over the real planet, and made up complicated games involving travel and the specific features of locale. Internet citi-zenship wasn't new either. A growing subset of the population considered themselves dual citizens of some real nation, plus an on-line virtual world. Since the economies of virtual nations could be bigger than many real-world countries, such citizen-ship wasn't just an affectation. It could be more economically important than your official nationality.

It wasn't a big step to imagining an ARG-based nationality. So Gennady said, "I don't see what's significant here."

"Read the next message," said Veen. She sat back, chew-ing a fingernail, and watched him as he read the next in what looked like a string of emails pasted into the page:

Mom, weren't those remappings amazing? Oversatch is so incredibly vibrant compared to the real world. Even Hong Kong's overlays don't cut it next to that. And the participatory stuff is really intense. I walked away from it today with over ten thousand satch-mos in my wallet. Sure, it's only convertible through this one anon-ymous portal based out of Bulgaria—but it is convertible. Worth something like five hundred dollars, I think, if I was stupid enough to cash it in that way. It's worth a lot more if I keep it in the ARG.

Veen leaned over to scroll the paragraphs past. "This one," she said, "two weeks later."

Gennady read.

It 2.0 is this overlay that remaps everything in real-time into Oversatch terms. It's pretty amazing when you learn what's really happening in the world! How the sanotica is causing all these pressures on Europe. Sanotica manifests in all sorts of ways— just imagine what a self-organizing catastrophe would look like! And Oversatch turns out to be just a gateway into the remappings that oppose sanotica. There's others: Trapton, Allegor, and Cilenia.

"Cilenia," said Gennady.

Fraction sat up to look at the book. He nodded and said, "Oversatch is a gateway to Cilenia."

"And you?" Gennady asked him. "You've been there?"

Fraction smiled. "I live there."

Gennady was bewildered. Some of the words were familiar. He was vaguely familiar with the concept of geographical overlays, for instance. But the rest of it made no sense at all. "What's sanotica?" he asked Fraction.

Fraction's smile was maddeningly smug. "You have no language for it," he said. "You'd have to speak *it 2.0.* But Sanotica is what's really going on here."

Gennady sent an appealing look to Lane Hitchens. Hitchens grunted. "Sanotica may be the organization behind the plutonium thefts," he said.

"Sanotica is not an organization," said Fraction, "anymore than *it 2.0* is just a word."

"Whatever," said Lane. "Gennady, you need to find them. Miranda will help, because she wants to find her son."

Gennady struggled to keep up. "And sanotica," he said, "is in…far Cilenia?"

Fraction laughed contemptuously. Veen darted him an annoyed look, and said to Gennady, "It's not that simple. Here, read the last message." She dragged it up from the bottom of the page.

Mom: Cilenia is a new kind of 'it.' But so is sanotica; a terrifying thought. Without that it, without the word and the act of pointing that it represents, you cannot speak of these things, you can't even see them! I watch them now, day by day—the walking cities, the countries that appear like cicadas to walk their one day in the sun, only to vanish again at dusk...I can't be an observer anymore. I can't be me anymore, or sanotica will win. I'm sorry, Mom, I have to become something that can be pointed at by 2.0. Cilenia needs me, or as many me's as I can spare.

I'll call you.

Gennady read the message again, then once more. "It makes no sense," he said. "It's a jumble, but..." He looked to Hitchens. "It two-point-oh. It's not a code, is it?"

Hitchens shook his head. He handed Gennady a pair of heavy-framed glasses like Veen's. Gennady recognized the brand name on the arms: *Ariadne AR,* the Swiss augmented reality firm that had recently bought out Google. Veen also wore Ariadnes, but there was no logo at all on Fraction's glasses.

Gennady gingerly put them on and pressed the frames to activate them. Instantly, a cool blue, transparent sphere appeared in the air about two feet in front of him. The glasses were projecting the globe straight onto his retinas, of course; orbiting around it were various icons and command words that only he could see. Gennady was familiar with this sort of interface. All he had to do was focus his gaze on a particular command and it would change color. Then he could blink to activate it, or dismiss it by looking somewhere else.

"Standard software," he mumbled as he scanned through the icons. "Geographical services, Wikis, social nets...What's this?"

Hitchens and Veen had put on their own glasses, so Gennady made the unfamiliar icon visible to all of them, and picked it out of the air with his fingers. He couldn't feel it, of course, but was able to set the little stylized R in the center of the table where they could all look at it.

Danail Gavrilov nodded, mimicking a satisfied smile for whoever was riding him. "That's your first stop," he said. "A little place called *Rivet Couture.*"

Hitchens excused himself and left. Gennady barely noticed; he'd activated the icon for *Rivet Couture* and was listening to a lecture given by a bodacious young woman who didn't really exist. He'd moved her so she appeared to be standing in the middle of the room, but Miranda Veen kept walking through her.

The pretty woman was known as a *serling*—she was a kind of narrator, and right now she was bringing Gennady up to speed on the details of an Alternate Reality Game called *Rivet Couture.*

While she talked, the cameras and positional sensors in Gennady's classes had been working overtime to figure out where he was and what objects were around him. So while the serling explained that *Rivet Couture* was set in a faux gaslight era—an 1880 that never existed—all the stuff in the room mutated. The walls adopted a translucent, glowing layer of floral wallpaper; the lamp sconces faded behind ghostly brass gas fixtures.

Miranda Veen walked through the serling again and, for a second, Gennady thought the game had done an overlay on her as well. In fact, her high-necked blouse and long skirt suddenly seemed appropriate. With a start he saw that her earrings were actually little gears.

"Steampunk's out of style, isn't it?" he said. Veen turned, reaching up to touch her earlobes. She smiled at him, and it was the first genuine smile he'd seen from her.

"My parents were into New Age stuff," she said. "I rebelled by joining a steam gang. We wore crinoline and tight waistcoats, and I used to do my hair up in an elaborate bun with long pins. The boys wore pince-nez and paisley vests, that sort of thing. I drifted away from the culture a long time ago, but I still love the style."

Gennady found himself grinning at her. He *understood* that— the urge to step just slightly out from the rest of society. The

223

pocket-watch Veen wore like a necklace was a talisman of sorts, a constant reminder of who she was, and how she was unique.

But while Miranda Veen's talisman might be a thing of gears and armatures, Gennady's were *places:* instead of an icon of brass and gears, he wore memories of dripping concrete halls and the shadowed calandria of ruined reactors, of blue-glowing pools packed with spent fuel rods...of an unlit commercial freezer where an entire herd of irradiated reindeer lay jumbled like toys.

Rivet Couture was not so strange. Many women wore lingerie under their conservative work clothes to achieve the same effect. For those people without such an outlet, overlays like *Rivet Couture* gave them much the same sense of owning a secret uniqueness. Kids walked alone in the ordinary streets of Berlin or Minneapolis, yet at the same moment they walked side by side through the misty cobblestoned streets of a Victorian Atlantis. Many of them spent their spare time filling in the details of the places, designing the clothes and working out the history of *Rivet Couture*. It was much more than a game; and it was worldwide.

Miranda Veen rolled her bags to the door and Fraction opened it for her. They turned to Gennady, who was still sitting at the devastation of the breakfast table. "Are you ready?" asked Miranda.

"I'm coming," he said; he stood up, and stepped from Stockholm into Atlantis.

Rivet Couture had a charmingly light hand: it usually added just a touch or two to what you were seeing or hearing, enough to provide a whiff of strangeness to otherwise normal places. In the elevator, Gennady's glasses filtered the glare of the fluorescents until it resembled candle-light. At the front desk an ornate scroll-worked cash register wavered into visibility, over the terminal the clerk was using. Outside in the street, Gennady heard the nicker of nearby horses and saw black-maned heads toss somewhere out in the fast-moving stream of electric cars.

Stockholm was already a mix of classical grandeur and high modernism. These places had really been gaslit once, and many streets were still cobbled, particularly outside such romantic landmarks as the King's Palace. *Rivet Couture* didn't have to work very hard to achieve its effects, especially when the brilliant, star-like shapes of other players began appearing. You could see them kilometers away, even through buildings and hills, which made it easy to rendezvous with them. RC forbade certain kinds of contact—there were no telephones in this game—but it wasn't long before Gennady, Miranda and Fraction were sitting in a cafe with two other long-time players.

Gennady let Miranda lead, and she enthusiastically plunged into a discussion of RC politics and history. She'd clearly been here before, and it couldn't have just been her need to find her son that propelled her to learn all this detail. He watched her wave her hands while she talked, and her Lussebullar and coffee grew cold.

Agata and Per warmed quickly to Miranda, but were a bit more reserved with Gennady. That was fine by him, since he was experiencing his usual tongue-tanglement around strangers. So, listening, he learned a few things:

Rivet Couture's Atlantis was a global city. Parts of it were everywhere, but their location shifted and moved depending on the actions of the players. You could change your overlay to that of another neighborhood, but in so doing you lost the one you were in. This was generally no problem, although it meant that other players might blink in and out of existence as you moved.

The game was free. This was a bit of a surprise, but not a huge one. There were plenty of open-source games out there, but few had the detail and beautiful sophistication of this one. Gennady had assumed there was a lot of money behind it, but in fact there was something just as good: the attention of a very large number of fans.

The object of the game was power and influence within Atlantean society. RC was a game of politics and most of its moves happened in conversation. As games went, its most ancient ancestor was probably a twentieth-century board game called *Diplomacy.* Gennady mentioned this idea, and Per smiled.

"The board game, yes," said Per, "but more like play-by-mail versions like *Slobovia,* where you had to write a short story for every move you made in the game. Like the characters in Slobovian stories, we are diplomats, courtesans, pickpockets and cabinet ministers. All corrupt, of course," he added with another smile.

"And we often prey on newbies," Agata added with a leer.

"Ah, yes," said Per, as if reminded of something. "We will proceed to do that now. As disgraced interior minister Puddleglum Phudthucker, I have many enemies and most of my compatriots are being watched. *You* must take this diplomatic pouch to one of my co-conspirators. If you get waylaid and killed on the way, it's not my problem—but make sure you discard the pouch at the first sign of trouble."

"Mm," said Gennady as Per handed him a felt-wrapped package about the size of a file folder. "What would the first sign of trouble look like?"

Per glanced at Agata, who pursed her lips and frowned at the ceiling. "Oh, say, strangers converging on you or moving to block your path."

Per leaned forward. "If you do this," he whispered, "the rewards could be great down the line. I have powerful friends, and when I am back in my rightful portfolio I will be in a position to advance your own career."

Per had to go to work (in the real world) so they parted ways and Gennady's group took the Blue Line metro to Radhuset Station, which was already a subterranean fantasy and, in *Rivet Couture,* became a candlelit cavern full of shadowy strangers in cowled robes. Up on the surface they quickly located a stuffy-looking brokerage on a narrow side street, where the reception-ist happily took the package from Gennady. She was dressed in a Chanel suit, but a tall feather was poking up from behind her desk, and at Gennady's curious glance she reached down to show him her ornate Victorian tea-hat.

Out in the street he said, "Cosplay seems to be an important part of the game. I'm not dressed for it."

Miranda laughed. "In that suit? You're nearly there. You just need a fob-watch and a vest. You'll be fine. As to you..." She turned to Fraction.

"I have many costumes," said the cyranoid. "I shall retrieve one and meet you back at the hotel." He started to walk away.

"But—? Wait." Gennady started after him but Miranda put a hand on his arm. She shook her head.

"He comes and goes," she said. "There's nothing we can do about it, though I assume Hitchens' people have him under surveillance. It probably does them no good. I'm sure the places Fraction goes are all virtual."

Gennady watched the cyranoid vanish into the mouth of the metro station. He'd also disappeared from *Rivet Couture*. Unhappily, Gennady said, "Let's disappear ourselves for a while. I'd like to check on my reindeer."

"You may," said Miranda coolly, "but I am staying here. I am looking for my son, Mr. Malianov. This is not just a game to me."

"Neither were the reindeer."

As it turned out, he didn't have to leave RC to surf for today's headlines. There was indeed plenty of news about a crackpot terrorist ring being busted, but nothing about the individual agents who'd done the field work. This was fine by Gennady, who'd been briefly famous after stopping an attempt to blow up the Chernobyl sarcophagus some years before. He'd taken that assignment in the first place because in the abandoned streets of Pripyat he could be utterly alone. Being interviewed for TV and then recognized on the street had been intensely painful for him.

They shopped for some appropriately steampunk styles for Gennady to wear. He hated shopping with a passion and was self-conscious with the result, but Miranda seemed to like it. They met a few more denizens of Atlantis through the afternoon, but he still hung back, and at dinner she asked him whether he'd ever done any role-playing.

Gennady barked a laugh. "I do it all the time." He rattled off half a dozen of the more popular on-line worlds. He had multiple avatars in each and in one of them he'd been cultivating his character for over a decade. Miranda was puzzled at his awkwardness, so finally Gennady explained that those games allowed him to stay at home and let a virtual avatar doing the roving. He had many different bodies, and played as both genders. But an avatar-to-avatar conversation was nothing like a face to face conversation in reality—even an alternate reality like *Rivet Couture*'s.

"Nowadays they call it social phobia," he said with reluctance. "But really, I'm just shy."

Miranda's response was a surprised, "Oh." There was a long silence after that, while she thought and he squirmed in his seat. "Would you be more comfortable doubling up?" she asked at last.

"What do you mean?"

"Riding me cyranoid-wise, the way that Fraction rides Danail. Except," she added wryly, "it would only be during game interactions."

"I'm fine," he said irritably. "I'll get into it, you'll see. It's just...I expected to be home in my own apartment right now, I wasn't expecting a new job away from home with an indefinite duration and no idea where I'll be going. I'm not even sure how to investigate; what am I investigating? Who? None of this is normal to me; it's going to take a bit of an adjustment."

He resented that she thought of him as some kind of social cripple who had to be accommodated. He had a job to do and, better than almost anybody, he knew what was at stake.

For the vast majority of people, 'plutonium' was just a word, no more real than the word 'vampire.' Few had held it; few had seen its effects. Gennady knew it—its color, its heft, and the uses you could put it to.

Gennady wasn't going to let his own frailties keep him from finding the stuff, because the mere fact that somebody wanted it was a catastrophe. If he didn't find the plutonium, Gennady would spend his days waiting, expecting every morning to turn on the news and hear about which city—and how many millions of lives—had finally met it.

That night he lay in bed for hours, mind restless, trying to relate the terms of this stylish game to the very hard-nosed smuggling operation he had to crack.

Rivet Couture functioned a bit like a secret society, he decided. That first interaction, when he'd carried a pretend diplomatic pouch between two other players, suggested a physical mechanism for the transfer of the plutonium. When he'd talked to Hitchens about it after supper, the Interpol agent had confirmed it: "We're pretty sure that organized crime has started using games like yours to move stuff. Drugs, for instance. You can use two completely unrelated strangers as mules for pickups and hand-offs, even establish long chains of them. Each hop can be a few kilometers, by foot even, avoiding all our detection gear. One player can throw a package over his country's border and another find it by its GPS coordinates later. It's a nightmare."

Yet *Rivet Couture* was itself just a gateway, a milestone on the way to "far Cilenia." Between *Rivet Couture* and Cilenia was the place from where Miranda's son had sent most of his emails: Oversatch, he'd called it.

If *Rivet Couture* was like a secret society operating within normal culture, then Oversatch was like a second-order secret society, one that existed only within the culture of *Rivet Couture*. A conspiracy inside a conspiracy.

Hitchens had admitted that he hated Alternate Reality Games. "They destroy all the security structures we've put in place so carefully since 9/11. Just destroy 'em. It's 'cause you're not you anymore—hell, you can have multiple people playing one character in these games, handing them off to one another in shifts. Geography doesn't matter, identity is a joke…

everybody on the planet is like Fraction. How can you find a conspiracy in *that?*"

Gennady explained this insight to Miranda the next morning, and she nodded soberly.

"You're half-right," she said.

"Only half?"

"There's so much more going on here," she said. "If you're game for the game today, maybe we can see some of it."

He was. Dressed as he was, Gennady could hide inside the interface his glasses gave him. He'd decided to use these factors as a wall between him and the other avatars. He'd pretend out in the open, as he so often did from the safety of his room. Anyway, he'd try.

And they did well that day. Miranda had been playing the game for some weeks, with a fanatical single-mindedness borne of her need to find her son. Gennady found that if he thought in terms of striking up conversations with strangers on the street, then he'd be paralyzed and couldn't play; but if he pretended it was his character, Sir Arthur Tole, who was doing the talking, then his years of gaming experience quickly took over. Between the two of them, he and Miranda quickly developed a network of contacts and responsibilities. They saw Fraction every day or two, and what was interesting was that Gennady found himself quickly falling into the same pattern with the cyranoid that he had with Lane Hitchens: they would meet, Gennady would give a report, and the other would nod in satisfaction.

Hitchens' people had caught Fraction carrying one of the plutonium pieces. That was almost everything that Gennady knew about the cyranoid, and nearly all that Hitchens claimed to know as well. "There's one thing we have figured out," Hitchens had added when Gennady pressed. "It's his accent. Danail Gavrilov doesn't speak English, he's Bulgarian. But he's parroting English perfectly, right down to the accent. And it's an *American* accent. Specifically, west coast. Washington State or thereabouts."

"Well, that's something to go on," said Gennady.

"Yes," Hitchens said unhappily. "But not much."

Gennady knew what Hitchens had hired him to do and he was working at it. But increasingly, he wondered whether in some way he didn't understand, he had also been hired by Fraction—or maybe the whole of the IAEA had? The thought was disturbing, but he didn't voice it to Hitchens. It seemed too crazy to talk about.

The insight Miranda was promising didn't come that first day, or the next. It took nearly a week of hard work before Puddleglum Phudthucker met them for afternoon tea and gave a handwritten note to Miranda. "This is today's location of the *Griffin Rampant*," he said. "The food is excellent, and the conversation particularly...profitable."

When Puddleglum disappeared around the corner, Miranda hoisted the note and yelled in triumph. Gennady watched her, bemused.

"I'm so good," she told him. "Hitchens' boys never got near this place."

"What is it?" He thought of bomb-maker's warehouses, drug ops, maybe, but she said, "It's a restaurant.

"Oh, but it's an *Atlantean* restaurant," she added when she saw the look on his face. "The food comes from Atlantis. It's cooked there. Only Atlanteans eat it. Sociologically, this is a big break." She explained that any human society had membership costs, and the currency was *commitment*. To demonstrate commitment to some religions, for instance, people had to undergo ordeals, or renounce all their worldly goods, or leave their families. They had to live according to strict rules—and the stricter the rules and the more of them there were, the more stable the society.

"That's crazy," said Gennady. "You mean the *less* freedom people have, the happier they are?"

Miranda shrugged. "You trade some sources of happiness that you value less for one big one that you value more. Anyway, the point is, leveling up in a game like *Rivet Couture* represents commitment. We've leveled up to the point where the *Griffin* is open to us."

He squinted at her. "And that is important because...?"

"Because Fraction told me that the *Griffin* is a gateway to Oversatch."

They retired to the hotel to change. Formal clothing was required for a visit to the Griffin, and so for the first time Gennady found himself donning the complete *Rivet Couture* regalia. It was pure steampunk. Miranda had bought him a tight pinstriped suit whose black silk vest had a subtle dragon pattern sewn into it. He wore two belts, an ordinary one and a leather utility belt that hung down over one hip and had numerous loops and pouches on it. She'd found a bowler hat and had ordered him to slick back his hair when he wore it.

When he emerged, hugely self-conscious, he found Miranda waiting in what appeared to be a cast-iron corset and long black skirt. Heavy black boots peeked out from under the skirt. She twirled an antique-looking parasol and grinned at him. "Every inch the Russian gentleman," she said.

"Ukrainian," he reminded her; and they set off for the *Griffin Rampant.*

Gennady's glasses had tuned themselves to filter out all characteristic frequencies of electric light. His earbuds likewise eliminated the growl and jangle of normal city noises, replacing them with Atlantean equivalents. He and Miranda sauntered through a city transformed, and there seemed no hurry tonight as the gentle amber glow of the streetlights, distant nicker of horses and pervasive sound of crickets were quite relaxing.

They turned a corner and found themselves outside the *Griffin*, which was an outdoor cafe that filled a sidestreet. Lifting his glasses for a second, Gennady saw that the place was actually an alley between two glass-and-steel sky-scrapers, but in *Rivet Couture* the buildings were shadowy stone monstrosities festooned with gargoyles, and there were plenty of virtual trees to hide the sky. In ordinary reality, the cafe was hidden from the street by tall fabric screens; in the game, these were stone walls and there was an ornately carved griffin over the entrance.

Paper lanterns lit the tables; a dapper waiter with a sly expression led Gennady and Miranda to a table, where—to the surprise of neither—Fraction was lounging. The cyranoid was drinking mineral water, swirling it in his glass in imitation of the couple at the next table.

"Welcome to Atlantis," said Fraction as Gennady unfolded his napkin. Gennady nodded; he did feel transported somehow, as though this really was some parallel world and not a downtown alley.

The waiter came by and recited the evening's specials. He left menus, and when Gennady opened his he discovered that the prices were all in the game's pretend currency, Atlantean deynars.

He leaned over to Miranda. "The game's free," he murmured, "so who pays for all this?"

Fraction had overheard, and barked a laugh. "I said, welcome to Atlantis. We have our own economy, just like Sweden."

Gennady shook his head. He'd been studying the game, and knew that there was no exchange that translated deynars into any real-world currency. "I mean who pays for the meat, the vegetables—the wine?"

"It's all Atlantean," said Fraction. "If you want to earn some real social capital here, I can introduce you to some of the people who raise it."

Miranda shook her head. "We want to get to the next level. To Oversatch," she said. "You know that. Why haven't you taken us straight there?"

Fraction shrugged. "Tried that with Hitchens' men. They weren't able to get there."

"Oversatch is like an ARG inside *Rivet Couture*," Gennady guessed. "So you have to know the rules and people and settings of RC before you can play the meta-game."

"That's part of it," admitted Fraction. "But *Rivet Couture* is just an overlay—a map drawn on a map. Oversatch is a whole new map."

"I don't understand."

"I'll show you." The waiter came by and they ordered. Then Fraction stood up. "Come. There's a little store at the back of the restaurant."

Gennady followed him. Behind a screen of plants were several market-stall type tables, piled with various merchandise. There was a lot of clothing in Atlantean styles, which all appeared to be hand-made. There were also various trinkets, such as fob watches and earrings similar to Miranda's. "Ah, here," said Fraction, drawing Gennady to a table at the very back.

He held up a pair of round, antique-looking glasses. "Try them on." Gennady did, and as his eyes adjusted he saw the familiar glow of an augmented reality interface booting up.

"These are—"

"Like the ones you were wearing," nodded Fraction, "but with some additions. They're made entirely in 3-D printers and by hand, by and for the people of Oversatch and some of their Atlantean friends. The data link piggy-backs on ordinary internet protocols: that's called *tunneling*."

Fraction bought two pair of the glasses from the smiling elderly woman behind the counter, and they returned to the table. Miranda was chatting with some of the other Atlanteans. When she returned, Fraction handed her one pair of glasses. Wordlessly, she put them on.

Dinner was uneventful, though a few of *Rivet Couture*'s players stopped by to network. Everybody was here for the atmosphere and good food, of course, but also to build connections that could advance their characters' fortunes in the game.

When they were finished, Fraction dropped some virtual money on the table, and as the waiter came by he said, "My compliments to the chef."

"Why thank you." The waiter bowed.

"The lady here was highly impressed, and she and her companion would like to know more about how their meal came about." Fraction turned his lapel inside out, revealing a tiny, ornate pin carved in a gear pattern. The waiter's eyes widened.

"Of course, sir, of course. Come this way." He led them past the stalls at the back of the restaurant, to where the kitchen staff were laboring over some ordinary-looking, portable camp stoves. Several cars and unadorned white panel vans were parked in the alley behind them. The vans' back doors were rolled up revealing stacks of plastic skids, all piled with food.

The waiter conferred with a man who was unloading one of the vans. He grunted. "Help me out, then," he said to Gennady. As Gennady slid a tray of buns out of the back of the van, the man said, "We grow our own produce. They're all fancy with their names nowadays, they call them *vertical farms*. Back when I got started, they were called grow-ops and they all produced marijuana. Ha!" He punched Gennady on the shoulder. "It took organized crime to fund an agricultural revolution. They perfect the art of the grow-op, we use what they learn to grow tomatoes, green beans and pretty much anything else you can imagine."

Gennady hoisted another skid. "So you, what?—have houses around the city where you grow stuff?"

The man shrugged. "A couple of basements. Mostly we grow it in the open, on public boulevards, in parks, roofs, ledges of high-rise buildings...there's hectares of unused space in any city. Might as well do something with it."

When they were done unloading the skids, Gennady saw Fraction waving to them from one of the other vans. He and Miranda walked over to find that this vehicle didn't contain food; rather, the back was packed with equipment. "What's all this?" Miranda asked.

Gennady whistled. "It's a factory." They were looking at an industrial-strength 3-D printer, one sophisticated enough to create electronic components as well as screws, wires, and any shape that could be fed into it as a 3-D image file. There was also a 3-D scanner with laser, terahertz and x-ray scanning heads; Gennady had used similar units to look for isotopes in smuggled contraband. It could digitize almost anything, from Miranda's jewelry to consumer electronic devices, and the printer could print out an almost perfect copy from the digital file. From a scan alone the printer could only copy electrical devices at about the level of a toaster, but with the addition of open-source integrated circuit plans it could duplicate anything from cell phones to wireless routers—and, clearly, working pairs of augmented reality glasses.

Fraction beamed at the unit. "This baby can even reproduce itself, by building its own components. The whole design is open-source."

Miranda was obviously puzzled. "*Rivet Couture* has no need for something like this," she said.

Fraction nodded. "But Oversatch—now that's another matter entirely." He sauntered back in the direction of the restaurant and they followed, frowning.

"Did you know," Fraction said suddenly, "that when Roman provinces wanted to rebel, the first thing they did was print their own money?" Gennady raised an eyebrow; after a moment Fraction grinned and went on. "Oversatch has its own money, but more importantly it has its own agriculture and its own industries. *Rivet Couture* is one of its trading partners, of course—it makes clothes and trinkets for the game players, who supply expensive feedstock for the printers and labor for the farms. For the players, it's all part of the adventure."

Miranda shook her head. "But I still don't understand why. Why does Oversatch exist in the first place? Are you saying it's a rebellion of some kind?"

They left the restaurant and began to make their way back to the hotel. Fraction was silent for a long while. Normally he affected one pose or another, jamming his hands in his pockets or swinging his arms as he walked. His walk just now was robotically stiff, and it came to Gennady that Danail Gavrilov's rider was missing at the moment, or at least, wasn't paying attention to his driving.

After a few minutes the cyranoid's head came up again and he said, "Imagine if there was only one language. You'd think only in it, and so you'd think that the names for things were the only possible names for them. You'd think there was only one way to organize the world—only one kind of 'it.' Or...take a city." He swept his arm in a broad gesture to encompass the cool evening, the patterns of lit windows on the black building facades. "In the Internet, we have these huge, dynamic webs of relationships that are always shifting. Meta-corporations are formed and dissolved in a day; people become stars overnight and fade away in a week. But within all that chaos, there's whirlpools and eddies where stability forms. These are called *attractors*. They're nodes of power, but our language doesn't have a word to point to them. We need a new word, a new kind of 'that' or 'it.'

"If you shot a time-lapse movie of a whole city at, say, a year-per-second, you'd see it evolving the same way. A city is a whirlpool of relationships but it changes so slowly that we humans have no control over how its currents and eddies funnel us through it.

"And if a city is like this, how much more so a country? A civilization? Cities and countries are frozen sets of relationships, as if the connection maps in a social networking site were drawn in steel and stone. These maps look so huge and immovable from our point of view that they channel our lives; we're carried along by them like motes in a hurricane. But they don't have to be that way."

Gennady was a bit lost, but Miranda was nodding. "Internet nations break down traditional barriers," she said. "You can live in Outer Mongolia but your nearest net-neighbor might live in Los Angeles. The old geographic constraints don't apply anymore."

"Just like Cascadia is its own city," said Fraction, "even though it's supposedly Seattle, Portland and Vancouver, and they supposedly exist in two countries."

"Okay," said Gennady irritably, "so Oversatch is another online nation. So why?"

Fraction pointed above the skyline. In reality, there was only black sky there; but in *Rivet Couture,* the vast upthrusting spires of a cathedral split the clouds. "The existing online nations copy the slowness of the real world," he said. "They create new maps, true, but those maps are as static as the old ones. That cathedral's been there since the game began. Nobody's going to move it; that would violate the rules of the alternate world.

"The buildings and avenues of Oversatch are built and move second by second. They're not a new, hand-drawn map of the world. They're a dynamically updated map of the Internet. They reflect the way the world really is, moment-by-moment. They leave these," he slapped the side of the skyscraper they were passing, "in the dust."

They had arrived at the mouth of another alleyway, this one dark in all worlds. Fraction stopped. "So we come to it," he said. "Hitchens and his boys couldn't get past this point. They got lost in the maze. I know you're ready," he said to Miranda. "You have been for quite a while. As to you, Gennady,..." He rubbed his chin, another creepy affectation that had nothing of Danail Gavrilov in it. "All I can tell you is you have to enter Oversatch together. One of you alone cannot do it."

He stood aside, like a sideshow barker waving a group of yokels into a tent. "This way, then, to Oversatch," he said.

There was nothing but darkness down the alley. Gennady and Miranda glanced at one another. Then, not exactly hand in hand but close beside one another, they stepped forward.

Gennady lay with his eyes closed, feeling the slow rise and fall of the ship around him. Distant engine noise rumbled through the decking, a sound so constant that he rarely noticed it now. He wasn't sleeping, but trying, with some desperation, to remind himself of where he was—and what he was supposed to be doing.

It had taken him quite a while to figure out that only six weeks had passed since he'd taken the Interpol contract. All his normal reference points were gone, even the usual ticking of his financial clocks which normally drove him from paycheck to paycheck, bill to bill. He hadn't thought about money at all in weeks, because here in Oversatch, he didn't need it.

Here in Oversatch...Even the 'here' part of things was getting hard to pin down. That should have been clear from the first night, when he and Miranda walked down a blacked-out alleyway and gradually began to make out a faint, virtual road leading on. They could both see the road so they followed it. Fraction had remained behind, so they talked about him as they walked. And then, when the road finally emerged into Stockholm's lit streets, Gennady had found that Miranda was not beside him. Or rather, *virtually* she was, but not physically. The path they had followed had really been two paths, leading in separate directions.

When he realized what had happened Gennady whirled, meaning to retrace his steps, but it was too late. The virtual pathway was a pale translucent blue stripe on the sidewalk ahead of him—but it vanished to the rear.

"We have to keep going forward," Miranda had said. "*I* have to, for my son."

All Gennady had to do was take off the glasses and he would be back in normal reality; so why did he feel so afraid, suddenly? "Your son," he said with some resentment. "You only bring him up at times like this, you know. You never talk about him as if you were his mother."

She was silent for a long time, then finally said, "I don't know him very well. It's terrible, but...he was raised by his father. Gennady, I've tried to have a relationship with him. It's mostly been by email. But that doesn't mean I don't care for him..."

"All right," he said with a sigh. "I'm sorry. So what do we do? Keep walking, I suppose."

They did, and after half an hour Gennady found himself in an area of old warehouses and run-down, walled houses. The blue line led up to the door of a stout, windowless brick building, and then just stopped.

"Gennady," said Miranda, "my line just ended at a brick wall."

Gennady pulled on the handle but the metal door didn't budge. Above the handle was a number pad, but there was no doorbell button. He pounded on the door, but nobody answered.

"What do you see?" he asked her. "Anything?" They both cast about for some clue and after a while, reluctantly, she said, "Well, there is some graffiti..."

"What kind?" He felt foolish and exposed standing here.

"Numbers," she said. "Sprayed on the wall."

"Tell them to me," he said. She relayed the numbers, and he punched them into the keypad on the door.

There was a *click,* and the door to Oversatch opened.

When the door opened a new path had appeared for Miranda. She took it, and it had been over a week before he again met her face to face. In that time they both met dozens of Oversatch's citizens—from a former high school teacher to a whole crew of stubbled and profane fishermen, to disenchanted computer programmers and university drop-outs—and had toured the farms and factories of a parallel reality as far removed from *Rivet Couture* as that ARG had been from Stockholm.

The citizens of Oversatch had opted out. They hadn't just left their putative nationalities behind, as Miranda Veen had when she married a mechanical engineer from Cascadia. Her

husband had built wind farms along the city's ridges and m
taintops, helping wean the city off any reliance it had once
on the national grid. Miranda worked at one of the vertical fai
at the edge of the city. A single block-wide skyscraper given o
to intense hydroponic production could feed 50,000 people, a
Cascadia had dozens of the vast towers. Cascadia had opt
out of any dependence on the North American economy, ar
Miranda had opted out of American citizenship. All very logica
in its own way—but nothing compared to Oversatch.

Where before Gennady and Miranda had couriered pack
ages to and fro for the grand dukes of *Rivet Couture,* now they
played far more intricate games of international finance for
nations and with currencies that had no existence in the "real"
world. Oversatch had its own economy, its own organizations
and internal rules; but the world they operated in was an ephemeral place, where nodes of importance could appear overnight.
Organizations, companies, cities and nations: Oversatch called
these things "attractors." The complex network of human activities tended to relax back into them, but at any given moment, the
elastic action of seven billion people acting semi-independentl'
deformed many of the network's nodes all out of recognition. A
the end of a day IBM might exist as a single corporate entity, bi
during the day, its global boundaries blurred; the same was tri
for nearly every other political and economic actor.

The difference between Oversatch and everybody el
was everybody else's map of the world showed only the attr;
tors. Oversatch used the instantaneous map, provided by int
net work analysis, that showed what the actual actors in
world were up to at this very moment. They called this may
2.0.' Gennady got used to reviewing a list of new nations in
morning, all given unique and memorable names like "Don
duckia" and "Brilbinty." As the morning rolled on Overs
players stepped in to move massive quantities of money
resources between these temporary actors. As the day end
one part of the world it began somewhere else, so the pro
never really ended, but locally, the temporary deformati

the network would subside at some point. Great Britain would reappear. So would Google, and the EU.

"It *is* like a game of Diplomacy," Miranda commented one day, "but one where the map itself is always changing."

When they weren't focused outward, Gennady and Miranda scanned objects and printed them from Oversatch's 3-D printers; or they tended rooftop gardens or drove vans containing produce from location to secret location. Everything they needed for basic survival was produced outside of the formal economy and took no resources from it. Even the electricity that ran the vans came from rooftop windmills built from Oversatch printers, which were themselves printed by other printers. Oversatch mined landfill sites and refined their metals and rare earths itself; it had its own microwave dishes on rooftops to beam its own data internally, not using the official data networks at all. These autonomous systems extended far past Stockholm—were, in fact, worldwide.

After a week or so it proved easier and cheaper to check out of the hotel and live in Oversatch's apartments, which, like everything else about the polity, were located in odd and unexpected places. Gennady and Miranda moved to Gothenburg on the West coast, and were given palatial accommodation in a set of renovated shipping containers down by the docks— very cozy, fully powered and heated, with satellite uplinks and sixty-inch TVs (all made by Oversatch, of course).

One bright morning Gennady sauntered up to the cafe where Hitchens had asked to meet him, and tried to describe his new life to the Interpol man.

Hitchens was thrilled. "This is fantastic, Gennady, just fantastic." He began talking about doing raids, about catching the whole network red-handed and shutting the damned thing down.

Gennady blinked at him owlishly. "Perhaps I am not yet awake," he said in the thickest Slavic accent he could manage, "but seems to me these people do nothing wrong, yes?"

Hitchens sputtered, so Gennady curbed his sarcasm and gently explained that Oversatch's citizens weren't doing

anything that was illegal by Swedish law—that, in fact, they scrupulously adhered to the letter of local law everywhere. It was national and regional economics that they had left behind and, with it, consumer society itself. When they needed to pay for a service in the so-called "real world," they had plenty of money to do it with—from investments, real estate, and a thousand other legitimate ventures. It was just that they depended on none of these things for their survival. They paid off the traditional economy only so that it would leave them alone.

"Besides," he added, "Oversatch is even more distributed than your average multinational corporation. Miranda and I usually work as a pair, but we're geographically separated...and most of their operations are like that. There's really no "place" to raid."

"If they just want to be left alone," asked Hitchens smugly, "why do they need the plutonium?"

Gennady shrugged. "I've seen no evidence that Oversatch is behind the smuggling. They don't seal the packages they send—I snoop so I know—and I've been carrying my Geiger counter everywhere. Whoever is moving the plutonium is probably using *Rivet Couture*. They *do* seal their packages."

Hitchens drummed his fingers on the yellow tablecloth. "Then what the hell is Fraction playing at?"

The implication that this idea might not have been preying on Hitchens' mind all along—as it had been on Gennady's—made Gennady profoundly uneasy. What kind of people was he working for if they hadn't mistrusted their captured double-agent from the start?

He said to Hitchens, "I just don't think Oversatch is the ultimate destination Fraction had in mind. Remember, he said he came from some place called 'far Cilenia.' I think he's trying to get us there."

Hitchens ran his fingers through his hair. "I don't understand why he can't just *tell us* where it is."

"Because it's not a place," said Gennady, a bit impatiently. "It's a protocol."

He spent some time trying to explain this to Hitchens, and as he walked back to the docks, Gennady realized that he himself *got it.* He really did understand Oversatch, and a few weeks ago he wouldn't have. At the same time, the stultified and mindless exchanges of the so-called 'real world' seemed more and more surreal to him. Why did people still show up at the same workplace every day, when the amount of friction needed to market their skills had dropped effectively to zero? Most people's abilities could be allocated with perfect efficiency now, but they got locked into contracts and 'jobs'—relationships that, like Fraction's physical cities and nations, were relics of a barbaric past.

He was nearly at the Oversatch settlement in the port when his glasses chimed. *Phone call from Lane Hitchens*, said a little sign in his heads-up display. Gennady put a finger to his ear and said, "Yes?"

"Gennady, it's Lane. New development. We've traced some plutonium packets through *Rivet Couture* and we think they've all been brought together for a big shipment overseas."

Gennady stopped walking. "That doesn't make any sense. The whole point of splitting them up was to slip them past the sensors at the airports and docks. If the strategy was working, why risk it all now?"

"Maybe they're on to us and they're trying to move it to its final destination before we catch them," said Hitchens. "We know where the plutonium is now—it's sitting on a container ship called the *Akira* about a kilometer from your bizarre little village. I don't think that's a coincidence, do you?"

So this was what people meant when they said "reality came crashing back," thought Gennady. "No," he said, "is unlikely. So now what? A raid?"

"No, we want to find the buyers, and they're on the other end of the pipeline. It'll be enough if we can track the container. The *Akira* is bound for Vancouver; the Canadian Mounties will be watching to see who picks it up when it arrives."

"Do they still have jurisdiction there?" Gennady asked. "Vancouver's part of Cascadia, remember?"

"Don't be ridiculous, Gennady. Anyway, it seems we won't need to go chasing this 'far Cilenia' thing anymore. You can come back in and we'll put you on the office team until the investigation closes. It's good money, and they're a great bunch of guys."

"Thanks." *Euros,* he mused. He supposed he could do something with those.

Hitchens rang off. Gennady could have turned around at that moment and simply left the port lands. He could have thrown away the augmented reality glasses and collected his fee from Interpol. Instead he kept walking.

As he reached the maze of stacked shipping containers, he told himself that he just wanted to tell Miranda the news in person. Then they could leave Oversatch together. Except... she wouldn't be leaving, he realized. She was still after her estranged son, who had spoken to her mostly through emails and now wasn't speaking at all.

If Gennady abandoned her now, he would be putting a hole in Oversatch's buddy-system. Would Miranda even be able to stay in Oversatch without her partner? He wasn't sure.

He opened the big door to a particular shipping container— one that looked exactly like all its neighbors but was nothing like them—and walked through the dry, well-lighted corridor inside it, then out the door that had been cut in the far end. This put him in one of a number of halls and stairways that were dug into the immense square block of containers. He passed a couple of his co-workers and waved hello, went up one flight of portable carbon-fiber steps and entered the long sitting room (actually another shipping container) that he shared with Miranda.

Fraction was sitting in one of the leather armchairs, chatting with Miranda who leaned on the bar counter at the back. Both greeted Gennady warmly as he walked in.

"How are you doing, Gennady?" Fraction asked. "Is Oversatch agreeing with you?"

Gennady had to smile at his wording. "Well enough," he said.

"Are you ready to take it to the next level?"

Warily, Gennady moved to stand behind the long room's other armchair. "What do you mean?"

Fraction leaned forward eagerly. "A door to Cilenia is about to open," he said. "We have the opportunity to go through it, but we'll have to leave tonight."

"We?" Gennady frowned at him. "Didn't you tell us that you were from Cilenia?"

"*From*, yes," said the cyranoid. "But not *in*. I want to get back there for my own reasons. Miranda needs to find her son; you need to find your plutonium. Everybody wins here."

Gennady decided not to say that he had already found the plutonium. "What does it involve?"

"Nothing," said Fraction, steepling his fingers and looking over them at Gennady. "Just be in your room at two o'clock. And make sure the door is closed."

After that cryptic instruction, Fraction said a few more pleasantries and then left. Miranda had come to sit down, and Gennady only realized that he was still standing, holding tightly to the back of the chair, when she said, "Are you all right?"

"They found the plutonium," he blurted.

Her eyes widened; then she looked down. "So I guess you'll be leaving, then."

He made himself sit down across from her. "I don't know," he said. "I don't...want to leave you alone to face whatever Cilenia is."

"My white knight," she said with a laugh; but he could tell she was pleased.

"Well, it's not just that." He twined his hands together, debating with himself how to say it. "This is the first time I've ever been involved with a...project that...*made* something. My whole career, I've been cleaning up after the messes left by the previous generation. Chernobyl, Hanford—all the big and little accidents. The rest of it, you know, consumer culture and TV and movies and games...I just had no time for them. Well, except the games. But I never bought *stuff*, you know? And our whole culture is about *stuff*. But I was never a radical environmentalist, a, what-do-you-call it? Treehugger. Not a back-to-the-lander, because there's no safe land to go back to, if we don't clean up the mess. So I've lived in limbo for many years, and never knew it."

Now he looked her in the eye. "There's more going on with Oversatch than just a complicated game of tax evasion, isn't there? The people who're doing this, they're saying that there really can be more than one world, in the same place, at the same time. That you can walk out of the 21st Century without having to become a farmer or mountain man. And they're building that parallel world."

"It's the first," she admitted, "but obviously not the last. Cilenia must be like Oversatch, only even more self-contained. A world within a world." She shook her head. "At first I didn't know why Jake would have gone there. But he was always like you—not really committed to *this* world, but unwilling to take any of the easy alternatives. I could never see him joining a cult, that was the point."

Gennady glanced around. "Is this a cult?" he asked. But she shook her head.

"They've never asked us to believe in anything," she said. "They've just unlocked doors for us, one after another. And now they've unlocked another one." She grinned. "Aren't you just the tiniest bit curious about what's on the other side?"

He didn't answer her; but at two o'clock he was waiting in his room with the door closed. He'd tried reading a book and listening to music, but the time dragged and in the end he just waited, feeling less and less sure of all of this every second.

When something huge landed with a crash on the shipping container, Gennady jumped to his feet and ran to the door—but it was already too late. With a nauseating swaying motion, his room was lofted into the air with him in it and, just as he was getting his sea legs on the moving surface, the unseen crane deposited his container somewhere else, with a solid thump.

His door was locked from the outside. By the time it was opened, hours later, he had resigned himself to starving or running out of air in here, for by that time the container ship *Akira* was well under way.

So he lay with his eyes closed, feeling the slow rise and fall of the ship around him. Behind his own eyelids was an attractor that he needed to subside into, at least for a while.

Eventually there was an insistent chirp from beside his bed. Gennady reached for the glasses without thinking, then hesitated. Mumbling a faint curse, he put them on.

Oversatch sprang up all around: a vast, intricate glowing city visible through the walls of the shipping container. Today's map of the world was all crowded over in the direction of China; he'd find out why later. For now, he damped down the flood of detail and when it was just a faint radiance and a murmur, he rose and left his room.

His was one of many modified shipping containers stacked aboard the Akira. In Oversatch terms, the containers were called *packets*. Most packets had doors that were invisible from outside, so that when they were stacked next to one another you could walk between them without going on deck. Gennady's packet was part of a row of ten such containers. Above and below were more levels, reachable through more doors in the ceilings and floors of some containers.

The packets would all be unloaded at their destination along with the legitimate containers. But in a rare venture into illegal operations, Oversatch had hacked the global container routing system. Officially, Oversatch's shipping containers didn't even exist. Offloaded from one ship, they would sooner or later end up on another and be routed somewhere else, just like the information packets in an internet. They bounced eternally through the system, never reaching a destination, but constantly meeting up and merging to form temporary complexes like this one, then dissolving to recombine in new forms somewhere else. Together they formed Oversatch's capital city—a city in perpetual motion, constantly reconfiguring itself, and at any one time nearly all of it in international waters.

The shipping container where the plutonium was stowed wasn't part of this complex. You couldn't get there from here; in fact, you couldn't get there at all. Gennady had skulked on deck his first night on board, and found the contraband container way up near the top of a stack. It was a good thirty feet above him and it took him ten minutes to climb precariously up to it. His heart was pounding when he got there. In the dark, with the slow sway of the ship and the unpredictable breeze, what if he fell? He'd inspected the thing's door, but it was sealed. The containers around it all had simple inspection seals on them: they were empty.

He hadn't tried to climb up to it again, but he kept an eye on it.

Now he passed lounges, diners, chemical toilets and work areas as he negotiated the maze of Oversatch containers. Some Swedes on their way to a holiday in Canada waved and shouted his name; they were clearly a few drinks into their day, and he just grinned and kept going. Many of the other people he passed were sitting silently in comfortable lounge chairs. They were working, and he didn't disturb them.

He found his usual workstation, but Miranda's, which was next to his, was empty. Another woman sat nearby, sipping a beer and having an animated conversation with the blank wall.

Somewhere, maybe on the far side of the world, somebody else was waving their hands, and speaking this woman's words. She was *riding* and that distant person was her cyranoid.

Yesterday Miranda and Gennady had visited a bus station in Chicago. Both were riding cyranoids, but Miranda was so much better at it than Gennady. His upper body was bathed with infrared laser light, allowing the system to read his posture, gestures, even fine finger motions, and transmit them to the person on the other end. For Gennady, the experience was just like moving an avatar in a game world. The physical skills needed to interpret the system's commands lay with the cyranoid; so in that sense, Gennady had it easy.

But he had to meet new people on an hour-by-hour basis, and even though he was hiding thousands of miles away from that point of contact, each new encounter made his stomach knot up.

At the bus depot he and Miranda had done what countless pimps, church recruiters and sexual predators had done for generations: they looked for any solitary young people who might exit the buses. There was a particular set to the shoulders, an expression he was learning to read: it was the fear of being alone in the big city.

The cyranoids he and Miranda rode were very respectable-looking people. Together or separately, they would approach these uncertain youths, and offer them work. Oversatch was recruiting.

The results were amazing. Take one insecure eighteen-year-old with no skills or social connections. Teach him to be a cyranoid. Then dress him a nice suit and send him into the downtown core of a big city. In one day he could be ridden by a confident and experienced auditor, a private investigator, a savvy salesman and a hospital architecture consultant. He could attend meetings, write up reports, drive from contact to contact and shift identities many times on the way. All he had to do was recite the words that flowed into his ears and follow the instructions of his haptic interface. Each of the professionals who rode him could build their networks and attend to business there and, through other cyranoids, in many different cities in one day. And by simple observation the kid could learn tremendous amounts about the internals of business and government.

Gennady was cultivating his own network of cyranoids to do routine checks at nuclear waste repositories around the world. These young people needed certification, so he and Oversatch were sponsoring them in schools. While they weren't at school Gennady would ride them out to waste sites where they acted as representatives for a legitimate consulting company he had set up under his own name. His name had a certain cachet in these circles, so the six young men and three women had a foot in the door already. Since he was riding them they displayed uncanny skill at finding problems at the sites. All were rapidly blossoming.

He sat down under the invisible laser bath and prepared to call up his students. At that moment the ship gave a slight lurch—a tiny motion, but the engineer in Gennady instantly calculated the quantity of energy that must have gone through the vessel. It was a lot.

Now he noticed that the room was swaying slowly. The *Akira* rarely did that because not only was it huge to begin with, it also had stabilizing gyroscopes. "Did you feel that?" he said to the woman next to him.

She glanced over, touching the pause button on her rig, and said, "What?"

"Never mind." He called up the hack that fed the ship's vital statistics to Oversatch. They were in the Chukchi Sea, with Russia to starboard and Alaska to port. Gennady had been asleep when the *Akira* crossed the north pole, but apparently there hadn't been much to see, since the open Arctic Ocean had been fogbound. Now, though, a vicious storm was piling out of the East Siberian Sea. The video feed showed bruised, roiling skies and a sea of giant, white-crowned pyramidal waves. Amazing he hadn't felt it before. Chatter on the ship's comm was cautious but bored, because such storms were apparently as regular as clockwork in the new ice-free arctic shipping lanes. This one was right on schedule, but the ship intended to just bull its way through it.

Gennady made a mental note to go topside and see the tempest for himself. But just as he was settling back in his seat, the door flew open and Miranda ran in.

She reached to grab his hands, stopped, and said, "Are you riding?"

"No, I—" She hauled him to his feet.

"I saw him! Gennady, I saw Jake!"

The deck slowly tilted, then righted itself as Gennady and Miranda put their hands to the wall. "Your son? You saw him here?"

She shook her head. "No, not here. And I didn't exactly see him. I mean, oh, come on, sit down and I'll tell you all about it."

They sat well away from the riding woman. The shipping container was very narrow so their knees almost touched.

Miranda leaned forward, clasping her hands and beaming. "It was in Sao Paolo. You know Oversatch has been sponsoring me to attend conferences, so I was riding a local cyranoid at an international symposium on vanishing rain forest cultures. We were off in an English breakaway session with about ten other people, some of whom I knew—but of course I was pretending to be a postdoc from Brasilia, or rather my cyranoid was—you know what I mean. Anyway, they didn't know me. But there was one young guy...Every time he talked I got the strangest feeling. Something about the words he chose, the rhythm, even the gestures...and he was noticing me, too.

"About half an hour in he caught my eye, and then leaned forward quite deliberately to write something on the pad of paper he was using. It was so low-tech; a lot of us had noticed he was using it but nobody'd said anything. But at the end of the session when everybody was standing up, he caught my eye again, and then he balled up the paper and threw it in a trash can on the way out. I lost him in the between-session crowd, so I went back and retrieved the paper."

"What did it say?"

To his surprise, she took off her glasses and set them down. After a moment, Gennady did the same. Miranda handed him her notebook, which he hadn't seen since the first day they met.

"I've been keeping notes in this," she whispered, "outside the glasses. Just in case what we do or say is being tracked. Anyway, I had to snapshot the paper through my cyranoid, but as soon as I could I downloaded the image and deleted the original out of my glasses. This is what was on the paper."

Gennady looked. It said:

Cilenia, 64° 58' N, 168° 58' W.

Below this was a little scrawled stick-figure with one hand raised. "That," said Miranda, pointing at it. "Jake used to draw those as a kid. I'd recognize it anywhere."

"Jake was riding cyranoid on the man in your session?" Gennady sat back, thinking. "Let me check something." He put his glasses on and polled the ship's network again. "Those numbers," he said, "if they're longitude and latitude, then that's almost exactly where we are now."

She frowned, and said, "But how could that be? Was he saying Cilenia is some sort of underwater city? That's impossible."

Gennady stood up suddenly. "I think he's saying something else. Come on." The unpredictable sway of the ship had gotten larger. He and Miranda staggered from wall to wall like drunkards as they left the room and entered one of the lengthwise corridors that transected the row of packets. They passed other workers doing the same, and the Swedes had given up their partying and were all sitting silently, looking slightly green.

"I've been checking on the, uh, other cargo," said Gennady as they passed someone, "every day. If it's bound for Vancouver there'll be a whole platoon of Mounties waiting for it. That had me wondering if they wouldn't try to unload it en route."

"Makes sense," called Miranda. She was starting to fall behind, and a distant rushing and booming sound was rising.

"Actually, it didn't. It's sealed and near the top of a stack—that's where they transport the empties. But it's not *at* the top, so even if you did a James Bond and flew over with a skycrane helicopter, you couldn't just pluck it off the stack."

They came to some stairs and he went up. Miranda puffed behind him. "Couldn't they have a trick door?" she said. "Like in ours? Maybe it's actually got inside access to another set of packets, just like ours but separate."

"Yeah, I thought about that," he said grimly. He headed up another flight, which dead-ended in an empty shipping container that would have looked perfectly normal if not for the stairwell in the middle of its floor. The only light up here was from a pair of LEDs on the wall, so Gennady put his hands out to move cautiously forward. He could hear the storm now, a shuddering roar that felt like it was coming from all sides.

"One problem with that theory," he said as he found the inside latch to the rejiggered container door. "There's a reason why they put the empty containers on the *top* of the stack." He pushed down on the latch.

"Gennady, I've got a call," said Miranda. "It's *you!* What—" The bellow of the storm drowned whatever else she might have said.

The rain was falling sideways from charcoal-black clouds that seemed to be skipping off the ocean's surface like thrown stones. There was nothing to see except blackness, whipping rain and slick metal decks lit intermittently by lightning flashes. One such flash revealed a hill of water heaving itself up next to the ship. Seconds later the entire ship pitched as the wave hit and Gennady nearly fell.

He hopped to the catwalk next to the door. They were high above the floor of the hold here, just at the level where the container stack poked above deck. It kept going a good forty feet more overhead. When Gennady glanced up he saw the black silhouette of the stack's top swaying in a very unsettling manner.

He couldn't see very well and could hear nothing at all over the storm. Gennady pulled out his glasses and put them on, then accessed the ship's security cameras.

He couldn't make out himself, but one camera on the super-structure showed him the whole field of container stacks. The corners of a couple of those stacks looked a bit ragged, like they'd been shaved.

He returned the glasses to his shirt pocket, but paused to insert the earbuds.

"Gennady, are you online?" It was Miranda's voice.

"Here," he said. "Like I said, there's a reason they put the empties at the top. Apparently something like fifteen thousand shipping containers are lost overboard every year, mostly in storms like this. But most of them are empties."

"But this one isn't," she said. He was moving along the deck now, holding tight to a railing next to the swaying container stack. Looking back, he saw her following doggedly, but still twenty or more feet back.

Lightning day-lit the scene for a moment, and Gennady thought he saw someone where nobody in their right mind should be. "Did you *see* that?" He waited for her to catch up and helped her along. Both of them were drenched and the water was incredibly cold.

Her glasses were beaded with water. Why didn't she just take them off? Her mouth moved and he heard "See what?" through his earbuds, but not through the air.

He tried to pitch his voice more conversationally—his yelling was probably unnecessary and annoying. "Somebody on top of one of the stacks."

"Let me guess: it's the stack with the plutonium."

He nodded and they kept going. They were nearly to the stack when the ship listed particularly far and suddenly he saw bright orange flashes overhead. He didn't hear the bangs because suddenly lightning was dancing around one of the ship's masts, and the thunder was instantaneous and deafening. But the deck was leaning way over, dark churning water meters to his left and suddenly the top three layers of the container stack gave way and slid into the water.

They went in a single slab, except for a few stragglers that tumbled like match-boxes and took out the railing and a chunk of decking not ten meters from where Gennady and Miranda huddled.

"Go back!" He pushed her in the direction of the superstructure, but she shook her head and held on to the railing. Gennady cursed and turned as the ship rolled upright then continued to list in the opposite direction.

One container was pivoting on the gunwale, tearing the steel like cloth and throwing sparks. As the ship heeled starboard it tilted to port and went over. There were no more and the other stacks seemed stable. Gennady suspected they would normally have weathered a heavier storm than this.

He rounded the stack and stepped onto the catwalk that ran between it and the next. As lightning flickered again he saw that there was somebody there. A crewman?

"Gennady, how nice to see you," said Fraction. He was wearing a yellow hard-hat and a climbing harness over his crew's overalls. His glasses were as beaded with rain as Miranda's.

"It's a bit dangerous out here right now," Fraction said as he stepped closer. "I don't really care, but then I'm riding, aren't I?" As blue light slid over the scene Gennady saw the black backpack slung over Fraction's shoulder.

"You're not from Cilenia, are you?" said Gennady. "You work for somebody else."

"Gennady! He's with sanotica," said Miranda. "You can't trust him."

"Cilenia wants that plutonium," said Fraction. "For their new generators, that's all. It's perfectly benign, but you know nations like ours aren't considered legitimate by the attractors. We could never *buy* the stuff."

Gennady nodded. "The containers were rigged to go overboard. The storm made handy cover, but I'd bet there was enough explosives up there to put them over even if the weather was calm. It would have been automatic. You didn't need to be here for it."

Fraction shifted the pack on his back. "So?"

"You climbed up and opened the container," said Gennady. "The plutonium's right here." He pointed at the backpack. "Ergo, you're not working for Cilenia."

Miranda put a hand on his shoulder. She was nodding. "He was after the rest of it himself, all along," she shouted. "He used us to track it down, so he could take it for sanotica."

Danail Gavrilov's face was empty of expression, his eyes covered in blank, rain-dewed lenses. "Why would I wait until now to take it?" Fraction said.

"Because you figured the container was being watched. I'm betting you've got some plan to put the plutonium overboard yourself, with a different transponder than the one Cilenia had on their shipping container....Which I'm betting was rigged to float twenty feet below the surface and wait for pickup."

Fraction threw the bundle of rope he'd been holding, then stepped forward and reached for Gennady.

Gennady side-stepped, then reached out and plucked the glasses from Danail Gavrilov's face.

The cyranoid staggered to a stop, giving Gennady enough time to reach up and pluck the earbuds from his ears.

Under sudden lightning, Gennady saw Gavrilov's eyes for the first time. They were small and dark, and darted this way and that in sudden confusion. The cyranoid said something that sounded like a question—in Bulgarian. Then he put his hands to his ears and roared in sudden panic.

Gennady lunged, intending to grab Gavrilov's hand, but instead got a handful of the backpack's tough material. Gavrilov spun around, skidded on the deck as the backpack came loose— and then went over the rail.

He heard Miranda's shout echoing his own. They both rushed to the railing but could see nothing but black water topped by white streamers of foam.

"He's gone," said Miranda with a sudden, odd calm.

"We've got to try!" shouted Gennady. He ran for the nearest phone, which was housed in a waterproof kiosk halfway down the catwalk. He was almost there when Miranda tackled him. They rolled right to the edge of the catwalk and Gennady almost lost the backpack.

"What are you doing?" he roared at her. "He's a human being, for God's sake."

"We'll never find him," she said, still in that oddly calm tone of voice. Then she sat back. "Gennady, I'm sorry," she said. "I shouldn't have done that. No, shut up, Jake. It was wrong. We should try to rescue the poor man."

She cocked her head, then said, "He's afraid Oversatch will be caught."

"Your son's been riding you!" Gennady shook his head. "How long?"

"Just now. He called as we were coming outside."

"Let me go," said Gennady. "I'll tell them we stowed away below decks. I'm a God-damned Interpol investigator! We'll be fine." He staggered to the phone.

It took a few seconds to ring through to the surprised crew, but after talking briefly to them Gennady hung up, shaking his head. "Not sure they believe me enough to come about," he said. "They're on their way down to arrest us, though."

The rain was streaming down his face, but he was glad to be seeing it without the Oversatch interface filtering its reality. "Miranda? Can I talk to Jake for a second?"

"What? Sure." She was hugging herself and shaking violently from the cold. Gennady realized his own teeth were chattering.

He had little time before reality reached out to hijack all his choices. He hefted the backpack, thinking about Hitchens' reaction when he told him the story—and wondering how much of Oversatch he could avoid talking about in the deposition.

"Jake," he said, "what is Cilenia?"

Miranda smiled, but it was Jake who said, "Cilenia's not an 'it' like you're used to, not a 'thing' in the traditional sense. It's not really a place either. It's just…some people realized that we needed a new language to describe the way the world actually works nowadays. When all identities are fluid, how can you get away with using the old words to describe anything?

"You know how cities and countries and corporations are like stable whirlpools in a flood of changes? They're *attractors*— states the network relaxes back into, but at any given moment they might not really be there. Well, what if human beings were like that too? Imagine a driver working for a courier company. He follows his route, he talks to customers and delivers packages, but another driver would do exactly the same thing in his place. While he's on the job, he's not *him,* he's the company. He only relaxes back into his own identity when he goes home and takes off the uniform.

"*It 2.0* gives us a way to point at those temporary identities. It's a tool that lets us bring the *temporarily real* into focus, even while the outlines of the things we *thought* were real—like countries and companies—are blurred. If there could be an *it 2.0* for countries and companies, don't you suppose there could be one for people, too?"

"Cilenia?" said Gennady. Miranda nodded, but Gennady shook his head. It wasn't that he couldn't imagine it; the problem was he *could*. Jake was saying that people weren't even people all the time, that they played roles through much of the day representing powers and forces they often weren't even aware of. A person could be multiple places at once, the way that Gennady was himself and his avatars, his investments and emails and website, and the cyranoids he rode. He'd been moving that way his whole adult life, he realized, his identity becoming smeared out across the world. In the past few weeks the process had accelerated. For someone like Jake, born and raised in a world of shifting identities, *it 2.0* and Cilenia must make perfect sense. They might even seem mundane.

Maybe Cilenia was the new 'it.' But Gennady was too old and set in his ways to speak that language.

"And sanotica?" he asked. "What's that?"

"Imagine Oversatch," said Jake, "but with no moral constraints on it. Imagine that instead of looking for spontaneous remappings in the healthy network of human relationships, you had an '*it 3.0*' that looked for disasters—points and moments when rules break down and there's chaos and anarchy. Imagine an army of cyranoids stepping in at moments like that, to take advantage of misery and human pain. It would be very efficient, wouldn't it? As efficient, maybe, as Oversatch.

"That," said Jake as shouting crewmen came running along the gunwales, "is sanotica. An efficient parasite that feeds on catastrophe. And millions of people work for it without knowing."

Gennady held up the backpack. "It would have taken this and...made a bomb?"

"Maybe. And how do *you* know, Mister Malianov, that you don't work for sanotica yourself? How can I be sure that plutonium won't be used for some terrible cause? It should go to Cilenia."

Gennady hesitated. He heard Miranda Veen asking him to do this; and after everything he'd seen, he knew now that in his world power and control could be shifted invisibly and totally moment by moment by entities like Oversatch and Cilenia. Maybe Fraction really had hired Hitchins' people, and Gennady himself. And maybe they could do it again, and he wouldn't even know it.

"Drop the backpack in the bilges," said Jake. "We can send someone from Oversatch to collect it. Mother, you can bring it to Cilenia when you come."

The rain was lessening, and he could see that her cheeks were wet now with tears. "I'll come, Jake. When we get let go, I'll come to you."

Then, as Jake, she said, "Now, Gennady! They're almost here!"

Gennady held onto the backpack. "I'll keep it," he said.

Gennady took the glasses out of his pocket and dropped them over the railing. In doing so he left the city he had only just discovered, but had lately lived in and begun to love. That city—world-spanning, built of light and ideals, was tricked into existing moment-by-moment by the millions who believed in it and simply acted as though it were there. He wished he could be one of them.

Gennady could hear Jake's frustration in Miranda's voice, as she said, "But how can you know that backpack's not going to end up in sanotica?"

"There are more powers on Earth," Gennady shouted over the storm, "than just Cilenia and sanotica. What's in this backpack is one of those powers. But another power is *me*. Maybe my identity's not fixed either and maybe I'm just one man, but at the end of the day I'm bound to follow what's in here, wherever it goes. I can't go with you to Cilenia, or even stay in Oversatch, much as I'd like to. I will go where this plutonium goes, and try to keep it from harming anyone.

"Because some things," he said as the crewmen arrived and surrounded them, "are real in *every* world."

ACKNOWLEDGEMENTS

The Editor (that's me) would like to acknowledge Steve Feldberg of Audible.com, for initially proposing the anthology, guiding it through production on the audiobook side, acting as a spot copy-editor for the text, being a huge cheerleader for the anthology and its writers all the way through the process, and also being cool enough to allow the anthology to have a print version as well. To not give him vast amounts of credit for the creation of all of this would be to do him a grave disservice. Thanks, Steve.

Thanks to everyone at Subterranean for their typical excellent work (and please note the fact that it's typical is exceptional in itself), with particular thanks to Anne KG Murphy for copy-editing, Edward Miller for the fine cover, Gail Cross for her usual stunning design, and to Bill Schafer, Tim Holt and Yanni Kuznia.

Most of all, I'd like to thank Elizabeth Bear, Tobias Buckell, Jay Lake and Karl Schroeder. This project has been one of the most fun of my professional career, and it's because they were part of it. They are good friends, great writers, and awesome collaborators. Thanks, guys.

—JS